The MOON CHILD

The MOON CHILD

Cate Cain

templar

For my father, John Cain, who loves ships.
And for my godsons, Henry Wells and Jasper Parsons.

January 1667

The mirror was tall and very old. The pitted surface was crazed with a network of blackened spider-leg lines that looked like veins running through the glass.

"I cannot see you." There was a rustling sound as the woman took a step closer. The gilded fruits and vines of the mirror frame seemed to quiver and reach out to her as she leaned forward.

"Do not touch the glass!" The distorted voice came from somewhere far away – as if from the bottom of the ocean.

"But I cannot… Ah, I have you now." The woman in the gold silk dress cocked her head to one side as she stared at the smoke-grey shadow behind her own reflection in the mirror.

She adjusted the jewelled patch over her left eye and peered into the depths of the glass. "I have prepared, my lord. Everything is ready, as you commanded. Your house is… much changed. But the journey is so…'

"Good. I am pleased with you." The distant, bubbling voice cut across her words.

The woman smoothed her skirts and pulled at the frothy lace cuff so that her left hand was completely hidden. She bit her lip as she looked up and into the glass again.

"You will keep your promise as we discussed?"

"Of course, Madame. I always ensure those loyal to me get exactly what they deserve, do I not?"

The woman nodded, more to herself than to the shadow in the mirror. "Soon then, my lord." She took a step back, and gently closed and locked the wooden doors of the great armoire so that the hideous mirror was shut away once again. Then she pushed the key into the high, ruffled collar of her bodice and left the room.

"Soon." In the darkness the crooning voice repeated the word, but it sounded more like the hissing of a snake. And then the laughter began…

CHAPTER ONE

"Never drop your guard!"

A sharp pain shot from Jem's wrist right up to his shoulder as the blunt-tipped practice sword flew from his hand, arcing gracefully into the air before clattering to the cobbles of the courtyard.

Jalbert brought his own weapon down to his side and shook his head. "You are good. One day you may even be a great swordsman, but right now you are always too hasty. Remember what I told you. This is like a game of chess. Speed and strength are important, but the battle is won here." The tall, lean-faced man tapped his head. "Now, again. Please retrieve your weapon and this time fight with your brain as well as your heart."

Jem rubbed his aching wrist and scowled. He was angry – not at Master Jalbert, but at himself. He knew the fencing teacher was right: he had momentarily lost focus, lashing out blindly, and Jalbert had found his weak spot.

For the last two months, Jem's regular fencing

lessons with William Jalbert had been the highlight of his week. The fact that this quiet, watchful and undeniably brilliant man had been specially selected to teach him the art of swordplay by Jem's father, King Charles II, made the sessions even more important. Even though they shared the same dark curling hair, brown eyes and tall lanky frame, the King had never publically acknowledged Jem to be his son. At first Jem was disappointed, but at least the weekly lessons made him feel that his father thought about him, occasionally.

Jalbert looked up at the flat, grey January sky. "We have another hour at most before dark. Take up your sword and we will begin again."

Jem nodded enthusiastically. "Can we try the heavy sword, please, William – before you go?"

The man raised an eyebrow. "Always so eager. We'll see. If you can knock the short sword from my hand, as I have just done from yours, we might think about it." He paused and his brown eyes twinkled. "But if you can't, then next week we will have to go back to wooden sticks and start all over again."

"That is not going to happen!" Jem grinned and loped across the cobbles to collect his sword.

His mother's voice rang out across the yard. "Jem!

You must come in now. It's getting late." Sarah appeared at an arched doorway at the top of a small flight of stone steps. Two serving girls stood behind her, one of them carrying a steaming jug.

Five miles outside the city of London, Goldings House had once belonged to Sarah's father, Lord Verrers. Surrounded by a fine park, the rambling old mansion was topped by an extravagant array of twisted chimneys. There were so many Jem could never count them properly. He thought there were probably twenty-seven, but each time he tried to number them, he'd discover another one, tucked away on a slanting roof or behind a tottering red-brick stack.

It saddened him to think that he had never met his grandfather. When he and his mother had first returned together to Goldings on a sunny day four months ago now, in the autumn of 1666, she had taken him to a long wood-panelled gallery that ran the whole width of the second floor. Above a massive stone fireplace, halfway down the gallery, hung a huge painting covered in grey cloth.

Sarah had pulled at the cloth, dust filling the air as it slumped down into the empty hearth, making them both cough.

The man in the painting over the fireplace had a

13

grimly handsome face with piercing blue eyes. He wasn't wearing a hat and his thick straight hair was very fair, almost white. The man was standing next to a table full of papers, his right hand resting on a globe. Jem thought he seemed dressed for a battle – he could see the edge of a breastplate glinting beneath the man's cloak.

Sarah was quiet for a moment as she stared at the portrait, then she spoke. "That is my father – your grandfather, Jem. Lord Edward Verrers was a good man, but…" she bit her lip and looked down at the hearth, "…he supported Parliament during the long war and he disowned both me and my brother Jamie when we… chose another path."

Jem darted a look at his mother. She had a brother? So he had an uncle?

She turned her face away as she continued. "Jamie died fighting for the old king and I think that broke my father's heart."

She moved across the gallery and stood stiffly with her back to Jem as she looked out of the tall window. "Now you and I are the only Verrers left. One day, this house and this estate will be yours."

She made a noise that sounded like a choked sob. Jem walked over to stand beside her. He watched through the milky glass for a moment as a small tabby cat padded round the corner of a brick gatepost on the far side of the circular gravel drive. The cat seemed very much at home.

He caught his mother's hand and squeezed it. She turned to look at him. "It must be the dust. It catches in my throat. The house has been shut up and abandoned for so long that we'll have to clean it from top to bottom to make it habitable." She smiled, but Jem had seen tears glittering in her eyes.

Now, four months later, Goldings was full of life again. Sarah had tracked down the sons and daughters of the servants she had known as a child and offered them employment. The ancient house had been thoroughly aired and cleaned, dusty cloths had been removed from the heavy old-fashioned furniture, herb-strewn fires burned in the great chambers and the sound of chatter and laughter could be heard as people went about their business.

Despite tedious lessons with his new tutor, Dr Speight, which made him long to be outside on even the bitterest of days, Jem felt at home for the first time in his life. There was just one thing – or more precisely, two people and a small black-and-white monkey – missing.

Master Jalbert bowed low as Sarah bustled down the steps and picked her way across the yard. She skirted carefully past a couple of ice-crusted puddles and tapped Jem lightly on the shoulder.

"Inside – now." Her breath misted the air. She nodded to the fencing teacher and smiled. "I am sorry, Master Jalbert, I meant to send word to postpone the lesson today. Jem is needed indoors. Eliza has prepared hot chocolate for you. I hope you will take some before you leave us."

"But that's not fair! William's come all the way from Whitehall and there's still at least an hour of daylight left. I suppose you want me to spend the rest of the afternoon in the schoolroom working on more of Dr Speight's pointless 'mathematical conundrums'?" Jem mimicked the weedy voice of his tutor. Dr Speight always referred to lessons as his "puzzles", "quizzes", "teasers" or "conundrums". As far as Jem was concerned it didn't matter what the little man called them, they were all a form of torture.

"Well, I won't," he continued angrily, waving the sword at the sky. "It's not late at all. There's plenty of light left to practise in. That's right, isn't it, William?"

Master Jalbert reached across and took the sword

gently from Jem's hand. "I think your mother is right, hothead. It is time for me to go."

"But what about the sticks?" Jem was indignant. "I'm not going back to them next time, am I?"

William laughed. "Of course not. You are doing very well. In fact, you'll soon get the better of me, I fear!" He turned to Sarah and made a small bow again. "Your son is a natural – like his father."

Sarah's cheeks flushed pink for a moment and Jem couldn't tell if she was pleased or embarrassed. He felt his own face redden too, but that was because he still wasn't used to praise.

Master Jalbert gathered up his cloak and swords from the cobbles, and ruffled Jem's dark hair. "You might want to think about getting this trimmed, lad. An expert swordsman needs to be able to see where he's aiming." He swapped a small smile with Sarah, adding, "That chocolate sounds good, my lady."

"Eliza has it ready. Take it in the hall before you leave us. Thank you, Master Jalbert. I know how much your lessons mean to my son."

Jem scowled as his fencing master crumped back across the frosted cobbles and climbed the steps. Then he folded his arms and kicked at a loose pebble.

"So why, exactly, I am needed inside? I'm not going

17

to the schoolroom. It's Twelfth Night tomorrow and you promised I wouldn't have to look at Dr Speight or his stinking, mouldy books until Christmas was over. There's still one more day."

"Precisely." Sarah grinned. "But we have a lot of things to do before we hold our Twelfth Night feast to celebrate our return to Goldings... and before your friends Tolly and Ann arrive with Mr Jericho and all his players."

"They're coming here?"

Sarah nodded. "Tomorrow. Eliza and the others are making ready for them."

Jem was rooted to the spot for a second. Then he beamed, spun about and skidded across the courtyard to the steps.

"What can I do to help?" he shouted as Eliza bustled into the house after Master Jalbert.

CHAPTER TWO

Jem kneeled on the window seat in the highest room of the north turret and scanned the road for the hundredth time. His breath fogged up the square pane and the glass squeaked as he cleared the view with his palm. It was late afternoon. Although it had been a bright, crisp day, the sun was low in the sky, and the turrets and chimneys of the west wing of Goldings cast long fingers of shadow across the meadow beyond the house.

Surely they should be here by now?

Jem had thrown himself into the preparations for the Twelfth Night celebrations with such enthusiasm that, when he was helping the servants knot together garlands of holly to drape over the rafters of the great hall, Sarah had remarked tartly that it was a pity he didn't apply himself with such industry to his lessons.

He had ignored her.

Every time he thought about seeing his friends again he felt a warm glow in the pit of his stomach.

He had last seen them at the end of September after the terrible fire that had burned old London to a city of skeletal, blackened carcasses and gaping voids.

He wondered where they had been since then and what they had been up to. While he was stuck in a gloomy schoolroom stumbling over Latin and Greek, Tolly, Ann and Cleo (the little monkey) had been touring the Eastern counties with Gabriel Jericho and his extraordinary, colourful, easy-going players.

After all that they had been through together, Jem had desperately wanted his friends to come and live at Goldings. It would be a new start for them all, a real home where they could forget about Count Cazalon. Even now, months after that terrifying confrontation in the catacombs beneath the old burning cathedral, Jem could still hear the ancient sorcerer's cracked voice and smell his rotting flesh. Every day he struggled to keep Cazalon out of his thoughts and he wondered if Ann and Tolly felt the same. If they had been living here at Goldings he could have asked them.

But when he'd made the suggestion as the players were about to leave London, Ann gently explained that she didn't think she and Tolly could ever live in an old house again, not after what had happened at

Malfurneaux Place.

"Besides, you are not a scullery boy any more. You are a gentleman now, Jem." Ann had scrambled up next to Tolly on the slatted seat at the front of one of Gabriel Jericho's huge wagons, before adding, "And I'm afraid that probably means you are going to have to learn how to be one."

"She's right, as usual!" Tolly had grinned down at him, Cleo on his shoulder. "Don't worry. We'll come and see you soon. And who knows, you might even be allowed to come travelling with us occasionally – if your mother agrees." The dark boy had looked anxiously at Sarah who was standing in the street next to Jem.

She'd nodded and laughed. "Of course. I know he will always be among friends if he is with you and Mr Jericho, but he… *we* have responsibilities now."

A shout had come from somewhere ahead. The horses had jerked their heads and the wagon lurched forward. "But remember," Sarah had called, as the giant wheels rumbled and clattered on the uneven stones, "you will always be welcome in our home. Always."

Tolly had waved and flicked the reins, while Cleo chirruped and leaped deftly from his shoulder to the curved canvas roof of the wagon. Ann had leaned out and reached down for Jem's hand. She didn't look at him, but she gripped tightly. He'd run alongside for a little way, feeling the delicate bones of her fingers curled in his. Then, eventually, he'd dropped her hand and stood watching as Gabriel Jericho's Theatrical Circus rumbled away in a cloud of dust.

He'd raised his hand and waved, but found he couldn't make a sound.

Jem banished the memory from his mind and concentrated on the view from the window. Was that a shadow on the road?

Boom!

A giant crack of something like thunder sounded overhead and the tiles on the turret roof rattled. Then the sky was suddenly filled with the most brilliant and extraordinary array of colours – a rippling, rainbow-like curtain that danced and shimmered in the air above the meadow. Amazed, Jem watched the lights flicker and saw that little flecks of gold and silver were coming to rest on the stone windowsill in front of him.

Down in the yard, several servants were gathered, gazing upward, open-mouthed, at the dazzling display. Eliza the chambermaid put out her hand and tried to catch the falling, fluttering glitter.

Jem looked up again and back at the road. He

narrowed his eyes – now there was a definite shape in the distance. Another huge blast sounded overhead and more vivid colours whirled about in the sky. He loosened the catch and pushed the window open, leaning out a little way for a better view. He made sure his knees were tucked firmly against the back of the window seat and gripped the frame tightly. His fear of heights had not improved.

The freezing air made him gasp, but now he was grinning from ear to ear as the shadow on the road sharpened into a familiar sight.

"I know that's you, Gabriel!" he thought to himself as the air popped and crackled and thousands of golden lights fizzled above the wagons that approached Goldings House. "You always know how to make an entrance."

Jem took in a deep gulp of sharp, smoky air laced with bonfire and gunpowder and thought he had never tasted anything so good. Before he had the chance to pull the window shut, he heard excited voices from below and the clatter of feet on the stairs.

"They are here. Make ready – the players have arrived!"

CHAPTER
THREE

"… and in Norwich we performed in the Market Square and some of the women mistook Cleo for a very hairy child. Do you remember what they said?"

Tolly grinned at Ann and nodded. "That if she belonged to them they'd shave her face at least, 'the poor little mite'." Tolly mimicked the soft country burr of the Eastern folk and leaned across to tickle Cleo's head. The small monkey was curled neatly in Jem's lap. "Can you imagine doing that to her, or getting her to sit still to try!"

They laughed and Cleo looked up at each of them in turn, her clever, black-button eyes gleaming in the firelight.

The three children and "the poor little mite" were sitting cross-legged in front of a crackling hearth in a square, wood-panelled room just off the Great Hall. They had been banished from the preparations for the celebrations because Cleo had taken a liking to the holly garlands – most specifically, the berries. She had been picking them off and throwing them, very accurately, at the people busy in the hall below.

Jem stroked Cleo's rounded back and looked at his friends. Ann's pale hair shone in the firelight and her green eyes were bright and merry. Instead of the desperate, hollow-cheeked waif he had known, she now glowed with health and happiness. Tolly was different too: he seemed taller than ever, confident and contented. Jem knew why – among the players Tolly had found a home and a family.

For a moment the image of Malfurneaux Place seared into his mind. The hideous ancient building with its twisted, carved timbers and watchful black windows loomed over him. The double doors swung silently open…

Jem shook his head roughly to make the picture go away. No wonder Tolly and Ann had changed. When they were the prisoners of Count Cazalon, it was as if his house – Malfurneaux Place – was slowly sucking the life out of them. He shuddered involuntarily. Despite the heat of the fire it seemed the room had suddenly grown cold. Ann pulled her red shawl around her shoulders, leaned forward and poked the log glowing on the hearth with an iron. Golden sparks flew upwards.

"There. That's better," she said, settling back.

"Don't think about it." Tolly's voice was warm and calm. "We have a pact never to talk about that place or that man. If you let those things come creeping back into your mind it gives them a power – makes them come alive again. I know it's hard, but it is the best thing to do."

Jem looked across at Tolly and nodded, then realised what his friend had just done. "So you're still an excellent mind-reader? I bet that's useful for Gabriel!"

Ann clapped her hands and leaned forward. "He's brilliant, Jem, not just with the animals – you remember how he was with the lions? – well, it turns out that Tolly is a marvellous actor as well. Gabriel says he could be a new star in the making. Next year he's going to give him some leading roles. That's right, isn't it?"

"I'm nothing special. Gabriel's just being kind." Tolly shifted position and stretched his long legs out in front of him.

"That's not true and you know it! Gabriel Jericho is a businessman through and through. If he says you're good, you are!"

Jem felt a pang of envy. His friends were out on the road living the sort of life he had always dreamed of. They were free while he was stuck in the schoolroom with Dr Speight and his fusty books and musty robes. Even his weekly fencing lessons with Master Jalbert seemed dull in comparison.

"And what about you, Jem? Have you seen your father?" Tolly asked.

Jem realised, guiltily, that Tolly had picked up his thoughts again. He chewed his lip and fondled Cleo's ears. "No, I haven't seen him since we came back here. He… he has sent a fencing master to teach me and I am to have my pick of the new foals in the royal stable in the spring because I am going to learn to ride like a proper gentleman, not like a farm hand. But…" He faltered. The truth of the matter was that beyond a couple of brief letters – clearly dictated to a court scribe – he had heard nothing from his father, the king.

"He must be very busy. I'm sure he thinks about you often." Ann spoke gently. She smiled and cocked her head to one side so that her long white hair brushed the painted wooden floor. "We all have different paths to follow." She looked around and up at the intricate plaster ceiling overhead. Jem often thought the plump white fruits and curling vines looked like one of Pig Face's confectionery creations.

He didn't know where the Duke of Bellingdon's fat cook was now, but he was glad that little Simeon, the kitchen boy at Ludlow House, and the only person Pig Face had bullied as much as Jem, was here at Goldings and would one day be his steward. The days when he and his mother had been servants themselves in the Duke's old mansion in the City of London seemed such a long time ago now. To Jem it felt like a different life lived by a different boy.

"Jem, you are training to be a gentleman, and I know you will be a very good one. You'll have to take care of all this…" Ann gestured at the ceiling and the panelled walls, "… and your people too."

As if on cue, a huge laugh came from the hall beyond and Eliza's broad, red-cheeked face appeared around the door. "Your friend Mr Jericho is a very wicked man, Master Jeremy. I hope you know what you and your mother are letting us all in for this evening. I've never heard such… Ooh!"

Eliza jumped as Gabriel sidled past her and into the room. He was wearing a broad-brimmed hat with a huge red feather and a trailing travel cloak.

"So this is where you've all been hiding, is it?" He thumped over to the fire and plonked himself down next to Jem, stretching his hands out to the flames.

"Lovely place you have here. Bit of a surprise to find you own all this, eh?"

Jem grinned broadly as the burly showman swept off his hat, loosened his cloak and began to pull off his boots. "Gabriel! It's so good to see you!"

"Well, we've missed you too, lad. I'm always saying to these two it's not the same without you. Even if you are a lordling, there's always a place for you with us – if you've a mind to it."

"It's true, he often says you would have made a good player." Tolly reached across to brush a glowing cinder that had popped from the fire away from the end of Cleo's tail.

Jem spluttered, "But I wasn't much of an actor!"

"Never you mind that – you're a fine-looking lad and that's what the girls come to see a play for these days." Gabriel's brown eyes twinkled mischievously. "What do you say, Ann?"

Her pale cheeks flushed. For the first time ever, as far as Jem could remember, she seemed to be stuck for words.

Gabriel laughed and the deep, hearty sound made Jem smile from ear to ear. He felt warmth tingle through every part of his body and he knew it wasn't from the heat of the fire. "I am so glad you've all come. My mother kept it secret until yesterday. I don't know how she did it."

"You couldn't hold a proper Twelfth Night feast in the old style without players! Of course your mother wanted us here. We're the finest mummers in the country." Gabriel slapped Jem's back. "And she knew how important it was to you, lad. We are your Twelfth Night gift."

Jem sighed contentedly, stretched his arms out behind him and leaned back, beaming at his friends.

"I have another gift for you too, Jem," Ann said. "I've been making costumes for us." Cleo chirruped and jumped into the midst of the group. "Costumes for all four of us," Ann continued, laughing at the monkey's enquiring expression. "Really, Tolly, I swear that sometimes she's a better mind-reader than you!"

Gabriel shuffled back from the fire on his large bottom. Jem heard the big man's knees crack as he stood up. "Mind-reading, is it? I'll tell you three something in confidence now…" He tapped a finger against the side of his nose. "I've got something rather special prepared for this evening – a surprise, and that's all I'm going to say." He narrowed his eyes and looked pointedly at Tolly. "And before you, or that monkey, go rummaging around in my head to try to find out what it is, I'm going to leave you."

He plonked the feathered hat back on his head, gathered up his boots and padded in his thick woollen socks back towards the door to the Great Hall.

Jem leaped to his feet. "You can't go now! You have to tell us more. What's going to happen tonight?"

Gabriel removed his hat again and performed a sweeping theatrical bow.

"All I'm going to say, Lord Jeremy, is this: tonight Goldings House will witness something so extraordinary, something so marvellous, something so completely, stupendously amazing that by dawn tomorrow Gabriel Jericho and his Theatrical Circus will be the toast of the county. And now, if you'll excuse me, I have lions to see to."

The showman clapped his hat back on his head, pulled his cloak around him and swept from the room.

CHAPTER FOUR

"Jem, this is wonderful!"

Sarah's blue eyes sparkled as she and Jem watched the celebrations in the hall below from their vantage point halfway up the wide oak staircase. The air was full of the sound of music and laughter, and thick with the scent of spices and burning wood. In the great hearth a giant Yule log cut from an old apple tree filled the hall with the comforting smell of fruit-sweetened smoke.

Hundreds of fat candles balanced carefully on beams and in every nook and cranny flooded the hall with a soft golden glow. As guests and players moved around, their colourful costumes – some strewn with sequins or tiny glittering mirrors – threw shimmering points of light onto the panelled walls.

"It's just as it was when I was a girl," Sarah continued. "Jamie and I loved the Twelfth Night feast. My grandfather, your great-grandfather, kept it in the old way and people came from all over the county to celebrate with us. But when he died and my father inherited Goldings, he changed things. He didn't approve of the past, you see. He…" Sarah stopped herself and pointed with her delicate bird-head mask. "Look – the cockatrice!"

Jem followed her gaze. Four men carrying a broad silver platter on their shoulders entered the hall. Through the crowd, he couldn't quite make sense of the peculiar, feathered shape sitting on top of the platter.

"What is it?" he asked as the men swayed towards them.

"It's for the feast. My grandfather always had our cooks prepare a cockatrice to feed as many people as possible. It's a mythical beast like a dragon – but, of course, dragons don't exist so our Goldings cockatrice has the head of a stag, the body of a pig, the wings of a cockerel, the front legs of a sheep and the haunches of a bull. I told the cook exactly how to make it. Look, here it is. Isn't it splendid?"

Jem looked down in silence. The men paused and dipped respectfully in front of Sarah and Jem before setting the edible monster down at the centre of a long table piled high with tarts, pastries, meats, cheeses and bread.

Everyone burst into whoops of delight as the

strange creature took prime position, but all Jem could think of at that moment were the strange, deformed creatures that Count Cazalon had created for his own amusement – the poor, wretched, sewn-together things he had seen inside Malfurneaux Place.

"Don't, Jem!" Tolly's voice sounded clearly in his head. "Remember what I said earlier. Don't let the bad thoughts in."

Jem looked down at the hall, but he couldn't see Tolly anywhere.

A masked golden figure at the centre of the hall waved at him and the voice came again. "I'm here and Ann's waiting outside with your costume. Come on."

Grateful to get away from the cockatrice, Jem turned to Sarah. "Can I go with Tolly? Ann has my costume – it's a surprise."

"Of course. I wonder what you'll be? Come and show me."

He took a step down but then Sarah called out, "Wait, I almost forgot. I wanted to give you this tonight." She felt into the folds of her dress and held out her hand. "It belonged to my grandfather – my father never wore it. He said it was ungodly, but Jamie always wore it about his neck."

Jem stepped back up to be level with her again.

"What is it?" He had to shout because the jolly music was becoming louder. People were dancing now.

Sarah shook her head and smiled. "I'm not sure. It's very old, that's all I know. It was always worn by the eldest Verrers boy – until… Now it's yours. Wear it."

She reached up to loop the golden chain over his head and Jem took the heavy, coin-sized medal in his hand. It was studded with rough jewels and around the edge was an inscription in letters he didn't recognise.

"Keep it safe, Jem. Now, I must go. One of us, at least, must attend to our guests." Sarah reached up to affectionately ruffle his hair. She grinned as he pulled a face. "One day soon I won't be able to do that. You are growing so tall!" She raised the neat feathery mask to her face and stepped down the stairs. As she moved into the throng, people began to clap and call her name.

Jem tucked the medal into his shirt and watched with delight as Gabriel, dressed in a magnificent breastplate and helmet, caught his mother's hand, kissed it and whisked her off into a group of swirling dancers. Tonight was going to be wonderful. He knew it.

Ann made a final adjustment to the hem of the cloak. "You have definitely got taller, Jem – just like Tolly. You two are sprouting like birch trees!" She stood up, brushed her skirt and surveyed her handiwork. "You look wonderful. I knew that red and gold would be right. What do you think, Tolly?"

Tolly shuffled back on the bunk in the curved caravan so that he could see Jem from head to foot and nodded. "You look like a prince from the old tales my father used to tell. Is it heavy?"

Jem shook his head. "No, it's very easy to move around in. And the sword is wonderful." He patted the hilt of the curved blade, which was carved into the head of a falcon with glinting red glass eyes. It hung from a thick golden band at his waist.

"Gabriel found that in his stores. It's only painted wood. This is the final touch." Ann reached up to a shelf above the bunk. The candle lantern swayed as she produced a feathered turban made from twisted lengths of brilliantly patterned silk.

"It's not a crown exactly – not like your father's, anyway – but I thought that a king from the East wouldn't wear one like that. Try it."

Jem took the turban and pushed it down over

his springy black curls. It felt as if he was wearing a bolster on his head. He hoped he wouldn't have to wear it all night. Jem looked across at Tolly on the bunk. The dark boy grinned and winked.

"She's worked really hard. I've been her dummy for the past two weeks. I had to model your costume."

"And it's perfect!" Ann reached up to brush a speck from Jem's shoulder. "So, now do you see? Tonight at the Twelfth Night feast we will be the Magi – the three kings. What do you think of Tolly's costume?"

Jem looked at the horned lion mask sitting beside his friend. Cleo was curled up inside it, her long tail poking out. The little monkey had clearly decided to make it her nest.

When Tolly put the mask on, it covered half of his face so that only the tip of his nose and his mouth showed. The mane, which hung over his shoulders and stretched halfway down his back, was made from hundreds of overlapping golden discs that jingled when he moved.

"It's brilliant – I didn't recognise him in the great hall. Did you make the mask too?"

Ann nodded. "Along with the rest of his costume – the toga and the winged sandals. He is the king of the desert lands."

She knelt beside the bunk, reached down and pulled out something wrapped in cloth. "And, finally, I am to be the king of the forests." Carefully she unfolded the bundle to reveal an incredibly delicate silver crown – a lattice of curling twigs and vines. Tiny golden acorns and leaf-green jewels quivered gently as Ann held the crown up to catch the lamplight. Jem thought it was almost like a living, growing thing.

Ann placed the crown at the foot of the bunk bed and began to wind her thick white hair into a tight ball at the back of her head. She kicked the little door of her caravan open with her foot and it swung back to reveal Goldings House across the courtyard – every window glowing with light.

The sound of fiddles and pipes and the scent of roasting meat wafted across the snow. Jem's mouth began to water. He had completely forgotten the cockatrice.

"Now, you two must wait outside for a moment while I change." Ann grinned and her words misted in the sudden inrush of midwinter air. "A king doesn't wear a dress!"

"Do you think that's what Gabriel meant when he told us about the surprise?"

Jem gasped as an acrobat dangling from a trapeze swooped above his head. The grinning man was carrying flaming torches in both hands. As he swung back, the man curled up on himself, twisted in mid-air and tossed the torches to another performer swinging from the opposite side of the hall. The crowd below cheered and clapped.

Ann ducked involuntarily as the acrobats overhead performed their routine for a third time. "I know that Saro and Cornelius have been practising in secret for the last couple of weeks. Even on Christmas Day they went up on the ropes in the camp and everyone was forbidden to watch. But we've seen this before, haven't we, Tolly?"

Tolly took a huge bite out of the roasted chicken leg in his hand and nodded. "It's their usual routine. There must be more to come." He licked his fingers. "This is truly excellent, Jem. You must dine like a lord every day now!"

Jem looked up at the acrobats and felt another small stab of envy as he thought of his friends. This amazing display must be as commonplace for them as Dr Speight and his lessons were for him.

A sudden trumpet blast sounded, clear and high.

The hall fell silent as the double doors leading out to the kitchens opened to reveal a huge multi-layered cake standing on a wheeled wooden board. As tall as a man and broad as an ox, the massive pyramid of icing sugar was pushed slowly to the centre of the room by a party of beaming servants, Simeon among them.

There were murmurs of appreciation as the cake juddered to a halt.

Jem waved at Simeon and the small boy scurried over. "It was Eliza's idea, Jem, er… sir," he whispered. "In the old days, when Sarah… sorry, when the mistress was a girl here, they always had a Twelfth Night cake. There's a golden bean hidden in there somewhere and whoever finds it is the king of the feast. For the rest of the night they can tell everyone what to do. We all get a piece so it doesn't matter who finds it." Simeon gazed admiringly at the towering cake. Jem was able to read Simeon's mind at that moment as easily as Tolly could.

Gabriel Jericho led Sarah towards the cake. The showman raised his hands and the murmuring stopped. "Now, everyone," he began in a deep voice that carried to every corner of the hall, "I'm sure we are very grateful to our hosts this evening for this fine food and the wonderful old-style celebrations." People cheered and Jem saw his mother blush with pleasure. Gabriel raised his hands again and continued. "And to show our appreciation, and to bring good fortune to this house and its people, we will sing the old Twelfth Night song while the cake is divided." He turned, bowed to Sarah and handed her a knife.

She hesitated for a moment and then took a step towards the cake. She began to saw away at the lowest tier until the icing sugar crumbled and the delicious dark fruit was revealed. Gabriel began to sing and very soon all the older folk in the hall were joining hands and singing with him.

"We have travelled far and wide,
to bring you cheer on this dark night.
We link our hands and raise a cry
to turn away the evil eye.
Let no malice harm this place
for we celebrate with grace.

Come share our food, come share our ale

to welcome New Year with wassail.
Now moon and stars shine bright and clear
to banish bane and welcome cheer."

Jem didn't recognise the song, but after hearing it repeated several times as the cake was handed about the hall, he, Tolly and Ann began to sing too. Something about the simple tune made him feel safe and protected. Like everyone else, he linked hands, Tolly and Ann on either side of him, and only broke the chain when a portion of cake came to him. He crammed the spiced fruit into his mouth and continued to hum along to the song. The cake was delicious. Ann bent down to feed some of her slice to Cleo who was staring imploringly up at the three of them in turn.

"Here you are, little one."

Cleo chirruped and plucked the morsel from Ann's fingers. Pausing briefly to smell it, she pushed the cake greedily into her mouth. She shrieked immediately and spat it out. There on the floor in front of her was a rounded golden bean.

Cleo prodded it suspiciously and then looked accusingly at Ann. The people around the children began to laugh.

"We can't have a monkey for a king," an old man

chuckled. "'T'int right."

Cleo chirped again and took the bean in her paw. She cocked her head from side to side and looked up at Jem, then at Tolly and then jumped onto Ann's shoulder and dangled the bean in front of her nose.

The old man spoke again. "Well, it looks like the little monkey has chosen for us. We have our Twelfth Night Queen."

Soon the cry was taken up by everyone in the hall. "A queen! We have a queen!"

The space in front of Ann cleared as if by magic as people parted to either side of the hall.

"What do I do now?" Ann's green eyes were huge as she looked at the expectant faces of the guests. Jem could tell that she was secretly thrilled.

"I think that's your throne." Tolly pointed to the far side of the hall where a heavily carved chair was set on a large box covered with red cloth. The back of the chair was decorated with ribbons and sprigs of holly.

"Go on then." He nudged her forward. "I think you'd better go and sit on it. That's what they're all waiting for."

"I'm not going without you two by my side." Ann took hold of Jem's right hand and Tolly's left. Jem felt a tingle of warmth shoot up his arm and across his shoulders as the three of them stood together. Then, amid the deafening sound of cheers, stamping and clapping, they walked through the parted crowd with Cleo following behind. The grinning boys made low bows as Ann clambered up onto the red box and turned to face the gathering. She smiled shyly, then, emboldened by the sight of the beaming faces about her, she tried a regal wave. The crowd cheered, there were even a couple of appreciative whistles. Ann grinned in delight. Candlelight sparked off the jewels set into her filigree crown and an escaped lock of silver-white hair shone like the moon.

For a moment Jem was reminded of something – no, *someone*. The painting of Ann's mother Elizabeth that had hung in the peculiar corridor at Malfurneaux Place framed itself in his mind. He thought again how much Ann resembled her. It must have been painted when they were about the same age.

Tolly nudged his arm. "Well, it certainly looks like Cleo made the right choice. Ann's loving this." Below his mask, Tolly's mouth curled into a generous smile. "Just look at her!"

"And what is your first command, so please Your Majesty?" Gabriel's deep, amused voice boomed from somewhere at the back of the hall. Ann shaded her eyes and went up on tiptoe, looking about. Gabriel spoke again. "Pray silence for our queen's first proclamation."

The shouting and clapping stopped and scores of eager faces turned towards her. Ann cleared her throat. "I... I..." She paused and looked down at Jem and Tolly. "What shall I say?" she whispered urgently.

Jem grinned mischievously. "Say whatever you like. You're usually very good at giving orders, so I'm sure it will come naturally to you!" He heard Tolly stifle a laugh.

Ann pulled a face at Jem and then looked out at the hall. Standing as straight and tall as she could, she swept aside her velvet cloak to reveal her costume of knee boots and sea-green breeches, planted her hands on her hips and took a deep breath.

"I... I command the dancing to continue. Musicians, play!"

The crowd roared its approval. As the pipers and fiddle players struck up a rowdy country tune, paper streamers were tossed into the air while the acrobats swung backwards and forwards, casting down handfuls of gilded nuts and currants.

Jem found himself caught by the hand and pulled into the centre of the hall. Through the swirling crowd he caught sight of Tolly's golden mask weaving backwards and forwards in the pattern of the dance. Ann was now seated happily on the throne, feeding the rest of her cake to Cleo, who perched on one of the arms. Jem decided that next time he whirled past he would drag Ann into the ring.

But just as he was about to loop back past the throne again, three echoing knocks sounded on the doors to the hall. The noise was loud and heavy that the thuds rang out above the music and laughter. The dancing came to a confused, ragged halt as the pounding came again and the musicians stopped playing.

Gabriel walked towards the doors. "Who's there?" he demanded.

There was a long silence before the answer came from what seemed like a hundred voices speaking at once. "We have come." The voices were cracked and whispery, making the hairs on the back of Jem's neck rise. "We have travelled far and wide. Will you open your doors to us this night?"

"Let them enter. I command it!" Jem turned to see Ann standing on the dais – her face alight with excitement. "Come on, Gabriel," she continued. "You can't keep us waiting any more. It won't be Twelfth Night for much longer, it's almost midnight. Open the doors."

Of course! Jem grinned. Gabriel's surprise! He turned back to Gabriel and was puzzled to see the big man hesitate for a second. Two other guests were already following Ann's royal command. The chuckling men swung back the great doors of Goldings House, calling out, "Welcome, friends!"

A sharp gust of bone-numbing air entered the hall and snow drifted across the threshold. A vast black shape filled the doorway. The crowd murmured as the shape paused and swayed for a moment before sweeping forwards, rustling into the very centre of the hall.

Jem tried to make sense of what he was looking at. The thing was oval – about eight feet long and fringed with layers of black shredded material like a beggar woman's skirts. It looked a little like a ship with a prow and a stern, but as Jem stared he realised that it was actually more like a creature with a pointed head and a trailing, knotted tail. Two crude circles were painted in white on the thing's black head to resemble eyes.

Behind it swarmed a troupe of actors dressed in

a patchwork of rags and dead leaves. Each one of them wore a mask – the horned skull of a massive stag. Four of the stag men carried staves with what looked like grinning human skulls mounted on the top. These men – who were taller than anyone else in the room – pushed through the crowd and positioned themselves watchfully in the corners while the others formed a ring around the black thing.

It stood stock still for a moment. Then it shook itself and little bells rang out from under the skirts. It began to revolve slowly, the "head" swaying from side to side as if the painted eyes were seeking something. When the creature's head was level with Ann's throne it stopped... and then it shivered, jangled and slowly tipped forward into a deep bow.

"Why 'tis an 'Oss!" An old woman standing beside Ann's throne grinned a toothless smile and shuffled forward. "I haven't seen one of these since I was a girl. It was always traditional, see, for the Twelfth Night mummers to bring in the 'Obby 'Oss for the luck of it. I never thought I'd live to see one again. I wonder who's under there tonight. It takes a strong man to dance under all that."

As if in agreement, the 'Oss shook itself and jingled again and music began to play. The pipers and fiddlers looked around in confusion – and Jem realised it wasn't coming from them.

The sound was low at first, but the strange music grew louder and faster, and the 'Oss began to slowly dip and spin, never moving from the centre of the hall. People gathered around it, swaying in time to the peculiar jagged rhythm. Some of them started to clap and stamp their feet. One of the stag men grabbed a woman's hand, pulled her from the crowd and whirled her around and around until she was standing in front of the black creature's head. It paused and swayed in front of her for a moment, then it reared up and swallowed her beneath its ragged black skirts.

People cried out as she was engulfed, but there was laughter moments later when she reappeared, pink-faced and chuckling. Gradually the music grew faster and wilder. Jem found himself stamping his feet and clapping along with everyone else.

But as he swayed on the fringes of the circle there was something... something...

Now the 'Oss was choosing its own partners, dipping low in front of them – rustling its skirts and jingling its bells in invitation. People were delighted to be selected, shrieking as the blackness folded over their heads only to be released seconds later, breathless and laughing on the far side of the circle.

The 'Oss spun round again. It came to a halt before Ann's throne once more, moving gently from side to side. Ann clapped her hands to her face and grinned, her green eyes sparkling as she stood up. Cleo leaped from her lap and cowered behind the chair. Jem rubbed his eyes – the air suddenly seemed thick and scented with something both sweet and rancid. The hall filled with a grey mist that shrouded all the colours in the room. He blinked hard – the shapes of the people around him seemed to be distorting and stretching. Jem's temples started to throb – surely this wasn't quite right? He looked for Tolly. Could he feel it too?

One of the stag men moved towards the throne and offered Ann his hand. Beneath the stag man's cloak Jem caught sight of something… something hideous, something that was gnarled and twisted like a claw.

Jem opened his mouth to shout a warning, but nothing came. At the same moment the stag man turned to stare at him. A single amber eye glinted coldly from the depths of the flaking bone mask.

"This is all wrong. We must stop her!" Tolly's

voice sounded in Jem's head. He tried to turn and find his friend in the crowd, but his body wouldn't obey him. He was still clapping and swaying in the circle around the 'Oss. On the far side of the circle he could see Gabriel doing exactly the same thing, but the tortured look on the showman's face sent a finger of ice down Jem's spine.

The stag man helped Ann down from the dais and escorted her the little way to the spot directly in front of the 'Oss. The music became screeching and discordant. Jem wanted to cover his ears but he couldn't make his hands do anything other than clap. Instead, he watched in horror as the stag man pushed Ann forward. Jem saw she wasn't smiling now, her eyes were wide with fear as the 'Oss reared up and raised its tattered skirts high above her head before swallowing her whole. For a moment the 'Oss froze, then it began to spin faster and faster until it was just a blurred shadow at the centre of the hall.

The music halted and the black creature stopped dead, hovering for just a second before falling flat to the floor. At exactly the same moment every light burning in the room was extinguished – every candle, every taper, every torch. Even the massive

Yule log in the hearth.

Blindly, Jem reached out through the darkness. He heard screams and shouts as terrified people around him bumped into each other. Then he felt a hand grip his arm.

"Jem, is that you? It's me, Tolly."

A light flared next to them – Gabriel, with a flaming torch in his hand. His expression was unreadable, his mouth set in a grim line. "This way, boys – over here."

Pushing through the confusion, he led them over to the flattened black oval of cloth. It looked like a wide dark pool at the centre of the hall. He tested it warily with his foot, but it didn't move, it just emitted a sweet, rancid smell like rotting meat. Gabriel muttered something under his breath then held the torch high above his head. He scanned the agitated crowd and Jem followed his gaze.

Outside, the bell in the tower over the stable block began to chime. It was midnight.

There was no doubt about it – Ann had vanished. And so had all the stag-headed mummers.

CHAPTER
FIVE

"Who were they?" Jem heard the tremor in his own voice.

"I think the question is *what* were they?" Tolly hugged a wriggling Cleo close to his chest. Everyone was silent now.

"I'll tell you what they weren't. They weren't part of the surprise.' Gabriel's voice was flat. 'Balthazar and Juno were to bring the elephant into the courtyard on the last stroke of midnight and I was supposed to lead everyone out to see it – not let anyone in." His torch showed the fear in their faces. The tang of something putrid lingered in the cold air, smothering the comforting fruit-wood scent of the fire.

"Why take Ann and no one else?" Tolly loosened his grip on Cleo, but now she buried herself into his neck. Jem noticed she was unusually still – even her tail hung limp and straight. Only her nose twitched at the rank smell in the hall.

"They can't have gone far with her. We must organise a search party. There are hunting dogs in the kennels behind the stables. Bess and Musket can follow any trail. What do you say?" Jem looked at Gabriel.

The showman was staring at the pool of black cloth at his feet.

"What do you think, Gabriel?" Jem asked again urgently. He was suddenly very sure that time was important. "We can't afford to waste a moment."

"I think Tolly is right." Gabriel clapped a hand to his head. "I was a fool! That was magic, Jem – the darkest I've seen in many a year. Twelfth Night is a time when the powers, be they good or bad, are strong - I should have been wary." He shook his head. "I'm not sure your dogs will pick up her trail, no matter how keen their noses are."

"We have to try something!" Jem kicked the material and the stench grew stronger. "We can't just stand here in the dark, we have to do something – and quickly. Tolly, what do you say?"

Tolly pulled off the golden mask. His dark skin was grey in the dim light and his eyes were huge. Cleo whickered mournfully and crept to his shoulder where she hunched low.

"Jem's right, Gabriel. Those things were… unnatural, but we have to do something. Animals sense things – Cleo always does. Using the dogs is as good a suggestion as any. It could be our only chance."

"Can you feel her?" Jem looked at Tolly hopefully, but his friend didn't reply.

Sarah stepped into the little circle of light cast by Gabriel's torch. "Wha…What just happened? My head… It feels as if it's about to split in two." She put her fingers to her temples. "It's all confused, like a hideous dream. Where's Ann?"

"The little one has vanished, ma'am." Gabriel took a deep breath. "The lads here are for organising a search, led by your dogs."

Sarah nodded. "Our head groom reckons Musket is the best tracker in the county."

"Exactly! We just need something to give them her scent…" Jem was already striding towards the door. "We can take something from the caravan. Tolly, come and help me choose." He glanced at Gabriel who was rubbing his stubbled chin, the network of crinkles around his eyes showing deeper than ever before. The showman looked as if he had aged ten years in the past five minutes.

"I should have known. I felt it was all wrong from that first knock. We shouldn't have let them in." He punched his left palm with his right fist. "This was my fault, lads."

Jem loped back across the stone floor and gripped Gabriel's arm. "No. This is my house – *I* should have protected her. We'll organise a search party from the troupe and the guests. Anyone willing to help should be ready to leave in five minutes. We'll gather in the courtyard. Tolly and I will bring up Bess and Musket."

The boys pounded towards the door. As Jem threw it open he paused. A shiver of doubt ran through him. Would they really be able to track Ann?

He squared his shoulders and stepped into the night, calling out in a voice that was much more confident than he felt, First edition "Make sure everyone is warmly dressed. It's snowing out here."

Ann's caravan was on the far side of the circle of carts in the courtyard. A red glass lamp still flickered above the small curved doorway.

"Her shawl – that would be best," said Tolly, leading the way up the painted steps.

As he pushed the door open, Cleo squealed and leaped from his shoulder. When Jem followed them both inside, the little monkey was scrabbling about in the bedclothes, sniffing and burrowing as if she hoped to find Ann hidden there.

Tolly moved to the back of the caravan where a

cupboard decorated with painted roses was set into the wall, forming an alcove over the bed.

"Ann's very tidy – she's always scolding me about the state of my own caravan. This is where she keeps her clothes." He reached up and opened the door. "Here it is. She wears it every day." He pulled down a roll of red woollen cloth and crushed it to his nose. "The dogs won't mistake her – and I can help them too. I'll try to… explain how important it is to find her."

"Of course!" Jem felt a first flicker of hope. "You can talk to animals, can't you? I'd forgotten about the lions. That first time when I visited Gabriel's camp you climbed into the cage with them! I'd thought you were mad and about to be eaten alive, but they did exactly what you asked them to do."

Tolly handed Jem the shawl. "I wouldn't call it *talking* exactly; it's more like the way I read people's thoughts. Not in words – *feelings* is more accurate. The closer I am to a person or creature the easier it is to see into their mind."

Jem nodded. "Well, whatever it is you do, Tolly, it must help. Come on!"

"No, wait a minute. I can't search dressed like this…" Tolly looked down at his golden winged sandals, his black toes poking out at the ends. "And nor can you,

57

Jem – we'll freeze to death before we've gone a mile. I'll fetch some travel clothes from my caravan. You can borrow some of mine. It will be quicker."

"Good idea."

The bell in the clock tower struck the quarter as if to remind them that time was slipping through their fingers.

Tolly dipped out through the door. Cleo watched from the middle of the bed as Jem threw his cloak into a corner and shrugged the tunic Ann had made over his head.

Moments later Tolly was back with a bundle of clothes in his arms.

"Here. There's a thick cloak for each of us, long breeches and other warm things. I brought some riding boots as well; one of the players gave them to me, though they're a bit big for my feet. I think they'll fit you."

The boys dressed speedily, their numb fingers fumbling at ties and laces. Jem gave up trying to fasten everything properly. Instead, impatient to leave, he just wrapped himself in the layers.

"Right. Let's get the dogs from the kennels. Gabriel should have everyone ready by now." He ducked through the doorway and jumped down to the snowy stones of the courtyard.

But Tolly didn't follow. "Come on!" Jem frowned, called again then climbed back up the steps.

"It's Cleo," Tolly said. "She won't come to me."

Cleo was now squeezed into the tiny gap between the top of the cupboard over Ann's bed and the canvas caravan roof. Her eyes gleamed in the soft lamplight.

"Here girl…" Tolly held out his hand gently so that she could smell his fingertips, but instead of jumping onto his arm as usual, Cleo whickered and plunged to the quilt, then dropped lightly to the boarded floor and disappeared under the bed.

"We'll have to leave her." Jem was anxious to be off. "She'll be safe here."

"No!" Tolly spun about, his eyes blazing. "I can't. She and Ann are all I…" He faltered. "Cleo has to come too. It's important."

Jem scowled. He wanted to shout about wasting time, but knew Tolly was deadly serious. He bit his lip as his friend knelt down and moved the trailing end of the quilt aside.

"Cleo – come to me, little one." Tolly spoke softly. There was a scuffling sound from beneath the bed and then a scraping, bumping noise as something rolled out across the boards.

It wasn't Cleo.

The boys stared at the object in horror.

"I can't believe Ann kept that thing!" Jem shuddered and moved the tip of his boot away from Count Cazalon's nubbled black staff. The crystal bird-head set at its tip glinted in the lamplight.

Jem remembered the first time he had seen the staff at Malfurneaux Place, when the count had interviewed him in front of the roaring fire. The count had said it was made from the spine of a shark. "Sharp-toothed wolf of the sea."

As he thought of the words, Jem felt a horribly familiar creeping sensation under his scalp. The Eye of Ra flared in his heel. He gasped and shifted the weight from his stinging foot – the place where Ann, in the form of a mouse, had once nibbled the ancient mark of protection into his skin. He tore his eyes from the crystal bird and looked at Tolly.

"I knew she had it, Jem. I just didn't know it was under the bed." A black-and-white ball of fur emerged from under the quilt edge. "Ah, come on, Cleo." Tolly reached to stroke her nose. "We have to go." He tried to catch hold of her, but she scampered aside, seating herself beside the end of Cazalon's staff. She stared at the boys in turn and made a low keening noise.

"This is ridiculous." Jem was angry and frustrated now. "Just grab her."

"No… she…" Tolly shook his head and held out a hand. Cleo wrapped her tiny digits round his thumb. "It's the staff, Jem. She's trying to tell us something about it. Only I can't quite…"

Cleo released Tolly's thumb and stretched her paw slowly towards the staff. She took a great gulping breath, trembled and touched it. Immediately she shrieked in pain, as if she had been burned. The scream turned into a long, low wail of terror, accompanied by a faint crackling, sizzling noise.

Cleo's eyes rolled back in their sockets so that only the whites showed. Her body bucked and quivered – but she didn't seem able to take her paw away from the staff.

Jem's nostrils clogged with the sickly sweet smell of burning fur and skin. He tried to kick the thing away from her, but his legs suddenly felt like lead.

Tolly lunged forward and snatched the staff up. He yelped in pain too, but managed to stagger to his feet and make for the door. Jem guessed his friend intended to hurl the thing into the snow, but at that moment the crystal bird's eyes started to pulse with a cold yellow light.

CHAPTER SIX

The caravan was filled with a low thrumming. Jem felt his whole body vibrate, from the centre of his chest to the tips of his fingers, making his stomach flip queasily. He brought his hands to his ears as the sound grew stronger.

The bird's eyes were glowing so brightly now that he blinked and looked to the floor to avoid the brilliant glare. As he did so, he caught sight of Cleo – a shivering ball of damp fur curled against a neat stack of books and papers at the foot of Ann's bed. She held her paw close to her chest and rocked back and forth.

"Drop it! Drop the staff, Tolly!" Jem tried to shout, but the words were caught in his mouth, coming out as a sort of mangled, stuttering gasp. With difficulty he forced himself to turn his head.

Tolly was rooted to the spot just in front of the door. The staff was clutched in his fist – its pointed tip wedged into a crack between the timber floor planks. He stared directly at the crystal bird-head, his eyes wide with terror.

"I can feel it... It's alive..." Tolly's body jerked as twin beams of light sprang from the crystal eyes. They shot through the air, searing into the wooden planks of the caravan wall just above Ann's bed. Jem could smell burning wood now and for a moment he was transported back to last September when Cazalon razed the timber buildings of old London from the face of the earth.

"It's e-evil. L-let go." Jem just managed to stammer out the words, but Tolly gritted his teeth and shook his head.

"Look." He pointed at the caravan wall.

The beams from the crystal eyes met at a single point that was now moving across the wood. It left a looping singed pattern in its wake that shimmered and shifted to form glowing words and shapes. Red and gold sparks flickered around the outlines of odd symbols and letters seared into the timbers. Then the burning words themselves began to move, squirming about on the wall, everything jostling and twisting to find a new place.

In the very centre, a single golden word suddenly flared brightly.

ANN

"What the...?" Jem managed to take a step forward, but Tolly caught his sleeve with his free hand.

"K-keep back. L-let it show us." His voice was cracked with pain.

Almost as soon as Ann's glowing name had appeared it faded, leaving dark marks in the plank. The burning point paused and then it veered off again, scorching madly until it had inscribed the fiery outline of a ship. The vessel seemed to glide across the wall, disappearing behind the cupboard over the bed. For a moment nothing moved, although the beam pulsed steadily like a beating heart. Then it was off again, this time twisting wildly upward and out across the ceiling.

The humming sound was now so loud the vibration was actually painful, each beat like a great kick to Jem's belly. He bent double, but couldn't tear his eyes from the canvas overhead where another single word blazed in the smouldering fabric for two seconds.

FORTUNA

He could smell something acridly familiar, though

he couldn't work out exactly what. Then the burning script zigzagged back from the ceiling to the point in the very centre of the wall where singed black letters forming *Ann* were still clear.

As he watched, the "A" burst into flames that ate into the wood until there was just a blazing circle there the size of an apple.

Every scorch mark on the wall pulsed with eerie greenish light now – and the letters began to move, coiling and rushing towards the place where the "A" had been. It was as if they were being swallowed by the glowing hole, which, in some peculiar way, seemed to stretch far beyond the wooden slats. Jem stared at the burning disc – so deep and unfathomable it was like looking into the centre of the universe.

A loose sheet of paper from Ann's stack of books whipped into the air and flattened itself against the caravan wall. It burst into flames and within seconds it was drawn into the flaming mouth. More papers began to fly and now whole books too – everything hurling itself against the wall to be devoured. Jem ducked as a woollen glove flew past his head, smacked into the wood and burst into brilliant blue flames.

At last he recognised the smell – burning flesh! Jem tore his eyes from the wall to glance at Tolly.

His hand still gripped Cazalon's staff just beneath the crystal head, but he was shaking. The boy's face was a mask of pain. His dark skin was the colour of ash and his lips were stretched back from his teeth in a rigid parody of a smile.

Jem scoured the caravan. A metal jug stood just beside the bed. Although it felt as if his limbs were moving through treacle, he forced himself to take it up. He turned to the wall and hurled the watery contents into the centre of the burning vortex.

It blinked once, like an eye, and instantly disappeared.

Tolly crumpled to the floor. There was a sickening crunch as his head caught the edge of the bed. The staff clanked as it fell to the boards.

Jem knelt beside him. "Tolly, can you hear me?" He took his friend's hand. It was hot, sticky and damp. When he looked down he was horrified to see Tolly's fingers were scalded raw, as if he had plunged his hand into a pan of boiling water. There was a deep gash above his right eyebrow and blood trickled down his cheek.

"Tolly?"

Cleo chirruped softly and shuffled across the planks to nudge her master's arm. Jem was relieved to see her concern. She, at least, seemed to have recovered. She picked at the wool scarf around Tolly's neck, all the while making little crooning noises. It did the trick.

"Cleo... Is that you? J... Jem?" Tolly opened his eyes and winced as he moved his head.

"I thought I'd lost you for a moment there." Jem dabbed at the blood on Tolly's face with his sleeve. "You'll have a nasty scar if we don't get some goose fat and nightshade on that. Eliza has some in the house."

Tolly grinned weakly. "That probably *would* kill me!" He struggled to sit upright, rubbed his head and yelped in sudden pain. He looked at his raw, blistered fingers, blinking in shock.

"When did that happen?"

"When you were gripping Cazalon's staff. First it burned Cleo, then you." Jem eyed the discarded object suspiciously. The crystal bird-head was turned away towards the underside of the bed. It was lifeless. "What was it, Tolly? What happened just now?"

"I don't know for sure. It was as if I could see things in my mind." Tolly sat up straight and stared at the wall. He frowned. "And then, as I thought them, they began to come to life... sort of. I saw a ship – well, the figurehead of a ship, anyway. I saw a red-haired woman with a star on her forehead. And I could sense Ann too, only… it wasn't her exactly. But I could see where she was."

He closed his eyes. "Danger. There is great danger. Every step is agony. There is a woman… No, a man… Feathers, bones, pestilence, flesh…"

As he spoke he swayed and his voice deepened.

"Blood. So much blood. Red everywhere covering the land – it is raining blood! Beware the man of shadows. He who walks between the worlds. He who —' Tolly began to choke. He brought his good hand to his mouth and hunched over as he hacked and spluttered. Uselessly, Jem thumped Tolly's back – there was no water to help, and Jem was worried his friend wouldn't stop.

Tolly's coughing finally lessened, and he took a ragged gulp of air. "S-something just stopped me talking. It got into my throat and…" He faltered and peered up at the wall. "What's that?"

Jem followed his gaze. The caravan wall was now almost completely bare. It was as if all the strange words had simply been scrubbed away. The only mark left was a blackened shape above the bed in the exact spot where the burning mouth had been.

He stood to examine it, tracing the scorched lines with the tip of his finger.

"What it is, Jem?"

"Er… I'm not sure. It looks like a man, but it's not. It's got the head of an animal of some sort – I don't know what exactly… It might be a dog? It's got a long snout and pointed ears?" He spun round. "I know – it's a sign! We must fetch the dogs and search for her. Do you feel well enough?"

Tolly nodded, wiped his mouth and struggled to his feet. He stared at the dog-man on the wall. "Where would you find hundreds of ships all moored together?"

"There isn't time for riddles!" Jem pulled the grey muffler tight around his neck. "Gabriel will have everyone ready in the courtyard. Come on, we need Bess and Musket."

"Wait, I'm serious, Jem. The image came into my head when I was holding the staff. Where would you see so many ships?"

Jem thumped the caravan wall in exasperation. "A port? The Pool of London is the greatest port in the world. I've seen hundreds of ships there all lined up across the river."

"Then we have to go to London – now – not waste

time searching with the dogs." Tolly swept Cleo up into his arms and kicked open the little door. "Ann is on a ship in the Pool. I'm certain of it."

CHAPTER
SEVEN

"How much further?"

Jem felt Tolly's grip tighten around his waist as the big horse clattered beneath an archway leading into the City. It was dark and very early in the morning.

"Not far. The Pool of London is that way." Jem pointed at the deserted, snowy crossroads ahead. To the right, the jagged stumps of buildings and shadowed gaps in the streets were bitter reminders of Cazalon's plot to destroy London.

"I hope you're right about this, Tolly." His breath froze on the night air. He couldn't feel the tips of his fingers curled about the reins.

There hadn't been time to tell anyone where they were going. Jem wasn't entirely sure they would have been able to explain it, and he was certain that his mother wouldn't have allowed him to take Titan. He glanced at the horse's alert, twitching ears. The creature was skittish and wary. Now they were alone in the dark city Jem began to wish he'd left a message to let his mother know where they'd gone.

He patted the horse's sweating flank. "Woah, there. Easy."

The boys had raced to the stables, avoiding the courtyard where they heard the chatter of the search party, saddled up the huge grey stallion and galloped off into the night. The ride to London had been wild and hard – and utterly exhilarating. Despite everything, a small, secret part of Jem was thrilled at the way he'd been able to manage the magnificent creature.

As Titan slowed to a trot, Jem wondered how long Gabriel and the search party had waited. Instantly he felt a pang of guilt.

"No one will mind when we bring Ann back." Tolly read his thoughts. "And don't worry. I *am* right about this. She's on a ship. I saw that very clearly."

Cazalon's staff thumped against the side of Jem's leg. Tolly had pushed it under the saddle and secured it with straps. Jem shifted. He didn't want to touch the thing, even if it was rolled in Ann's shawl.

"I still don't understand why we had to bring the staff with us." He twisted in the saddle to look back. Cleo was poking out from the thick folds of Tolly's cloak. There was a dusting of snow on her nose. "Cleo – yes, but that thing…"

"Ann always said it was important. It's why she

kept it. She was fascinated by it, but I think she was scared of it too." Tolly sighed. "Look, I don't understand it either. The staff hurt me tonight, but it helped us, didn't it?"

Jem grunted. He wasn't so sure.

"*The sharp-toothed wolf of the sea.*" Cazalon's singsong voice swam into his mind and Jem's mouth went dry. What if the count was still alive? What if he had taken Ann again?

"He cannot have survived." Tolly read his fear. "We both saw what happened in the cavern under St Paul's – veins erupted from the stone itself to bind Cazalon's body, and the chamber collapsed on top of him. You mustn't think those things. Remember what I said."

Jem scowled. "Well, you're thinking it too. Admit it. It's not so easy to forget what happened. And I'd thank you to stop poking around in my head."

He pulled his hood forward and stared at the silent streets ahead. To the left of the crossroads narrow timber houses that had escaped the fire were clustered together, their tottering storeys stacked one upon the other, as if the buildings were scrambling up to reach the light.

A church bell began to sound the hour. Four long

metallic notes lingered on the night air.

"That way, lad, walk on." Jem urged Titan forward and the hollow sound of hooves clopping on cobblestones echoed in the dark.

※ ⊥ ※

Titan bucked as a large sheeny-backed creature with beady, burning eyes disappeared into the shadows with a flick of its pink tail. Jem pulled hard on the reins. "Steady, lad. Did you see the size of it? They say that the ships here are alive with rats. Keep hold of Cleo; that one was twice her size."

"Don't worry, I've got her safe." Jem felt Tolly move in the saddle as he leaned out to get a better view. "There must be a hundred ships on the river. Where do we begin?"

"I hoped you'd know that." Jem scanned the quayside. The black walls of the Tower loomed to the left, casting a shadow over the wharves on the banks of the Pool of London. He could see a light moving high along the ramparts – probably the night watch. To the right, the wide black river was choked with tall-masted boats. He could hear the creaking of timbers and the sound of waves slapping against thick wooden hulls.

"On foot, then, I suppose – we can't take Titan any further. We'll have to tie him to the wall over there." He pointed at a dark passage between two tall stone warehouses set back from the quay. Jem patted the horse's arched neck. If Titan was stolen his mother would be furious and Smeaton the head groom would never speak to him again.

"Then we must find Ann as quickly as possible." Tolly slipped down from the saddle and landed lightly on the snow-crusted stones. "Sorry, I wasn't prying; it just happened," he added without looking up.

Jem flushed. He felt uncomfortable about what he'd said earlier, but sometimes he wondered how much Tolly really saw in his mind. He knew he had been rude.

"No, I should be the one to apologise. I'm sorry. It's just that everything tonight is so…"

"Wrong?" Tolly glanced up now.

Jem nodded grimly and dismounted. When they'd secured Titan by tying the reins to a metal loop in the passageway, Tolly rested his forehead against the horse's nose.

"I've told him to stay in the shadows if he can. I think he understood me. But we can't leave this." He loosened the saddle to free Cazalon's staff and tucked it under his cloak.

Jem didn't say anything. Instead he stared back along the quay. Some thirty yards away there was a long, low building with a torch burning over a central door. The Neptune Arms – its painted tavern sign showing the sea god spearing a fish with his trident swayed in the wind. It creaked as it moved backwards and forwards.

Despite the hour, every window blazed with light. Jem could hear laughter and music – the people inside were singing a raucous drinking song. The door swung open and a man sprawled out onto the quayside. The Pool of London was rough and rowdy and Jem knew it would be best to stay hidden from view. As the man cursed and scrambled to his unsteady feet, Jem pulled Tolly behind a pile of rope-bound boxes waiting to be loaded aboard a ship. They crouched low and Jem blew on his fingers.

"Where now?"

Tolly peered out through a gap at the ships moored in rows ten deep across the wide river. They creaked and moaned as the Thames moved around them.

"Can you sense her nearby?"

Tolly was silent for a moment. "Yes… and no.

I keep thinking that I've caught her, but then she dissolves and there's no trace." He pulled his hood up tight to make sure Cleo was hidden from view as a couple of sailors rolled past. They stopped on the other side of the stack and the boys shrank further back into the shadows.

"And ain't it the strangest fing?" The voice was weedy and shrill. "No one would set out on that course at this time of the year. Never been done. 'Tis madness, that's what it is."

"But the pay's good. They say Trevanion's offering four times the usual rate." The second voice was deeper with the butter-soft accent of the West Country.

"That what they say, is it?" the first man spoke again and burped loudly. "Well, let me tell you, friend, any ship chartered by a woman – and a French one at that – is a ship I'd give a wery wide berth. Anyway, you know what they say about a ship with a name like that, don'tcha?"

"No." The other man sounded confused.

"It ends in an 'A', don't it? Unlucky that is, wery unlucky. I don't know what you Devoners say, but here in London we wouldn't set one foot on a ship with a name like that."

The other man laughed. "Well, it doesn't matter

what we Devoners would say. Fact is the *Fortuna* is setting sail with the tide at sunrise today and I heard Captain Trevanion's got a full crew for the crossing. Come on, let's find ourselves a fireside."

Jem stared at Tolly. The *Fortuna*! The word they'd seen burned into the wall of Ann's caravan.

The two sailors crunched away across the icy cobbles of the quayside and the boys slipped out from behind the boxes.

"It's a ship – the *Fortuna* is a ship and it's here somewhere. That must be where Ann is."

"But there are more than a hundred ships here – where do we start?" Tolly sounded panic-stricken.

Jem squinted at the rows of groaning vessels moored across the river. "Well, if the *Fortuna* is setting sail at sunrise it must be making ready now. We just have to find the busiest ship in the pool."

Tolly nodded.

"Look!" Jem pointed at a pallet being pushed along the quayside by four burly men. They passed the boys and halted further along the quay. One of the men stepped forward and put his hands to his mouth.

"Last delivery for the *Fortuna*," he bellowed.

"Here!" came a voice from among the dark tangle

of masts. "Bring it up here alongside and we'll take it from there."

Jem gripped Tolly's arm. "We've found her!" He felt a surge of hope. "Now, let's get her back."

CHAPTER EIGHT

From their hiding place the boys watched the great black package swing up from the pallet and out over the glittering water. The delivery men puffed and wheezed as they hauled on ropes that guided the package upward until it was suspended over an open hole in the centre of the huge ship's deck. The package twisted in mid-air for a moment before it was lowered slowly into the darkness of the hold. Once the ropes had been cut free, two massive doors closed over the gaping mouth, making the deck smooth and whole again.

The boys had a clear view of the deck, but the ship's sharp prow and bulky stern with its tiers of lighted windows towered above them. The *Fortuna* was the biggest, blackest ship in the pool. Her ridged sides glistened like the skin of a reptile.

"Look." Tolly nudged Jem's shoulder and pointed.

Jem clutched the edge of the squat barrel that hid them and shifted position so that he could see more clearly.

Tolly's voice came from the darkness. "The

figurehead. That's what I saw."

Jem looked up and over to the left. The *Fortuna* rose and fell as the river waters sucked at the hull, but he could clearly see the carved wooden profile of a woman. She had one hand held out in front of her and the other, clenched into a fist, was clasped to her breast. From the light of the many lanterns strung along the side of the ship, Jem could see red tendrils of hair swept back from the woman's white-painted face. They curled in elaborate scrolls across the *Fortuna*'s prow.

As the ship dipped down again, he saw a silver star set into the scarlet scrolls just above the woman's forehead. The Eye of Ra began to prickle on his heel.

Tolly bumped Jem's shoulder and whispered urgently. "Look! She is *exactly* what I saw – a red-haired woman with a star on her forehead. Ann must be on board. Jem, did you hear me?"

Tolly nudged him again. With difficulty, Jem dragged his eyes away from the figurehead. He was sure the wooden woman had just opened her eyes. It must have been a trick of the lanternlight, he told himself, trying to clear the unsettling image from his mind.

Heavy footsteps sounded on the deck somewhere

to the right. "We ride the tide, shipmates. Less than an hour to go. Are you ready?"

"Aye." The ragged answer came from many voices speaking at once.

"Set the small sails."

A dozen pairs of feet thundered across the deck and the boys ducked even lower into the shadows behind the barrels. Suddenly the rigging above the ship was alive with crew swarming upwards. Some of them had small lanterns attached to their belts. Jem's stomach flipped as he watched the lights weaving like fireflies between the ropes, higher and higher.

A whumping noise filled the air as sheets of pale canvas tumbled down into the night, blocking the stars from view. Ropes began to creak and strain as the sails caught the wind and bulged. Instantly, the *Fortuna* seemed to buck forward, like a greyhound straining at the leash.

"Steady the jetty ropes! Foreyard and mizzen only until we reach the estuary." The harsh voice from the deck added, "The pilot boat will be with us at sunrise and then we sail."

Jem looked east along the river and saw the ink-black sky thinning, as if it was diluted with water. Very soon now it would be dawn.

"We have to go aboard and find her, Tolly." Jem clutched his friend's arm. "Look – there's a doorway in the side over there."

The boys watched the narrow, swinging gangway leading from the jetty to a small entrance set low into the wooden hull below the heavily carved, brightly lit windows of the great cabin.

With all the activity taking place on deck and in the rigging, no one was watching the gangway. "Come on!" Jem pulled at his friend but Tolly held back.

"I… I'm not sure I can go in there. I thought I could, but now… I'm sorry – I just can't." He faltered and Jem knew why. Many years ago Tolly and his entire family had been kidnapped by traders, chained together and taken up the Nile in the stinking bowels of a slaver's barge, only to be sold like cattle on the quayside at Alexandria.

That was when Tolly had been separated from his father, mother and sister, and bought by Count Cazalon.

In the gloom Jem could see the terror in the boy's wide-set eyes. Cleo, shrouded in the depths of Tolly's loose hood, made a soft crooning noise, as if she sensed her master's distress.

Jem pushed his springy black curls back from his

face so that Tolly could see him more clearly. "Look, I can't go in there alone. There's not enough time to search the ship as it is before it sails, and if it's just me in there I don't stand a chance. You're the one who can lead us to her, Tolly – like before at St Paul's? You can search with your mind for the smallest trace of her. It won't be like the barge. Please – you must try. Do this for Ann."

Tolly looked down at the wooden boards of the jetty and his shoulders slumped. Beneath them Jem could hear the river slapping against the underside of the planks.

Tolly drew a deep breath and straightened up. "For Ann," he said.

Jem gripped his friend's arm fiercely, understanding just how much those two words had cost him. "For Ann."

The boys took advantage of the shadows and slipped along the quay until they reached a set of steps to the jetty below. They waited until they were certain that they couldn't be seen and then crept down and slipped along the boards to the narrow door leading into the ship. Jem looked at the dark, sheeny water moving beneath the slats. Cleo slipped from Tolly's shoulder and loped along behind.

"I'll go first," Jem whispered. "Stay close."

"Wait!"

Jem turned, expecting his friend to have frozen in fear, but Tolly was looking up.

"I think we're being watched."

Jem looked too. High on the forecastle at the front of the ship a shadow moved in the lantern light. As Jem watched, the shadow became a man, a tall, thin man with what looked like a great shaggy mask covering his head and shoulders. The mask seemed to rise to two points above the man's head.

The figure began to turn slowly in their direction.

"Run!" Jem whispered urgently, and the boys and the monkey pelted across the narrow gangway and into the black heart of the *Fortuna*.

※ ⚓ ※

The smell hit Jem first. The air was thick with the scent of tar and wood interlaced with something briny, sharp and sour. Tolly brought his hand up to cover his nose and mouth, and even though he was no mind-reader, Jem knew exactly what was going through his friend's head.

He reached out to grasp Tolly's arm again. "Can you feel her?" he whispered, trying to distract him from his fear.

Tolly shook his head miserably. "No… not really." He closed his eyes and dipped his head forward, then, after a moment, he nodded and looked up. Jem was relieved to see a glint of hope in his friend's dark eyes. Tolly nodded again. "There *is* something – a trace of her, but it's not her. I don't understand. It's as if Ann's here, but not here."

Jem scanned the space around them. In the gloom he saw that they were in a long storage space running the length of the ship. The shadowy hold was cluttered with jumbled barrels, boxes, earthen jars, sacks and very large, oddly-shaped packages.

He stepped forward and pulled Tolly along behind him. "Perhaps we can get out over there? Look – there's a sort of glow…"

They negotiated their way past a mound of sacks. Jem looked up. Cracks of lamplight showed between the broad timbers overhead.

"I'm going to sling my hammock across here if that's all right with you, Spider?"

Jem and Tolly ducked instinctively at the sound of a boy's voice directly above them.

"That's fine by me, but you'll have Ned to deal with," came another boy's voice. "He's done four crossings now and by his reckoning that means he got rights to the best cot. I wouldn't argue with him, Pocket, he's bigger than you and me put together."

"Maybe you're right."

Jem heard bumping and the sound of something being dragged over the timbers above. The first boy spoke again. "And as we're all three going to be kipping here tighter than eels in a barrel, I wouldn't want to make an enemy of him."

Flakes of pitch fell from the timbers as the boys above shifted about. Jem quickly covered his nose and mouth to stifle a sneeze.

"What was that?" The second boy – Spider, was it? – spoke sharply.

"Nothing – probably just rats down in the hold below. This must be the worst place on the ship – it stinks of bilge water. Help me with this, will you?" More thumping came from overhead and the boards groaned.

Pocket spoke again. "They say she's bought a houseful of stuff on board with her. I'd like to take a look down below. Mind you, by the time we get there, the rats'll have eaten through all her fancy French goods. You seen her yet, Spider?"

"No. They came aboard in the early hours and went

straight to the cabin. We're to be shown to her at first light – all of us. You seen that 'orrible doorway up on deck yet? Well, it leads to the passengers' chamber and we're not to go there on pain of a flogging." Spider paused. "Master Grimscale says we're not to speak to them at any time. Though why she'd want to make the crossing at this time of year is beyond me."

"Me too," Pocket answered cheerfully. "But Ned reckons this is the biggest, grandest ship he's ever seen, so she'll get us across all right. Anyways, I'm content with my lot – the captain's a fair man, the pay's good and the grog ration is more than generous."

"Good thing too." Spider laughed. "We'll be needing that to see us through."

Clank!

Jem jumped at the sudden noise and spun around. He was horrified to find that the doorway behind them was sealed. The foul air became suddenly dense and smothering. He heard the heavy thud of boots as someone clumped away along the jetty outside.

Jem shot a glance at Tolly. His friend was rigid in the gloom, his right hand clutching Cazalon's staff. Cleo pulled nervously at Tolly's cloak, making little whickering sounds while staring up at his face.

Jem scanned the cluttered space around him.

How would they get out now?

He peered up at the cracks in the boards. Just to the left, the feeble light showed six metal rungs set into the side of the ship. He tested the first bar and hauled himself up. It was definitely a sort of ladder, but where did it lead?

Overhead there was a shout and the boards creaked as Spider and Pocket raced to answer a command. Jem waited for a moment until he was certain they were gone and then he clambered higher and reached up to test the wood overhead. His fingers traced the edges of a small hatch. He dropped back to the floor of the hold and felt the ship move beneath him, rocking in the water. He clutched the side of a leather-bound chest to steady himself.

"I think I've found a way out." He chewed his lip and looked up at the hatchway, wondering where it led. "Tolly, did you hear me?" He turned to his friend.

Tolly's eyes were tightly closed and he moaned softly. Jem wondered if he was having some sort of fit brought on by his fear. He reached forward to clasp his shoulder. "I'm here. I'm right here. It's all right." He knew the words sounded weak and meaningless.

Tolly's eyes flicked open. "It's not all right. In fact, it's very far from all right." He gripped Jem's hand so hard that it hurt. "Don't you feel it? We're moving. The *Fortuna* has set sail."

CHAPTER NINE

The black timbers of the *Fortuna* groaned and the floor moved. Jem steadied himself by wedging his foot beneath a canvas sack. The bottom of the sack felt damp. He looked down to see a thin layer of brown bilge water lapping across the toes of his boots.

He felt as if he and Tolly were in the belly of a vast sea creature – like the story of Jonah and the whale. It definitely smelled like the entrails of an old dead fish down here.

The *Fortuna* seemed to be alive. In the hold, the sounds of the ship were amplified and distorted. It moaned like a wounded animal as it rolled in the water.

"Jem, we have to get off!"

Jem crouched down next to Tolly, who was now crumpled against a sack with his arms wrapped tightly around his knees. "We're still on the river – we've only just set sail." He looked at the metal rungs. If they could climb up and get out onto the decks above without being seen, they could dive over the side and swim to the bank.

He clenched his fists – but what about Ann? They couldn't leave her.

Jem pushed his hair away from his eyes. If she really was on board then the only way to find her was to get out of the hold and search the ship. Then all four of them would have to swim back to shore.

He drew a deep breath. The water would be bone-achingly cold, but he knew he could do it. "Come on, Tolly. Wrap Cleo in your cloak. We're going up."

"And then what are we going to do?" Tolly's eyes were closed.

"First we're going to find Ann and then we'll all have to swim ashore. Cleo too." Jem hoped he sounded more confident than he felt.

Cleo's head shot up and her nose twitched. Jem frowned. "Er… can she swim, Tolly?"

The other boy was silent as Jem continued. "Look, one of us can hold Cleo safely when we jump in – she'd be happiest if it was you – and then, when we start swimming, she can cling on to your back."

Tolly started to laugh hollowly. "You've got it all worked out, haven't you?"

Jem was confused. Surely Tolly was as eager to

leave the *Fortuna* as he was? "I don't see what's funny about swimming ashore."

"Don't you?" Tolly opened his eyes. "It's not Cleo you should be worrying about – she'll be fine. It's me. *I* can't swim. If I jumped over I'd drown in seconds." He brought his hands up to cradle his forehead. "I'm stuck here – and no matter how badly I want to get away, I can't – even if we do find Ann."

Jem felt a cold, twisting feeling in the pit of his stomach. It was all going so wrong. He slumped down against the sack next to Tolly. Cleo leaped into his lap and Jem fondled her ears. He couldn't shake away the thought that he was responsible for everything that had happened. Ann had gone missing from under his very nose at his own home, at Goldings. He should have protected her. It was his duty.

What was Master Jalbert always saying? *"Never drop your guard!"* Well, it looked like he hadn't even learned that simple lesson. Beside him, Tolly was like a stone.

"I… I'm sorry. I got us into this."

Tolly didn't answer.

There had to be something they could do, some chink of hope. Jem thought hard.

"Listen, the men back there on the quay and

93

the boys with the hammock – the ones we heard overhead... They talked about making a crossing, didn't they? And they both said something about a French woman being on board. So, we must be crossing the English Channel over to France. Well, if that's true, we'll probably make a couple of stops on the south coast first, and even if we don't, France isn't so far. It might even be a good thing if it gives us time to make a proper search. What do you think?"

Jem knew his words sounded unconvincing. Even if they did find Ann aboard, that would make three people who needed to travel back from France. How would they pay for that? His fingers went to the medal hanging round his neck, the one given to him by his mother just a few hours earlier. Of course!

He started to speak again with a brighter tone. "If you're worried about paying for our passage back from France, don't be. I can sell this." He held the medal out from the neck of his shirt. "What do you say, Tolly?"

The other boy took a deep breath and raised his head. "I say please be quiet for a moment, Jem. I can feel her. Ann. She's here on the boat with us."

Jem straightened up and Cleo chattered excitedly in his lap. "How... Where? Tell me."

Tolly opened his eyes and stared blankly at the curved side of the ship. Jem saw his friend's eyes move across the tar-black, riveted timbers, taking in the details of a scene that only he could see. After a moment, he frowned. "I don't understand. It's not right – it's all blurred. There's a long window. I can see water now – moving water and sunshine glinting on the waves. I don't know why I'm here. I don't know who I am."

"But you do, don't you, Tolly?" Jem broke in excitedly. "It's Ann, isn't it? You're seeing through her eyes. She's here on the boat with us."

Tolly nodded slowly. "Yes… yes, I think she must be. But it's odd. All broken up. I can't understand why I can't speak to her and make her hear me – like we always used to. Even when we were in Malfurneaux Place I could talk to her wherever she was. This is different. It's like there's a fog between us."

Jem tried to crush the odd sensation that flared within him when he thought of the close bond between Tolly and Ann.

For the first time since Ann's disappearance, Tolly smiled. "You have to remember how it was for us back then," he said gently. "We forged a link – a strange one – but that's because we only had each other.

And Cleo here." He reached out to stroke the little monkey's curved back. She cocked her head to one side at the mention of her name and stared from one boy to the other, her bright black eyes questioning.

"The good thing – and as far as I can tell the only good thing about what's happened so far –" Tolly continued, "is that Ann must be with us on this ship. She's very close. Even if I can't communicate with her, I can sense her."

Jem felt a charge of excitement. "Then we must find her. Come on."

Glad to have something to do, he passed Cleo gently to Tolly and scrambled to his feet. Reaching out for the rungs, he climbed until he was directly under the hatch. He raised a hand and pushed at the boards above. The hatch shifted – it was unlocked. He let it fall quietly back into place and looked down at Tolly and Cleo.

"There's just one thing…" He frowned. "We can't go out now. It will be daylight up there and we're bound to be spotted. Can you bear waiting down here until it's dark again?"

Tolly scratched the top of Cleo's head between her black ears and she held his finger. He nodded. "It's getting better. If we can find Ann, then nothing else matters." He looked up and grinned ruefully. "And anyway – I don't think I've got much choice."

⚜ ☖ ⚜

Jem startled awake to the sound of cloth ripping. He blinked hard. He couldn't believe that he'd fallen asleep. Only pinpricks of dull light came from knotholes in the boards above them. He wrinkled his nose and stifled a cough as the smell of old fish, tar and stale, briny water caught at the back of his throat. Tolly was sitting upright next to him on a pile of sacking, examining his blistered fingers. The eerie sound of water slapping and sucking against the sides of the boat echoed around them.

"What time is it?" Jem whispered.

"I heard six bells just now. It's got dark. I'd forgotten all about my hand, but when I woke it was burning." Tolly bound a strip of material he had torn from his undershirt round his index finger. "There, that's better."

"So you slept too, then?" Jem felt almost guilty, but Tolly nodded.

"Of course I did. We haven't rested for hours. I woke just before you did."

Just then they heard the sound of footsteps and

voices. The darkness was suddenly illuminated by brighter lamplight streaming through the cracks in the boards overhead. Tolly put his finger to his lips and pointed upward.

The same voices as before came clearly from above.

"The master mate, Grimscale, is Tartar, right enough. You've sailed with him before, you say, Ned?" The light, familiar voice was Spider's. He was answered by a new and slightly deeper voice.

"Twice. You'll keep out of his way if you know what's good for you. They say he was sent to sea at the age of six. Most particular he hates us younger ones cos we remind him of the brothers he never had. He's as handy with the cat as you are with the deck scrubber. He's not a Swale man, that's for sure."

"It's not Grimscale who bothers me." This was Pocket. "It's that other one – him with all the bones in his hair and the tattoos. He don't say a word, he don't, just stares at you like he can see right under your skin into your soul. S'not right having one of them on board. I mean, it's bad enough having a woman."

"Well, you'd better get used to it – both of you." Ned's confident voice came again. "The only way to get through is to keep your head down and do your duties. After this crossing I'll be moving my hammock out from the bilge box to the mess deck. I'm going up in the world, I am, and if you two want to do the same you'd best keep your noses clean."

He was interrupted by something that sounded like the chimes of a cracked bell. "Grog's up – come on, you two. It'll keep the winter out of your bones." There was more thumping and creaking above as Ned, Pocket and Spider eagerly answered the tinny call.

Jem and Tolly waited for a minute until they were sure they were alone again.

"Now?" whispered Tolly.

Jem nodded and stood up. He paused beneath the hatchway, listening, and then he clambered up the rungs. He was just about to push at the board when Tolly caught his ankle.

"Wait – I almost forgot." He retrieved Cazalon's staff wrapped in Ann's shawl from beneath a roll of canvas. "We can't leave this here. I don't know why, but it's important."

Jem raised his eyebrows and turned back to the hatch. He pushed it up a little way so that he could see the space above. His eyes darted from left to right as he tried to make sense of the room. The hatch appeared to lead up into a small box-like space. The air was just as rank and unpleasant here as in the hold below. If anything it was worse.

Two candle lanterns stood on the floor, lighting three narrow hammocks. They were slung so closely together across the tiny space that if the occupant of one of them turned over he would surely tumble onto the tenant of the next. As far as Jem could make out, the only exit was upwards, where a spindly stepladder with a couple of missing struts led to another hatch.

Jem hauled himself into the dingy little space. "Come on. It looks like it'll lead us out." He reached down for the staff and then offered his friend a hand.

Tolly grimaced as he scrambled up through the hatch. "It's like a coffin in here." He clenched his fists and closed his eyes. His fingers scrabbled to loosen the cloak at his neck. "We have to get out of here. I… I can't breathe."

"We'll soon be out. Now, Cleo. Come on, girl… Where is she? I thought she followed you?" Jem dipped his head back down through the hatch and peered into the gloom.

The little monkey was cowering in front of a tall,

flat package propped against the wooden wall.

"Cleo," Jem called softly, but she didn't seem to hear him.

"I'll go and fetch her." He leaped nimbly back down and pushed past the barrels and boxes. The package before Cleo was wrapped in layers of grey oilcloth and tightly bound with red cord. There was a long, tattered gap in the front where the fabric was ripped. Cleo chattered and grabbed his foot. Her eyes were locked on the package.

"What's got into you? Come on, beauty." Jem leaned down to gather her in his arms but as he did so he thought he heard a hissing sound. He straightened up and looked around – ships always carried vermin, but did rats hiss?

He listened. Now he could hear a dry, rustling noise too.

He took a step back and looked up at the package. It was taller and broader than he was and it leaned back against the wall so that there was a gap behind it. Was something hiding there? Huddling Cleo close to his chest, he stepped to the side and bent to peer into the gap. Cleo whickered and wriggled in his arms. It was so gloomy he could hardly see and he wondered if maybe that was a good thing. Ship rats were said to be enormous.

He shook his head, straightened up and turned his back.

"*Ssssssooon*." The word sounded like the swish of a sword in the air.

Jem shuddered. It felt as if someone, or something, had traced a lump of jagged ice along every knobble of his backbone. He froze – had that been a voice? He listened for a moment but nothing more came. Perhaps it was just the distorted sound of the water sucking at the sides of the ship? Yes, that was what he'd heard… wasn't it? Without looking back he placed Cleo firmly on his left shoulder, swayed over to the metal rungs and clambered up through the hatch.

"So, there are two of you, are there?" The gruff, unfamiliar voice came from the left.

Momentarily confused, Jem looked up to see Tolly pinned to the wall by a lumpen man with a pockmarked face. He seemed to fill the room.

Tolly's breath was coming in wheezing gasps. There were beads of sweat on his forehead despite the cold and his eyes were shut.

The man grinned, revealing a mouth full of broken teeth and blackened gums. His tiny, watery eyes glittered in the lamplight. "And what you got there?

A monkey, is it?" He leaned forward to poke at Cleo and Jem shrank back as the man's fetid breath rolled over him. "They make good eating, they do. Not a lot of meat on them, mind, but very... toothsome."

The man's huge tattooed hand shot out to grip Jem's shoulder. "We'll see what Captain Trevanion has to say about stowaways. I've not seen a proper keelhauling for years." He began to laugh again and the tiny space fugged up with the stench of him.

"Perhaps it's your lucky day, lads. Or mine."

CHAPTER
TEN

Captain Trevanion flung his grey wig to the floor of the cabin and ran his fingers through the fine fair stubble on his scalp. He turned his back on the boys – held firmly on the shoulders by the huge man who'd discovered them – and began to spin the globe that stood behind his broad oak desk. After a moment he spoke.

"What I can't understand is how they came aboard in the first place. You are the master mate, Grimscale. Why weren't the watches doing their job?"

Grimscale flushed and the scarlet pockmarks across his nose and cheeks pulsed. He opened his mouth to answer, but Jem saw the big man's beady eyes narrow in a calculating way before he allowed himself to speak in anger.

"They were, sir. And we made all the usual searches. These two must have come aboard just afore we set sail. They were hiding in the hold – with the rest of the rats! We need to make an example of them – a flogging or maybe a keelhauling?" He grinned.

"That's the way to keep the crew in line."

"A keelhauling?" Captain Trevanion spun round. In the lamplight Jem saw there were deep furrows on his high forehead and crinkles around his grey eyes. "That's barbaric. Can't you see they're just boys?"

Grimscale's tattooed hand tightened its grip on Jem's shoulder. "What I see, sir, beggin' your pardon, is a pair of stowaways and they should be punished. Let me show them the cat at least?"

Trevanion shook his head. "If you had sailed with me before, you would know that I'd never allow such cruelty on a ship of mine. Leave us now. I'll deal with this."

Jem felt Grimscale stiffen beside him. He released the boys with a rough shove and took a heavy step forward, looming over the captain. Trevanion put his long, pale hands flat on the oak desk and leaned forward. "Do you have anything further to say, Master Mate?"

Grimscale balled his right hand into a fist – the blue-black lines across the back of his hand and around his wrist knotting to form a grinning skull.

The captain stared up at him. "Well?"

After a long moment Grimscale nodded. "Have it your way. But Madame won't be pleased. No one else was to make the crossing with her – that's what she said, wasn't it?" He smiled crookedly and once again Jem shrank from the foul stench of the man's tooth-rot breath. "I wonder what she'll say when she hears about these two? They weren't shown off to her with the rest of the crew."

Trevanion looked down at the charts unfurled on his desk. He smoothed back the one on the top and held the edge in place with an intricate golden instrument. "Then we must make it our business to make sure she doesn't hear about them, from you or from anyone else. Is that clear?" Grimscale grunted and the captain spoke again. "I said, is that clear, Master Mate?"

"As daybreak over the horizon, *sir*."

"You may go."

The big man turned and pushed angrily past the boys. As he did so, his eyes flickered over Cleo, who was curled in Tolly's arms. "The monkey – shall I give her to the cook? The men will be wanting all the fresh meat they can get in this weather. Keep their strength up, it will."

"Go." Trevanion didn't look up. 'And leave the monkey.'

Grimscale's face became purple and the cord-like

veins in his neck bulged. "I'll take this at least and store it in the hold. Ridiculous thing – and dangerous too. I'll warrant the Moor boy meant to beat someone's brains out with it." He snatched up the bird-headed staff from where it lay on the floor next to Tolly's feet and lumbered towards the door. While his back was turned, Jem retrieved Ann's shawl from the cabin floor and tucked it into his belt.

Trevanion waited until the furious man had squeezed his bull-like frame through the ornate narrow entrance of the cabin and slammed the door shut behind him. He looked up and studied the painted ceiling before he spoke again.

"I am afraid you have both made a very serious mistake coming aboard the *Fortuna*." Jem took in the deep lines of worry etched on the captain's long face. He was a thin man of middle age with sad, kind eyes. Cleo chirped in Tolly's arms and Trevanion frowned.

"What am I to do with you all? Grimscale is right. Madame de Chouette was most specific that no one other than paid crewmen were to be aboard – and she has seen all of them. They were paraded before her like cattle just before sunrise and made to declare their loyalty. I will have to return you both to the lower hold for the entirety of the crossing."

"No!" Tolly gasped.

Trevanion looked sharply at the terrified boy who was now clutching Cleo so tightly to his chest that only her head and white-tipped tail were visible through his crossed arms. "What else am I to do with the three of you? Don't worry, I'm not a monster. You'll be fed and watered, I promise that, but you cannot be seen by anyone except me and my most trusted men."

Jem's mind raced. "Please, sir – anything but going back to the hold. My friend can't go down there again. I… That is, we could pay for our crossing. I have this…" He reached into his shirt collar and pulled the golden medal over his head. "It must be worth something?"

Trevanion reached forward to take the chain. He turned the medal over in his fingers and his head shot up. His grey eyes were now hard and suspicious. "Where did you steal this from?"

"I didn't. It was my…" Jem thought back to the moment before the party at Goldings when Sarah had given him the medal. "It belonged to James Verrers of Goldings House and I am his nephew, Jeremy – people call me Jem."

Trevanion frowned. "Are you lying, boy? Tell me

the truth now or I'll call Grimscale back and let him deal with you."

"No – it's true. My mother gave it to me."

Trevanion's eyebrows shot up. "And her name is…?"

"Sarah, and her father was Edward, Earl Verrers. He fought for Parliament in the war, but my mother and Jamie, my uncle, sided with the old king. And the new king is my…" Jem faltered. If Trevanion didn't believe him to be the real owner of the medal, he certainly wasn't going to believe that King Charles was his father.

Jem pushed a hand through his thick black hair and his next words tumbled out in a desperate rush. "Please, it's true. My mother's name is Sarah and the medal was my uncle's, but he's dead. We live at Goldings House. I'm not lying – the medal is mine now. I…"

Trevanion raised a hand. "Slow down, boy. I believe you. I knew your uncle – we served together. Jamie Verrers wore this, always." He paused for a moment and weighed the chain in his palm.

Jem's mind flooded with questions he didn't dare to ask. The man standing in front of him had actually known his uncle? He was amazed and desperate to know more about Jamie. Trevanion sighed and handed back the medal. "You must keep this. He was a brave man and a loyal friend. When he died it was me who sent this to your mother – that's how I knew her name. But I thought she too had…" He stared hard at Jem. "How old are you – both of you?"

"I'm thirteen and Tolly, my friend here, is… about the same. We don't know for sure, do we?

Tolly shook his head. "No, sir." He glanced at Jem who nodded encouragingly. "I was taken from my land after six great floods and then I lived in London through seven great frosts. I believe I am of Jem's age."

Trevanion stared into Tolly's eyes and frowned. "Remarkable!" he muttered.

"Sorry, sir?" Tolly was confused.

The captain shook his head. "Nothing, it is nothing. You bear a passing likeness to someone my daughter was… *is* fond of – Tam, her companion." He drew a deep breath. "Now, what to do with you both?" He looked from one boy to the other and nodded as if he had made a decision. "You are tall, strong lads – that's something at least. You'll work as crew – hidden from Madame de Chouette in plain sight. It's the best I can do. She does not seem to relish the day, which should work in your favour.

Keep your heads down, keep your noses clean and we'll see…"

Cleo wriggled in Tolly's arms, freed herself and jumped to the captain's desk, plonking herself onto the middle of the unfurled chart. She held her head to one side and stared boldly up at Trevanion. Jem saw him smile for the first time. "Does the little beast have a name?"

"She is Cleo, sir." Tolly reached forward. "Come here, girl. Not on the map."

Trevanion watched as Cleo leaped from the desk to perch on Tolly's shoulder. "My daughter, Jane, is just a year younger than you two. She also loves animals. I gave her a little dog for her last birthday and she called it Bella. That was before…" His face clouded and the lines across his forehead deepened. "You may be the son of an old friend, boy, but nothing alters the fact that you have been found stowing away on my ship. What are you doing here? Was it some sort of game – a Twelfth Night dare?" He raised the golden instrument from the edge of the map so that it curled back into a roll. "Well?"

Jem looked at his feet and wondered how much to tell the captain. "It's no game, sir. We… we think our friend is hidden here. We came on board and thought we could scour the ship before it sailed. But we got trapped in the hold and then…"

"But why on earth would you think your friend is aboard the *Fortuna*?" As well as bafflement there was something else in the captain's voice – perhaps fear, or was it disgust?

Jem didn't know what to say next. How could he explain Tolly's visions? "We… We had good reason to believe, sir, that she'd been kidnapped and taken to a ship with this name."

"*She?*" Trevanion snorted and shook his head. "There is only one woman on board this ship and I doubt very much that she is your friend."

CHAPTER ELEVEN

"So, you two came aboard late then, that it? And the captain's doing your poor mother a favour?"

Spider scrubbed vigorously at the icy deck. Beside him Jem kept his head down and gave a grunt of agreement.

"I can't see why we didn't come across you earlier, seeing as how you're to be bunking down with us in the bilge box. And you weren't in the line-up for Madame the other morning, were you? I s'pose you had one last gentleman's meal with the captain and Mr V? Mind you, Ned's happy as a dolphin now that he's been sent up to billet on the mess deck. It was his lucky day when you arrived."

Jem grunted again. The more he said to Spider about their sudden appearance among the crew, the more difficult it would be to stick to the story Captain Trevanion had ordered Grimscale and Master Valentine, the ship's second-in-command, to put about.

He and Tolly were introduced to the crew at first

light by Master Valentine as distant acquaintances of the captain's family. Master Valentine, a young dark-haired gentleman mariner with merry eyes and a constant half-smile, hadn't questioned the captain when he "explained" their situation. Jem's mother had fallen on hard times, Trevanion said, and, as a favour, he had agreed to take the boy and his companion on with a view to training them up for a career at sea. They were to learn the ropes.

"From the bottom up," Grimscale told the assembled ship's company. "There's no job too difficult or too lowly for these two. Remember that." He'd been furious when Trevanion revealed the plan, but the captain had stood his ground, ordering the master mate to follow orders.

Jem rubbed his frozen nose with the back of his hand and glanced ahead to the prow where Grimscale was in conversation with a couple of the older deckhands. The hulking man laughed loudly and dipped a pewter mug into the grog barrel. Then, as if he was aware of Jem's gaze, he turned and raised the mug like a toast, twisting his thick lips into a cruel, mocking grin.

Spider nudged Jem's elbow. "I'd keep clear of him if I were you. He's not Swale-born like the most of us, including the captain. Truth be told, I don't rightly know why Captain T took him on, though I 'spose it was mortal hard to get a crew together at such short notice – and in winter too. I know that's one reason so many of us signed up – not much work in Swale for a sailor in the wintertime."

The boy sat back for a moment and scanned the busy deck. "Best sailors in the country, Swale men. For all that it's small, it's got a mighty reputation amongst them what know. Where you from?"

"London. We're both from London." Jem kept scraping at the ice and didn't look up.

"Your friend don't say much, does he?" Spider pointed his scrubber at Tolly. "Nice little monkey he's got there. Chloe, is it? Lots of sailors like to bring a pet on board. Pocket brung a mouse with him last time – kept giving it half his cheese. Thing was as round as an apple by the time we got to port again. Animals don't always last the going, though. Not when rations get low."

"Cleo. Her name's Cleo," said Jem. He looked over to where she was perched on the side of the ship watching her master work. Her tail was curled tightly around one of the ropes leading up into the rigging. Jem's eyes followed the cat's cradle of

115

blackened ropes zig-zagging high above him. His stomach heaved.

They'd been hard at it for the last two hours, starting from the stern end at the back and working forward to the prow. Over to the left – the starboard side, Spider called it – Tolly and the boy called Pocket were also down on their knees scraping ice from the timbers. Cleo had taken an instant liking to Pocket and he was clearly very taken by her. Unlike Spider, Pocket was a sturdy lad with cropped blond hair that stood upright on his head. Although he'd only known him for a few hours, Jem already knew Pocket's main interest in life was food. He talked about it constantly, loudly describing his mother's meat pies in such loving detail that one of the older crewmen asked him to "muffle it" because it was "making his guts rumble". Pocket was first in the queue when the biscuit barrel was opened at noon, but Jem saw him slip crumbs to Cleo when he thought no one was looking.

"We got to get the crust off, see?" Spider was saying. "Otherwise we'll have a man slipping overboard in no time. And none of us can swim – sailors can't as a rule. Only thing is, this time of year, the ice comes back as soon as we've scratched it off."

Spider rubbed his red-raw hands together. He was tiny – a twitching knot of bony arms and legs topped with a leathery face that was old beyond its years. He wore his lank brown hair tied back at the nape of his neck and a thin golden hoop glinted in the lobe of his right ear.

"Beats me why the fancy Madame's so keen to make the crossing in winter. Never been done before. Money's good, though, ain't it?" He winked at Jem. "You'll see your poor old mother right once we get back."

Jem thought guiltily of his mother back at Goldings, no doubt frantic with worry. "Er… How long… How long will it take to make the crossing?" Jem put down his brush and folded his arms across his chest, thrusting his numb fingers under his armpits for warmth. "Three days? Four? A week at most?"

Spider laughed and threw his own brush down. It clattered and skidded a little way across the deck. "Blimey, you're a puddle-duck, aren't you? A crossing to the new colonies – over the wild, wide Atlantic – takes at least two months, probably more at this time of year."

"The new colonies?" Jem was horrified. "I…

I thought we were crossing the Channel to France. The passenger, she's French, right?"

Spider nodded and grinned. He had a gap between his front teeth just like Ann's. Jem felt a wave of panic rise from the pit of his stomach as he thought about her. They hadn't even had a chance to look for her yet.

"That's right." The skinny boy stood and went to retrieve the brush. "She's French true enough, but she's going to see her estates in the northern colonies – urgent business. Says she couldn't find anyone in the Pool to take her, so she came to Swale and bought herself a captain and a crew. The *Fortuna* is her ship, that's why we sailed from London."

Spider knelt beside Jem again and waved the brush at the carved black timbers. "Now, she's a funny old thing – a real giantess. I've not seen one built quite like her before. Not in Swale, anyways. Must be foreign. Like that odd fellow with all the skulls in his hair – you seen him yet?"

Jem shook his head as Spider continued. "They say he's called Mingan. He's served before with Captain T and word is that he's a good shipmate, even if he looks a bit peculiar. This time he's going home to his own people. Ned reckons they don't wear proper clothes like we do – just animal skins. What do you make of that? Primitive, that's what I call it." The boy paused to wipe a quivering bulb of snot from his nose and bent back to the task in hand. "Anyways, the *Fortuna* will likely be his last ship."

Jem felt something twist in his gut – there was something ominous about the words "last ship". He looked up to take in the details of the vessel more closely. In the clear morning light he could see hundreds of figures carved into the creaking timbers around him. Faces and animals curled in the blackened wood, and sea creatures with looped tails, clawed hands and jagged fins. He turned round, assessing the square hatch in the timbers leading directly down to the stinking crew's quarters, above which lay a finely carved set of broad steps, more appropriate to a great house than a ship. These led up to a wide quarterdeck where there was a doorway to the passenger's accommodation.

Jem gasped and dropped his brush. Above the doorway there was a ghastly gilded mask with staring eyes. The face was surrounded by serpents which coiled down either side of the doorframe, fanning out into elaborately twisted knots and golden curlicues across the coal-black timbers. In the dead centre beneath the mask, the arched wooden door was like a gaping mouth. He'd seen something very like it before – at Malfurneaux Place.

"Pretty, ain't she?" Spider laughed again, but Jem felt the skin on his back prickle as he remembered Tapwick, Cazalon's steward, using those very same words.

Spider slid Jem's brush towards him. "Catch on. I reckon we'll know every knot and every wormhole in these timbers by the time we make land. If you want my opinion, I reckon it'll take a lot longer than eight weeks. We'll have to go far down south and up again to avoid the floating islands." Spider cocked his head to one side and squinted up into the sun. "I could be wrong. It won't be a bad thing if we get more days like this and there's a good wind up. The sails have got a bellyful. I've heard we're already making good time."

"But we'll be stopping to take on supplies before we start the actual crossing, won't we?" Jem struggled to keep the sound of panic out of his voice. "We'll go into a port on the south coast? Maybe Plymouth?" He did a hasty calculation in his head, wondering if it might be possible to make a thorough search of the ship in what, two, maybe three days?

"Ah well, that's interesting too, isn't it?" Spider started to scrub again. "We're not making any stops – another of Madame's orders. Our feet won't be touching dry land again now until we reach the new colonies. I wouldn't be surprised if we've got webbed feet by then. Look sharp – Jem, is it? Old Grimface is on his way over."

Jem followed Spider's lead and started to scrape furiously. As his hands scratched across the icy boards the skin of his knuckles tore, but he didn't feel a thing. All he could think about now was the fact that they were trapped on the *Fortuna* and were likely to remain so for weeks. It was all his fault. And what if Ann wasn't on board? As Jem pushed the horrible thought away his mother's face swam into his mind. He paused to wipe some stinging sea spray from his eyes.

The boys shuffled forward on their knees and worked the stiff, flat brushes into the icy deck. A pair of heavy boots came into view just beyond the tips of Jem's black, curly fringe. There was a cracking noise as Grimscale crouched beside him.

He flinched at the fetid smell of the man's grog-laced breath. "I'll be keeping a very close eye on you and your friend over there. Remember, one mistake and I'll be ready." The man kicked the brush out of Jem's frozen hand and laughed. "You might want to ask little Spider here what a keelhauling is. Just so that you're prepared."

CHAPTER
TWELVE

"And then you are tied up with your hands behind your back, lowered over the side and dragged underneath the ship from one side to the other. It probably takes about two minutes altogether, depending on who's pulling on the ropes. They draw lots to see which members of the crew take that job because no one in their right mind would want it. But Spider says it's not drowning you should worry about. No, it's the fact that the barnacles covering the bottom of the ship rip the skin off your back as you're scraped under the hull. He's never seen a keelhauling, but he reckons no one could survive it. It's like being flayed alive. And he says if there are sharks in the water and they get the scent of blood…"

Tolly winced and raised his bandaged hand. "Don't – I can't hear any more. It's disgusting. How could anyone invent something so cruel?" He drew his cloak about him and tucked Cleo deeper into the folds.

It was the first time Jem and Tolly had been able to speak properly all day. The knife-sharp air was salty on their faces as they huddled together halfway along the main deck. The *Fortuna* groaned as she rode the waves, rising like a bucking horse and then plunging down again into frothing, churning water. Jem gripped the rail to steady himself as the vast black ship ploughed forward.

It was late, and apart from the watch stationed high above in the lookout, all the other shipmates were making themselves as snug as possible in the gloomy warren of spaces below the deck.

"Have you managed to pick up anything at all – even the smallest whisper?"

Tolly nodded. "Ann's here on board with us. I'm certain of it. I keep seeing what she's seeing and feeling what she feels. She's frightened and confused. She's in a grand room, finely furnished with a wide window – and beyond the glass there's sea." He spoke without looking at Jem and his breath fugged the air. "But I can't connect to her. She doesn't know me. She can't hear me. It's as if I... *we* have been wiped clear from her mind. We know she's not in the hold and we've seen all the crew and their quarters – so that means she must be up there." He pointed at the steps to the passenger quarters. "But the crew aren't allowed into that part of the ship. Only the captain is permitted to speak to the passenger and there's a guard. Look."

Jem stared at the golden Medusa mask over the entrance to the grand cabins. Just below, in the shadow behind the broad steps, he could see a little point of glowing red. Someone – probably the guard – was smoking a pipe.

He shivered. "We must be careful, Tolly. I can't stay out here for long. Spider says she – the passenger, I mean – has given orders that no one is to go about on deck at night without permission after the watch has gone up. She didn't even want to allow that, but the captain insisted because of the floating islands. Do you know what they are?"

Tolly shook his head miserably. "Something horrible, I expect?"

"Ice – big lumps of it in the sea. Like the Thames last winter – but much bigger. If the ship runs into one of them she'll go down in minutes because they're as hard and jagged as rock. Some of the floating islands are the size of Wales – the country, I mean, not the sea beasts – that's what Spider says."

"Spider says a lot, doesn't he?" Tolly fed a nugget of dry ship's biscuit to Cleo. She didn't seem to like it very much, but there was little else to offer.

Jem decided to change the subject. "Are you and Cleo going to be all right up here on deck?"

"Well, I won't go below, so we don't have much choice, do we?" Tolly's voice was sharp, but then he must have seen Jem's face and continued more softly. "We're as comfortable as possible. I've made a sort of... *nest*, I suppose you could call it, inside the stacks up there." He pointed towards the prow where a mound of sailcloths and some fat bundles covered in oilskins were lashed to the foredeck. "Don't worry. No one will notice us. I'll be careful. And if anyone catches me, I'll say I'm out here for one of the essentials."

Jem nodded. He'd always thought that the servants' privies at Ludlow House were the foulest place on earth, but now he knew better. The hole cut into the side of the *Fortuna* for shipmates to relieve their bowels was not only revolting, but dangerous too. He couldn't believe his eyes when Spider had shown him where it was.

Tolly looked behind him and frowned. "The *Fortuna* is travelling fast."

"Spider said that too when we were scrubbing ice off the deck. We're making good time."

Tolly shook his head slowly. "No, that's not quite

right. We're moving unnaturally fast. Pocket said some of the experienced crewmates are nervous about it. Look back there, Jem. That's England slipping away from us in the dark. We shouldn't be here yet. We only left London yesterday morning. It can't be possible, and yet…"

The boys fell silent as they watched the winking lights gradually recede on the coastline far behind them. Ahead of them was a wall of black. Jem felt as if they were sliding over the rim of the world. He had always dreamed of going to sea, to seek adventures in distant lands, but not like this.

"What are we going to do, Tolly?"

"Well, we certainly can't swim for it, that's for certain. Even you couldn't make it to land now." Tolly's knuckles showed white as his brown hand tightened on the rail. He stared up at the stars.

Jem felt utterly trapped and defeated. He drew a deep breath and just for a second caught the rich, spiced tang of tobacco. He glanced back at the man guarding the entrance to the grand cabins.

Jem realised it must be the strange crewman Spider had spoken about earlier. Mingan – was that it? Jem had helped the tall, silent man to unfurl a sail on deck earlier that day. Grimscale had ordered them to check it over for tears.

Mingan didn't seem to feel the cold. His bare torso and arms were covered with elaborate tattoos, and he had peculiar ice-blue eyes that burned like the hottest part of a fire in the weathered skin of his face. But the most extraordinary thing of all about him was the mane of thick grey-black hair that fell to his waist, threaded with scores of tiny white skulls. Mouse skulls, Spider reckoned, "and maybe a couple of cats."

Tolly followed the line of Jem's gaze. "I can't read him," he said, after a moment. "Usually I pick up things – you know, just feelings – about people. But not him…" Tolly shook his head. "There's a wall around him."

Jem watched as Mingan leaned forward and raised the long pipe to his mouth again. The bowl of the pipe sparked and the scent of the man's tobacco wafted down to them once more. As he moved, the outline of his head was sharply silhouetted in the glow of the single lamp swinging from a chain beneath the Medusa. For a second, Jem saw the shadow of a huge, long-snouted dog. He blinked and the image was gone. A trick of the light.

"Spider says he's going home to his people. He's

served with the captain before. Trevanion trusts him."

"Does he?" Tolly's eyes narrowed. Cleo poked her head out from the folds of the cloak. "I think she's frightened of him. You know how she always has a nose for people? Well, when Mingan's near, she acts in an odd way. She doesn't run away exactly... it's more that she watches him – she's fascinated by him, but wary too. I don't understand it."

Jem thumped the rail. "Well, I don't understand any of this! The one thing I do know is that we have to search the ship. We have to find Ann, but with him keeping guard over there..." he nodded back to the entrance to the cabin, "we haven't got a hope of getting in and that's the only part of the *Fortuna* we haven't seen yet. Ann must be there..."

Jem stopped as a low, wailing noise filled the air. The eerie sound rose to a long melancholy note and then faded away. It began building again and Jem felt the sound coiling around him like a cobweb – it had a peculiar silky quality to it. He found himself brushing his face, trying to wipe invisible tendrils of sound away. Cleo covered her ears with her paws and burrowed deeper into Tolly's cloak.

"What on earth is that?" Jem held his hands over his own ears as the sound grew stronger. He peered over the side of the ship. "It's... It's coming from the sea."

Tolly didn't answer. He was looking back along the deck. Mingan was nowhere to be seen now, but there was a dark, hunched shape outlined against the golden light of the open doorway beneath the Medusa mask. "Look!" he whispered. "Is that Ann?"

The cloaked shape took a few steps forward and then seemed to float down the steps to the deck some twenty yards away from them.

It paused before moving to the side of the boat to look out over the water. Jem couldn't see who it was – the person had their back to them. "Can you feel anything – is it her?"

Tolly shook his head slowly.

Jem watched as the figure shrugged back a hood, revealing a mass of auburn curls which glowed in the light from the open door. He slumped against the rail. So it definitely wasn't Ann. Slowly, it raised its arms. The wailing stopped abruptly and a sudden gust of icy wind caught at the trailing cloak, making it billow and flap about like the unfurled wings of a great black bird.

The person turned and the beautiful, pointed chalk-white face sent a bolt through Jem. The woman wore a jewelled eye-patch which glittered in the lamplight pooling from the doorway.

"Duck!" He pulled Tolly down beside him and the boys crouched behind a couple of water barrels lashed against the rail. Jem watched through the sliver of space between the barrels. He didn't know why, but suddenly he was very sure that he didn't want to be seen by the one-eyed woman. There was something horribly familiar about her, but he couldn't remember when or where he had seen her before. As he wracked his memory he heard rustling as she came close to their hiding place... and passed on by. There were other sounds too – scratching, and a slow mechanical clicking.

Tolly shifted and leaned to the right so that he had a view.

"*Careful!*" Jem thought and Tolly nodded.

"*Don't worry, she's got her back to us.*" The words sounded clearly in Jem's mind.

Instantly, the woman paused and turned swiftly to stare at their hiding place. She arched her neck, raised her head and turned it from left to right like an adder about to strike.

Had the woman heard them? Jem shrank into a ball and kept very still in the shadows.

A buried image began to form in his mind.

A snake?

The woman moved to the far end of the ship and paused at the stack of goods and sailcloth where Tolly had made a nest for himself and Cleo. Once again she arched her neck and swayed from side to side before leaning down.

Jem couldn't see her clearly now, but he heard a dragging sound, as if a heavy package was being pulled across the boards. Moments later there was a loud splash. He wanted to shift for a better view, but he couldn't risk being seen. Instead he backed even further into the dark space between the barrels and the ship's rail, aware that beside him Tolly was gently stroking Cleo's head, willing her to stay silent.

"*Mange bien, mes soeurs. Mange tout.*" The hissed words carried on the biting air. Then the scraping, scratching, ticking and clicking came again as the woman swept past them and back along the deck.

At the Medusa doorway she turned and stared back towards the prow of the ship. Her red-painted lips curled into a cruel smile and the jewels sewn into the velvet of her eye-patch caught the light.

At last Jem realised where he had seen her before – in a portrait hanging in the long gallery leading to the library at Malfurneaux Place.

He thought back to the moment when he'd found himself drawn to the picture. The woman's single golden eye had glinted with malice as he reached out to the brilliantly painted material of her glistening black dress. The swirling fabric resembled thousands of sheeny reptilian scales sewn together and Jem had felt compelled to touch them. And he was about to do just that when he had caught sight of the woman's foot revealed by a parting in the fabric of her skirts, as if she was about to stride out of the picture.

The foot was the gnarled and blackened talon of a huge bird – and now, in a flash, Jem realised it was the same hideous, scaly, blackened claw he had seen beneath the hem of the gown of the mummer who had led Ann to the 'Obby 'Oss at Goldings.

CHAPTER
THIRTEEN

"I know her!" Jem waited until the strange woman had disappeared through the doorway back into the cabin. "She was with the mummers who took Ann – and in a painting." He stood up and grabbed at a rope to steady himself as the *Fortuna* creaked and rolled.

"What do you mean, 'in a painting'?" Tolly loosened his grip on Cleo and the little monkey jumped up to perch on one of the barrels that had shielded them from view. She flicked her tail and stared at the doorway.

"In the corridor to the library at Malfurneaux Place there were lots of peculiar paintings of men and women all dressed in strange costumes. You must remember it?"

Tolly nodded. "Of course I do. But I never looked at them. It was as if they were... alive. If I had to go there I always kept my head down. Ann said the paintings were evil. She warned me never to look directly into their eyes."

"She was right about that." Jem shuddered at the

memory. "There was one of a woman in a dress made of scales. She looked like a snake. I wanted to tear my eyes away but I couldn't. I was almost… drawn into the picture with her. It was her – the woman we've just seen. I'm sure of it. She wore an eye-patch too and in the painting she had claws instead of feet – like an eagle or a hawk. Remember the masked mummer who led Ann to the 'Obby 'Oss? When its cloak moved, I saw that same foot then."

Tolly's eyes widened, as Jem continued in a rush. "Did you hear the noise – the scraping? That was the sound of talons scratching on the wood. I'd know her anywhere. Who is she?"

"I don't think that's the right question." Tolly stared back at the doorway beneath the carved mask. "I tried to close my mind to her just now, when she seemed to sense us. It meant I couldn't read her, but at least it also meant she couldn't read me." He frowned. "The thing is, if that woman really was in a painting at Malfurneaux Place, then perhaps the question we should be asking is *why* is she here?"

"Because she has Ann?" Jem tightened his grip on the rail.

Tolly's eyes sparked with hope. "If you saw her at

Goldings with the mummers it must prove we're on the right track. But that's not exactly what I meant."

He looked around at the blackened, carved timbers of the *Fortuna* and then stared up into the forest of masts and ice-crusted ropes straining above them.

"No, the question is this: if she knew Count Cazalon, is the *Fortuna* a trap? And have we walked straight into it?"

⚜ ⚓ ⚜

Jem tried to find a comfortable position in the narrow, stringy hammock. Every time he closed his eyes he saw the woman standing in the doorway again, her lips curved into that mirthless smile. The expression reminded him a little of the way Wormald, the vicious steward who'd tormented Jem in his previous life as a kitchen hand, used to look at him before inflicting yet another undeserved punishment with his special serrated cane.

"*Mange bien.*" That was what the woman had said, wasn't it? Jem twisted about and found himself wishing for the very first time that he'd paid more attention to Dr Speight's French lessons. It was something about food, and "*bien*" meant good, didn't it? He wasn't sure.

In the dark next to him, Spider snored like an old bloodhound. Jem was surprised that such a skinny boy could make such an incredible noise. Pocket mumbled occasionally and smacked his lips; Jem caught the word "bacon" and something that sounded like "good mutton". He wondered how Tolly and Cleo were in their nest on the deck above and then he thought about their plan again. He had to get down into the hold without being seen, but if he tried now he'd need to light a candle lantern to see the way. He couldn't risk waking either of his companions.

It was Tolly's idea. If they could find Cazalon's staff, then perhaps they could use it again to show them precisely where Ann was hidden.

"If we know exactly where she is, that would be a start, Jem," Tolly had pressed him earlier when they stood on deck. "And besides, if we have to fight that… that woman, I've got a feeling the staff could be a powerful weapon. It was important to Cazalon, wasn't it? We don't know what it can really do."

Jem had nodded, but Tolly's words about the *Fortuna* being a trap had run through his mind. What if Ann wasn't on board at all?

"She is!" The words had been sharp.

Tolly had read his doubt. For some reason Jem had felt guilty, as if he'd been caught doing something wrong.

"She must be." Tolly had reached up to stroke Cleo, who'd perched on his shoulder. She'd whickered softly and nuzzled his neck.

He had rubbed a hand across his face and turned away to look out to sea, but not before Jem had noticed the glittering tears that brimmed in his friend's dark eyes.

After a moment Tolly had spoken gruffly. "When Count Cazalon bought me and took me to Malfurneaux Place, little Cleo here, and Ann, they... they became my family. I won't lose my family for a second time." He'd clutched the rail so tightly that the bandage over his fingers had split.

Jem had felt his stomach knot as he thought of his own mother, and Gabriel too. He wondered if he would ever see either of them again, along with Ann. He tried to swallow the lump in his throat as Tolly spoke again.

"We need the staff, Jem. From the moment I touched it in the caravan, I... I knew it was a key."

The boys had stood together in a miserable silence

as the black timbers of the *Fortuna* growled and wind lashed through the rigging overhead. It sounded like the swish of a score of swords.

"*Never drop your guard.*"

Jem turned in the hammock and Pocket muttered in his sleep again. He thought about everything his fencing master had taught him. Tolly was right. They needed every weapon they could lay their hands on, but there was more. They needed to use their brains too. There had to be a way to get into the hold without anyone knowing.

※ ⚓ ※

The sails billowed, their fat grey bellies straining as a fierce east wind drove the *Fortuna* on. Jem squinted as he looked up into the brilliant sunlight and tried to work out what time it was.

"You finished with that lot?" Spider pushed another coil of rope across the deck. "Remember, if any is frayed or torn it can't be used. It has to be unpicked and knotted again, otherwise it won't be safe up there – won't take the weight, see." The boy pointed upward, but Jem didn't look. He didn't like to think about the network of ropes strung out between the towering masts above them. Most particularly, he didn't like to think about the way the experienced crewmen clambered and swung between them. It was how Spider had got his name – he was particularly nimble on the ropes. His real name was John, but on his first voyage some of the older crewmates had nicknamed him Spider, impressed by his dexterity.

"You don't have a head for heights, Jemmie, do you?"

Jem didn't answer Spider's question.

"Pocket and me, we've noticed how you don't look up. It's no matter to us, we like it up there – the view and that." Spider sniffed. "Tell you what, if you get sent up, one of us'll do it for you. We'll swap chores." Jem glanced at Spider and nodded gratefully as the scrawny boy continued. "A word of advice – don't let old Grimface know you're feared."

As the *Fortuna* lurched, the boys were soaked by a deluge of freezing salty water that crashed over the side. "I'll tell you another fing, Jemmie." Spider rubbed the stinging water from his eyes with his raw, cracked hands. "You and your mate over there," he waved a bit of frayed rope end at Tolly, who was sitting cross-legged at the other end of the deck, working on a section of tattered sail alongside Pocket, "you've found your sea legs quick enough. I was sick as a dog first time out."

"How many trips have you made?" Jem wondered

what made a boy like Spider prefer the sea to the land.

"This'll be my third, same as Pocket. Never seen a ship go like this one, though." Spider grinned up at the bulging sails. "You've brought us first-timer's luck. That's what I told Ned this morning when he said we were riding a witch wind. As a general rule, I don't hold with that superstitious stuff and neither should you. If you ask me there's too much of that kind of talk."

Spider shuffled a bit closer. "A couple of the lads reckon they've seen an owl in the sky. Now, that's a bird of ill-omen, I'll grant you that, but what's it doing out here? If you want my 'pinion on the matter, they've been taking an unfair go at the grog rations. And that's not right."

Jem plucked at the rope as Spider lowered his voice to a confidential whisper. "You have to be careful with the grog. It's strong stuff for all it warms you up. Ned says someone's gone overboard already – slipped on the ice, I reckon. We're a man down, but you're not to say I told you that."

Another wave of ice-cold water slammed across the deck, but that wasn't why Jem shivered.

A man down? Was that the splashing sound he and Tolly had heard last night? He closed his eyes and ran the scene through his mind again – the eerie noises from the water, the way the woman had dragged something from beneath the sailcloth stack, the heavy splash…

"Oi! Wake up." Jem felt a sharp prod in the ribs. "If Grimface catches you napping on the job he'll have his cat out of the bag quicker than you can empty your grog can." Spider grinned. "You were nearly off there."

"I wasn't. I was thinking." Jem reached for another coil of rope as the other boy continued cheerfully.

"I don't hold with finking, me. Dangerous that is – slows the brain, clogs it up with all manner of rubbish. What was you finking about, anyway?"

Jem grinned now. "If you must know, I was *finking* about ways to stop your snoring. If I did nearly fall asleep just then – and I'm not saying I did – it's because I can barely sleep. At night you sound like a pig with its nose stuck in a bucket of swill."

Spider nodded amiably. "My brothers say that too. I daresay they'll be happy to have the bed to themselves at home now I'm at away sea on a permanent footing, like. I'm the oldest, but they'll be at sea themselves soon enough. It's what Swale men have done for a thousand years."

"How many brothers do you have?" Jem asked, wondering what it must be like.

"Six, and three sisters too."

"And you and your brothers all sleep in one bed?"

"Course. But we top to tail so there's plenty of room. Look sharp – grog's up." Spider leaped to his feet and scuttled to the prow end of the ship where Grimscale was prising the wooden top off a fat-bodied barrel. A queue of thirsty crewmates began to form along the deck, clanking their pewter mugs expectantly on the rail. Another crewman was handing out flat, stale biscuits from a second barrel. The porridge-coloured ovals were as hard as stone and tasted of dust, but Jem now knew that they were the best rations he could expect on board the ship.

His stomach rumbled as he watched the men chewing, their jaws bulged as they worked on mouthfuls of dry stuff. They needed the grog to get the disgusting, worm-riddled things down. Jem's mouth began to water. He was starving, but today he was going to have to go hungry.

This was the moment he had been waiting for. From now until the change of watch, everyone on the *Fortuna* would be allowed to leave their duties. Sometimes groups of the older men sang shanties, others smoked or played cards or dice. Captain Trevanion was very clear that recreation should happen every day, despite Grimscale's sour-faced mutterings.

Jem wrapped his cloak about him. He nodded at Tolly, who winked before turning to say something to Pocket. Standing up, Tolly gave a low whistle. Instantly Cleo leaped from his shoulder to the deck. Pocket laughed as she executed a string of perfect somersaults across the boards. Soon a knot of shipmates had gathered to watch, some of them kneeling to offer her crumbs from their biscuits.

Unnoticed, Jem stood up and crossed to the stern where the square hatch beneath the steps led down to the cramped crew quarters. He pulled on the metal ring to open it and slipped down.

CHAPTER FOURTEEN

Within a minute Jem was in the bowels of the *Fortuna* in the cramped and stinking space where he, Spider and Pocket slept above the hold. He felt for the little tinderbox and candle lantern stowed beside Pocket's hammock and struck a light. He didn't have time to feel his way around in the darkness down there. He had to find Cazalon's staff and get back up on deck quickly.

He paused for a second, straining his ears to check that no one had followed, then he raised the hatch in the planks beneath Spider's hammock and clambered down, gripping the lantern tightly. The air was thick with the scent of tar and foul water. Wrinkling his nose, Jem jumped from the lowest of the metal rungs and landed in a crouching position. There was a sudden scrabbling noise beside him. He raised the lantern and glanced down. Next to his hand a fat black rat squirmed into a gap between a couple of wooden crates. He could see its tiny red eyes watching him from the shadows.

Jem pushed his salt-matted fringe out of his eyes and straightened up. He didn't have long. Where would Grimscale have put the staff?

Jem thought hard. The master mate had been furious with the captain that night. He imagined the thwarted, red-faced man opening the hatch and roughly flinging the staff into the jumble of packages, boxes and barrels. It wouldn't have gone far, surely?

He held the lantern higher to scour the cluttered hold and blinked in surprise. There was another light down here too – a flickering golden glow like a candle flame halfway along the right-hand side. The light seemed to be coming from the large oblong package that rested against the wall – the one that had fascinated Cleo.

As Jem took a step forward, the ship lurched. The moaning of the timbers was magnified tenfold down here, accompanied by a hollow rhythmic booming as waves pounded at the hull. He steadied himself and picked his way carefully between the piles of sacks, leather trunks and crates until he was level with the package propped against the side of the hold. There was a jagged rip in the fabric wrapped around it. Ragged shreds of grey oilcloth flapped loosely over the crimson cords that bound it and something glowed within.

He placed the lantern and the tinderbox on a barrel and frowned. There was a mark on the wrapping cloth just above the rip – a small, reddish handprint. Jem reached out to touch the mark and scratched at the print. He brought his fingers to his nose and recoiled instantly from the familiar metallic tang.

Blood!

His heart began to hammer in his chest as he took a step back. A horrible thought seeped into his mind. Was this where Ann had been all the time? Was this why Cleo didn't want to leave the hold?

"Ann?" He whispered her name urgently and then repeated it more loudly. "Ann, are you down here?" He turned to scan the jumbled space and listened intently for the faintest answer. "It's me, Jem. If you can hear me, try to let me know." He fought to squash the awful thought that sprang suddenly into his mind. What if she was dead? What if Tolly was sensing her lifeless body hidden down here? He hadn't been able to connect with her since they first got on the ship, had he? If she was dead, it would make hideous sense. His hand went to the red shawl still tucked around his belt. It was all they had of her.

A crackling noise came from behind him and he spun round. The glow beneath the torn fabric was beginning to fade now. Jem grabbed the tattered shreds and ripped hard. The tear widened into a gash about a yard long and he yanked the cloth aside. He saw his own face reflected in a flat, glassy surface.

A mirror – a very old one.

The *Fortuna* dipped and Jem jerked forward, flattening his hand against the pitted glass. The surface was cold and dead. Any glimmer in its depths seemed to be a distorted, weirdly magnified reflection of the feeble lantern. He leaned closer, noticing more blood on the glass – not a handprint this time, but a series of delicate looping squiggles. He tried to make sense of what he saw, squinting to see if the shapes formed a word he recognised.

Something black moved swiftly over the surface – something ragged and huge. At the same moment the glass beneath Jem's fingers rippled. It was suddenly so cold that his hand burned with pain. He tried to pull away, but his bare flesh was frozen to the mirror as if stuck to a block of ice.

He felt something undulating against his palm. The hairs on the back of his neck prickled. He stared wildly into the glass. There was nothing there now, not even his reflection, just blackness. He tried to pull away, but as he struggled to free his hand the mirror bulged beneath his skin

He felt long, bony fingers slip between the gaps of his own splayed fingers. They curled over the back of his hand and sharp, claw-like nails dug into the skin below his knuckles, making him cry out. He tried to look but he couldn't move any part of his body. Just out of his eyeline and to the right, something like liquid silver was moving over his hand, dragging it into the mirror.

He felt a tremendous scorching sensation in his heel. The Eye of Ra – Ann's ancient mark of protection – flared so painfully that, involuntarily, he raised his foot and kicked out. There was a splintering sound and a crack slowly jagged up the glass until it reached the base of his flattened palm. Instantly his hand came free and he fell back. His heel burned, but worse were the four stinging red strips running down the back of his hand. The palm of his hand was bubbled and raw too. He looked up. The cracked mirror was completely black.

A tiny red point began to glow in the depths of the glass. The point pulsed and seemed to expand and unfurl until Jem realised he was looking at smouldering embers in a great hearth in a room beyond the mirror. The image sharpened and he saw a massive carved fireplace, the mantel supported by two grotesque horned figures.

He knew that room in the glass. He had stood in front of that fireplace before – in Count Cazalon's great chamber at Malfurneaux Place. He whipped his head round to look over his shoulder, but there was nothing behind him except for the muddle of shadowed, bulky objects in the hold. He looked back and the room was still there in the mirror.

It was impossible. Jem backed away and caught his ankle on the edge of a sack. He lost his footing and crumpled to the boards. The fire in the glass suddenly flared with such an intense, cold brilliance that he was forced to shield his eyes. When he looked again, the room had gone.

Now, in the cracked, pitted glass, Jem could just make out the dim, distorted reflection of his own terrified face as he knelt amid the sacks. There was a metallic tinkling sound and suddenly a thousand tiny vein-like crackles began to spread across the glass from the first fracture. A splinter of mirror the size of a hand fell out from the frame and shattered near Jem's knees. . The crackles zigzagged over the surface until Jem's face blurred beneath a network of tiny lines. For a second it was as if an old, old man was staring back at him.

Without thinking about the staff, he scrambled to his feet and blundered to the hatch. He had to get away.

CHAPTER FIFTEEN

Jem pushed the wooden hatch open a crack. The broad steps on the deck that led up to the grand cabin above shielded him from view, but they also meant he couldn't see everything clearly. He listened for a moment and caught the merry sound of a shanty being sung by men up at the other end of the ship. Cautiously, he pushed the hatch open a little wider and peered through the narrow gap. As far as he could tell no one was nearby.

He climbed up and out onto the deck, hunching his shoulders against a sudden blast of frozen air. He pulled his cloak tight, raised the collar of his jerkin, and buried his chin in the coarse-woven fabric. He winced as the movement pulled at the burned skin of his hand. He looked down at the red marks across his knuckles and shivered. He had to tell Tolly what he had seen in the mirror.

Keeping his head low, Jem stepped forward. He paused at the edge of the steps to the cabins and glanced up at the carved wooden Medusa mask. It was so very like the one at Malfurneaux Place, the carved snakes of her hair twisting and coiling to form a sort of canopy over the studded door.

"Now I've got you!"

A hand clamped down hard on his shoulder. Jem didn't even have to turn round to know that Master Grimscale was standing directly behind him. The man's rank breath made him gag.

"Been stealing from the crew quarters, have you? Sneaking around when you think no one's looking? Well, let me tell you something lad: Grimscale's always on the lookout."

Grimscale spun him about roughly and lowered his big, pitted face so that it was level with Jem's. The man grinned, revealing a fat grey tongue glistening in his black-gummed mouth. It wriggled like one of the pale old carp in the moat at Goldings. Grimscale stared into Jem's eyes. He was clearly delighted with his catch.

"Empty your pockets."

"I haven't taken anything." Jem felt nausea rise in his throat as a fresh wave of Grimscale's foul breath clogged his nostrils.

"*I haven't taken anything.*" Grimscale mimicked Jem's voice, before tightening his grip and continuing

153

more harshly. "Then what were you doing below deck at grog time when you knew no one would be watching, eh? Thief."

"I... I..." Jem clenched his fists as he tried to think of something to say. The sudden pain from the burned, scraped skin of his hand made him gasp, but it gave him an idea.

"I hurt my hand on the rope earlier." He held his right palm out to Grimscale, the skin blistered where it had been stuck to the mirror. "It got caught up – the rope, I mean. But when I pulled, it came free so fast that it tore across my palm. I just went below to find something to wrap around my hand, so that I could carry on working. But there was nothing to use."

Grimscale frowned, then he sniffed and licked the corner of his mouth, leaving a glob of yellow-tinged saliva in his reddish stubble. He grinned even wider. "A likely story. Come here, lad. I'm going to introduce you to my pets."

He gripped Jem's ear and dragged him out into the middle of the deck. Some of the sailors stopped singing and watched as Grimscale unhooked a baggy black leather sack from the main mast.

"This is where I keep my cats." He rummaged

in the bag and drew out a short wooden baton with several leather cords attached to the end. Jem flinched as he saw that at least three of the cords ended with a metal weight, like a shiny musket ball. Grimscale held the whip up in his right hand and turned around slowly, speaking loudly and steadily so that everyone could hear. Jem sensed that he was enjoying this very much indeed.

"My girls like to get out and have a good scratch every now and again. And it seems they've got just the chance they were looking for."

The deck fell completely silent. Jem saw a couple of the older men swap wary glances. Spider's face was grey as the sailcloths.

"He's just a lad. Leave him be, master," a gruff voice called out from the huddle of sailors gathered near the grog barrel and the biscuit rations. There was a mutter of agreement from all sides.

"'Tis not the way of Swale. Take him down to the captain. Let him decide," someone else called out.

"And why would I bother Captain Trevanion with a petty crime? No – I think I'll deal with this my way." A blast of wind made the ship plunge forward and a wave crashed across the boards. Jem stumbled and gripped the rail of the steps to steady himself.

He could taste salt on his frozen lips as he looked across at Grimscale. The man was standing with his feet planted wide apart. He was as broad as an ox and now he lowered his head ready to charge.

At the far end of the deck, near the prow, someone very tall stood up. Mingan.

His long grey hair flew up like a wild mane around his head as the wind caught at it. The bones plaited into the strands rattled and clicked as they flew about. Mingan took a step towards Grimscale. The tattoos on the strange man's torso rippled as he flexed his muscles. The markings seemed to come together to form something that looked like…

"*Aaarghffff!*"

Grimscale let out a cry of pain. He dropped the whip and clapped a hand to his right ear. A thin trickle of blood oozed through the master mate's fingers. Cleo squealed and raced from between Grimscale's splayed feet to the rigging on the side of the boat, clambering to a point several feet just above Tolly's head.

She clung on tightly and waved something golden and round in front of her nose – Grimscale's hooped earring.

"Why, you little… Ripped it from my ear, it

did!" The furious master mate lumbered over the deck, and jumped up and down, trying to snatch the object from her paw. But Cleo flicked her tail, climbed a little higher and continued to dangle the earring tantalisingly out of reach, all the while chattering mockingly.

With surprising agility for his size, Grimscale leaped onto the side of the ship and wound his big left hand into the rigging ropes. With the bloody right, he lunged at Cleo, but the little monkey was too fast for him, disappearing higher into the puzzle of ropes and sailcloths overhead. The burly man's face turned the colour of a freshly broiled salmon as he swore and took one last swipe at her disappearing tail.

On the deck below crewmen began to laugh. Some of them started to call out bets on how long it would take Grimscale to catch her. But at Captain Trevanion's voice, everyone fell silent.

"What the Devil is going on here?" Trevanion walked forward and paused when his boot caught against the whip Grimscale had dropped to the deck. He stared down, his face hardening into an expression of disgust. "What is the meaning of this?" He looked up at the master mate who was trying to extricate himself from the rigging. "Explain yourself, Grimscale. I thought I gave clear instructions that this… this thing," he kicked the whip aside, "was never to be used on board."

"That's as may be, sir. But when you find a thief you have to take a hard line." Grimscale heaved himself back onto deck and gripped Jem's shoulder – pushing him forward.

"A thief?" Trevanion's eyebrows shot up.

"That's not true, Captain. I'm not a thief. I went down into the ship to find something to bind this." Jem held his hand forward so that the captain could see the marks. "I've been working on the ropes all day, haven't I, Spider?"

A look of confusion crossed the skinny boy's face, but he glanced swiftly at Jem and nodded. "That's right enough, Captain, sir. And it can be sore hard work on the hands." He held up his own scratched fingers. "Red raw these are too."

Trevanion nodded. "Do you see that, Grimscale? No wonder the boy needed a bandage. This will end now."

Grimscale muttered something that sounded like a curse, but the captain didn't hear him, or chose not to. He looked back to the entrance to his own quarters beneath the passenger's cabin. There stood Master Valentine, frowning at the sky. His black wig was askew and there were spots of ink on the white linen cuffs of the shirt that showed beneath his long coat. He fiddled with a golden instrument in his hands. It was just like the device that Jem had seen on the charts in Trevanion's cabin and now he knew it was a quadrant used to plot their progress. The young man didn't come out on deck often – Spider said he was happiest at a desk, examining sea charts and star maps.

The captain drew a deep breath. "Now I want you all to go back to your duties. There's at least an hour of daylight left. Mr Valentine, will you come back in with me, please? I want you to check something again. Bring the quadrant with you. We'll try another of the charts. There must be an error."

The young man nodded and dipped through the doorway. The captain turned sharply on his heels to follow when a voice called out, "We're riding a witch wind, ain't we? We shouldn't be here yet. Not by rights."

Jem saw Trevanion's back stiffen, but he carried on without turning round or saying another word. When he was gone, groups of anxious crewmen formed around the deck. Jem heard them muttering together.

Grimscale jumped heavily down from the rail and pushed Jem aside. He walked over to the doorway to the captain's quarters and listened for a moment. The veins in the sides of his thick red neck bulged and his hands clenched and unclenched. After a moment he turned about slowly and looked at the crewmen who were watching him. He spat on the boards and stumped over to the grog barrel, helping himself to a large mugful.

Spider tugged at Jem's sleeve. "How did you really do that then?" He nodded down at Jem's hand.

There were footsteps on the deck behind them. "Did you get it?" Tolly tapped Jem's shoulder. Jem turned and flashed a warning with his eyes, indicating Spider, who was hidden from Tolly's view.

"No, I couldn't find anything…" he said, holding out his blistered palm and adding with heavy significance, "for my hand."

Tolly nodded. "Right. I'm sorry about that. I mean, I'm sorry about that… rope burn?" He looked questioningly at Jem, who was aware that their stilted conversation must seem very strange.

To cover the awkwardness Jem spoke quickly.

"Thank goodness for Cleo back then, Tolly. She saved me from Grimscale and his whip, that's for certain."

Spider pulled a face. "He's famous for his cat. Ned says he takes it with him everywhere he goes. First time I've seen it out of the bag though." He shuddered. "I wouldn't want to see it again."

There was a thumping sound on the deck behind them as Grimscale himself appeared.

"You – monkey boy – I'm going to make life very unpleasant for you and your pilfering pet." He spat the words and winced as he rubbed his torn ear. "For a start, you're going to go up the rigging to find it. But when you do, you're not going to bring it down…"

Grimscale took a swig from his mug and wiped his wet lips with the back of his tattooed hand. He seemed to be very pleased with himself now. "No, you're going to spend the night in the cradle with it. All night, mind, from dusk to dawn – maybe longer. I haven't decided yet. Anyway it will be just you and your little furry demon, a hundred feet up with only the stars for company."

Grimscale grinned and Jem winced as he caught another whiff of the man's sour breath. "Not that you'll see many stars tonight. By my reckoning there's a storm brewing. Within the hour this ship will be bucking like an unbroken stallion. We'll have to take sails in too. But not before you're aloft. Go to it."

Jem stared up at the lookout high above them. The ship was rocking and lurching in the heavy seas and the rickety little basket swayed wildly from side to side. He tried to drag his eyes away, but he couldn't. For some reason he was mesmerised by the sight of the soaring masts and flapping sails. His head began to spin, the backs of his legs tingled and he thought he might be sick.

"It's fine. I can do this." Tolly's voice sounded faintly in his mind. Jem tore his eyes from the mast-tops and looked across at his friend. Tolly's voice came again, but it was oddly muffled. Jem strained to hear the words and caught the end of a message "… not scared. Remember… Cleo with me."

Confused, he tried to shoot back an answer, but Grimscale had already taken Tolly firmly by the scruff of his neck and marched him over to the central mast. He pulled Tolly's cloak away and threw it to the side of the deck. "Can't have this flapping round your legs as you climb. See how thoughtful I am? Mind you, it'll be a cold night up there with just a candle lantern to warm your bones."

He grinned. "Up you go, then. I'll tell you when you can come down again. Remember this – if you aren't still up there at first light tomorrow, I'll roast that monkey of yours on a spit and suck out the marrow of its haunches. I'm missing the taste of fresh meat."

CHAPTER
SIXTEEN

It was no good. He couldn't sleep. Every time he closed his eyes the mirror in the hold beneath glinted in his mind. Jem shifted and swung his legs over the side of the hammock. Pocket snuffled and mumbled something about pottage. It sounded as if he was talking to his mother. He'd told Jem, in confidence, that he missed her very much – and the rich, meaty stews she made back in Swale. The ship lurched and Spider's hammock bumped against the wall, but the boys didn't stir.

Jem slipped to the timber floor and climbed the rickety ladder out of their shared coffin. All along the mess deck, crewmen snored in rows of lumpy hammocks. He moved softly to the steps leading up to the deck hatch, careful to avoid bumping into a swinging net and disturbing its occupant.

He needed to know that Tolly and Cleo were safe up in the cradle.

The deck was deserted – the only light came from a weak lantern bobbing at the prow and there was a glow overhead from the oval window set into the door leading to the passenger's cabin. Jem clung to the rail as the *Fortuna* rolled. Grimscale had been wrong about a storm coming. It was another clear night, but the bitter east wind driving the ship relentlessly forward tried to tear the hair from his head.

He wrapped his arms around himself, drew a deep breath and glanced up. The ropes whistled and vibrated with a low-pitched hum as the wind cut through the rigging. There was another sound too – Jem caught occasional snatches of song from somewhere high above. He strained his ears to listen as the sound came again.

There! A clear, melodious voice singing a song Jem didn't recognise, though it sounded like a lullaby. Tolly was singing to Cleo.

As the boat swayed, Jem caught sight of a tiny light, high overhead. He moved forward, gripping the rail tightly as he imagined himself to be up there with them. At least they were alive.

He craned his neck to track the flickering light of the lookout cradle through the tangle of ropes and sails. Long, thin icicles hung from the rigging, glittering in the moonlight like a score of crystal chandeliers. Spider had warned him to be wary of them. "Kill a man, they can. Spear you to the deck just like that." He'd clicked his fingers under Jem's nose, before adding, "That's what Ned says, anyhow."

Jem stared doubtfully at the vicious point of one of the longer icicles. Tolly would know if that was possible. He wondered if Tolly could sense his presence below. He closed his eyes and concentrated. "I'm down here. Are you two all right?"

Nothing. He tried again and again, but Tolly didn't answer.

Jem stayed there for a long time watching the light and catching soft snatches of song. The sound reassured him, a little.

It was gnawingly cold out on deck and he thrust his hands under the armpits of his jerkin for warmth. The rough material made the scars across his knuckles burn and that made him think about the mirror in the hold again. The Eye of Ra tingled on his heel. He tried to force the memory of that room in the glass out of his head.

He badly needed to communicate with Tolly. He needed to ask him about Ann. Was it possible that she might be… He bit his chapped lip and smothered the thought. Why couldn't his friend "hear" him?

Eventually, numbed to the core, Jem decided to go back to the bilge box. He could spend the rest of the night out here watching, but what good would it do? Tolly was right – he wasn't scared, and at least he and Cleo were together up there.

Jem bent his head against the wind and battled towards the hatch leading down to the crew quarters. When he was level with the steps, he glanced warily up at the Medusa canopy guarding the entrance. Was that where Ann was? If she was alive there was nowhere else she could be on this black monster. He was certain that Spider spoke the truth when he said he'd never seen a ship quite like it. There was something very wrong about the *Fortuna*. Even Jem could feel it.

He ducked low under the wide steps, and paused before pulling open the creaky hatch. He didn't want to draw attention to himself by making a noise. He listened for a moment, but there were no sounds from the deck. In fact, he realised that *no one* was standing guard to the passenger cabin. It was the chance he'd been waiting for. If he could sneak inside now while everyone was asleep he could search for Ann. He moved cautiously to the foot of the steps and looked up at the window, trying to see any shadow beyond the frosted panes.

A great slap of water crashed against the side of the ship. Jem stooped and closed his eyes to avoid the stingy, salty spray, but when he opened them again, someone barred his way. Someone with long, bare feet.

Jem's head shot up.

Mingan raised a finger to his lips and nodded his shaggy head up toward the Medusa doorway. He gripped Jem's shoulder roughly and propelled him into the darkness beneath the steps until the two of them were hidden from the deck.

Seconds later Jem heard a door slam, followed by the familiar scraping, scratching, ticking noise of the woman he and Tolly had watched the previous evening. The sound was lost on the wind as she moved down the steps towards the prow end of the ship, her cloak billowing around her once more.

Jem couldn't see her properly now; she was too far away. He strained forward, but Mingan pulled him further back into the gloom until the two of them were screened by the steps. Jem glanced up. The man shook his head and the tiny skulls plaited into his hair rattled. He raised his face and stared towards the prow. His odd, pale eyes narrowed and his nostrils flared.

Jem looked too. He couldn't see the woman at all now, but he was aware of a dense silence. The wind had died and the *Fortuna* was oddly still. He tried to catch the sound of Tolly's song, but there was nothing... at first.

Then the unearthly melancholy wailing began again. Just as before, the noise came from the sea. Jem's skin crawled as he felt the eerie sound twisting around him, brushing against his face like cobwebs. Mingan's grip tightened on his shoulder as the wailing rose and fell. Then the noise stopped abruptly.

The air began to vibrate with a weird energy. Blood pulsed in Jem's veins and made his temples ache. As the painful throbbing intensified, he felt that his head might burst open. He bent to cover his ears with his hands, but it didn't do any good.

Splash! The noise came from somewhere up ahead.

Instantly the peculiar atmosphere vanished. Jem straightened up and listened – nothing. He took a cautious step forward to get a glimpse of the woman at the prow. Immediately Mingan pulled him back, drawing him deep into the shadows once more.

At the same moment the *Fortuna* rolled and

reared up, throwing them both violently back against her side rail. Jem was winded as he lost his footing and crashed his spine against two wooden struts. He clung tight and watched in terror as the black deck of the ship began to rise in front of him. The timbers groaned and tremendous cracking, tearing sounds rang out as the prow rose higher and higher from the sea.

A stray bottle rolled back towards Jem, bouncing twice on the edge before disappearing over the side and into the water. Icicles cracked from the rigging and rained onto the deck like a shower of glass. A coil of ropes slid past and caught up in the rail struts by Jem's foot, the loose ends flailing over the side. The barrels next to him rumbled and juddered under their straps, and Jem knew that if they came free, he would be crushed.

His heart cannoned in his chest as he struggled to hang on. He thought about Tolly and Cleo, high above. Surely they would be hurled into the sea?

Beside him, through the gaps in the rail, he could see frothing white waves rising to meet the back of the ship. At any moment he and Mingan would be swept overboard. Jem wound his arms around two of the carved rail struts, squeezed his eyes shut and scrabbled madly to brace his feet against the rising deck planks. Just when he felt that he might lose his grip and slip into the foaming water, he felt Mingan's hand tighten over his right shoulder, keeping him safe.

Then, just as quickly as it had risen, the *Fortuna* slammed down into the waves and began to plough forward as if the Devil himself was filling her sails. The wind roared and Jem's ears popped as the ship powered ahead. He had to swallow hard to clear the muffling feeling.

"Wh-what just happened?" He gasped out the words and tried to struggle to his feet, but Mingan placed a hand firmly across his mouth.

The woman came back into view and Mingan withdrew his hand. He shrank deeper into the shadows behind the barrels, urgently motioning Jem to follow his lead. Jem obeyed. Neither of them moved or made a sound as she came closer. She didn't seem to be troubled by the wild motion of the ship. Despite the plunging and rolling, she moved in a direct line to the steps to her cabin, her black cloak swirling around her.

She almost seemed to be flying rather than walking, Jem thought, but as she neared the door he caught the familiar scratching, ticking sound. He pictured the talons beneath her cloak and knotted himself into a ball, praying that she wouldn't see him.

"Madame, I must ask you to return to your quarters. I am amazed to find you out here." Captain Trevanion had to shout to make his words carry over the wind. "It is not safe on deck. This gale is buffeting my ship about like a cork in a drain. Grimscale tells me that another man has gone missing today. I have lost *two* crewmen now. I'll not lose another soul."

The woman began to laugh. Jem tilted his head and saw the edge of the captain's shoulder, at the door to his cabin, strands of the man's grey wig flying about in the gale. A line of golden buttons glinted on Trevanion's sleeve as he held his hand behind his back and out of her view. As the weird, jagged sound of the woman's mirth carried on the air, Jem recognised the oval shape the man made with his thumb and index finger.

It was the old sign to ward off the evil eye.

The laughter stopped abruptly and the woman spoke. "I must thank you, Captain, for your concern for my... soul." She lingered on that last word, making it sound like the hiss of snake, before continuing. "Please do not worry yourself on my account. Nothing of earth can threaten me. I am not afraid of the air and I am not afraid of the water." She spoke in heavily accented English, her voice a soft purr, but the words seemed to be magnified, rather than swallowed by the storm. She gestured elegantly at the sky with a gloved hand and the dark cloak flew up around her, exposing flashes of emerald green lining. "Remember our bargain. I am impatient to reach my estates. We must make haste."

"I think you will find that we are making excellent time, Madame de Chouette." The captain's voice was clipped and strained.

She smiled more broadly and inclined her head. Jem thought again how beautiful she was, even with one eye, but it was the sort of beauty you might find in a wild creature. There was something cruel and dangerous about her. She moved out of view and then her voice came again, this time mocking. "And I think *you* will find, Captain, that this ship belongs to me. Come, we will look at the sea charts together in your quarters. I know how fascinated you are by our progress. I promised you, did I not, that this would be a voyage like no other?"

Trevanion stepped back to allow the woman

to go through the door first. He didn't follow immediately, but stepped forward, braced his feet against the rolling of the ship and turned slowly in a circle, staring intently up at the creaking masts and blackened timbers. Jem supposed that he was reassuring himself that after being hurled about on that huge wave the *Fortuna* was still seaworthy. The captain shook his head and turned back to the doorway. As light spilled onto the deck, Jem saw the man's face clearly. He seemed to have aged by a decade. The door slammed shut. Jem waited for a moment and then turned to Mingan.

He had gone.

CHAPTER SEVENTEEN

"It looks worse than it is." The thumb and first two fingers of Tolly's right hand were a peculiar mottled grey. "It was the cold last night. I thought my hand was on the mend, but it's made it worse again." He waggled his fingers and made a fist. "Look, I can still move them – I just can't feel anything at the moment. It will come back, won't it?"

Jem didn't answer. Years ago, one of the younger footmen at Ludlow House had foolishly gone out to a tavern during a snowstorm. When he didn't come back, they'd scoured the gardens and then the streets for him. It was two days before his frozen body was found crouching behind a yard wall. He'd been as stiff as a side of pork in the ice store. Jem couldn't help thinking that there was something about Tolly's frost-deadened fingers that reminded him of the sight of that footman when they'd brought him home.

Tolly frowned, wrapped the bandage back around his damaged hand and pulled his jerkin sleeve to cover it. "Luckily someone had left a blanket up there, but I don't think we would have survived another night, eh girl?" He huddled Cleo closer and she gripped the fabric of his cloak, nestling into the crook of his arm. "I think Grimscale hoped we both might die. I'm glad to have this back." Tolly shivered and pulled the woollen fabric around him.

"Pocket's up there tonight," said Jem. "But it's not a punishment this time. Spider says he actually likes it." His whole body went rigid at the thought. He glanced up at the lookout. Could Pocket see them down below? Jem thought it was unlikely. They were sitting in the space Tolly had cleared for himself at the foredeck of the ship. It wasn't exactly cosy, but it was covered overhead and enclosed on three sides, shielded from wind and from prying eyes. It reminded Jem of a cave.

He had to lean right out to see the tiny, moving point of light from Pocket's lantern. The other boy didn't have Cleo for company, but at least he was wrapped in a blanket and had taken a leather bottle of grog and a hunk of worm-riddled, salted meat with him. Jem wondered how long it would be before it was his turn to go aloft. The thought made his stomach lurch so he dragged his eyes down to the deck again. At the stern end of the ship he could just make out the pinprick glow of a pipe bowl. Mingan, perhaps? Some of the crew were still wary of the strange, silent man, but after the previous evening Jem didn't fear him.

Outside it was a clear, starry night and a crescent moon hung low in the sky. Thousands of unblinking stars arced overhead. Spider said sailors called them the eyes of the lost. Jem felt lost too as he looked up. He could almost feel himself dissolving as he thought about the vastness of nothing above and below the ship. The *Fortuna* was his world now, and it was a tiny one. He was a speck upon a speck.

The ship was slicing forward at an incredible pace, but tonight at least the glittering sea was calm. Another day had passed since they had been able to speak in private.

Jem moved the little lantern so that the candle was guarded from the wind and shifted on the sacking Tolly used as bedding. "Listen, there's not much time. I'll have to go back below deck soon. Grimscale is watching everything I do at the moment and it wouldn't surprise me if he snooped around the ship at night too. I couldn't find the staff, but something else happened. I don't know where to begin... Last night I saw..."

"Me too!" Tolly interrupted quickly. "You saw her again on deck?"

Jem nodded. "I didn't get a clear view..."

"Well, I did!" Tolly's eyes widened. "And I saw *exactly* what she did. Did you hear the noise again?"

"Yes... and I felt it, just like last time." Jem shuddered. "It comes from the sea?"

"No! It comes from things *in* the sea." Tolly shook his head. "Horrible scaly things – bald women covered in lumps and barnacles – mermaids, I suppose, although not beautiful like the legends say."

"But Cazalon told me that merfolk didn't exist." Jem thought back to Malfurneaux Place and the room where the count had kept the disintegrating results of his cruel experiments. Most horrible of all was a unicorn with a twisted horn bolted to its forehead. Jem swallowed hard. "He told me that himself. He said he had travelled the world to find creatures of myth and was disappointed to find they didn't exist. That's why he decided to make his own instead – the gryphon, the unicorn? That can't be right, you can't have seen —'

"I *saw* them in the water, Jem – dozens of them!" Tolly interrupted. "And they were as real as you or me. I had a clear view from the lookout. Their mouths are huge, half the size of their heads, running across their faces like open wounds and full of teeth – rows and rows of teeth." He paused as Cleo burrowed into his lap and squirmed to make herself comfortable.

"But that's not the worst thing. It's their eyes – they're round and completely black, as if there's nothing inside them, just hunger. Then I saw her as she stood at the prow, just above the figurehead, and pulled hairs from her head and cast them onto the water."

"She was *feeding* them her own hair?" At last Jem remembered what *mange* meant – to eat!

Tolly shook his head. "No – it's worse than that. I couldn't see everything because of the rocking of the ship, but when she threw her hair out into the sea, it was as if silver ropes began to… *grow* in the water. The merpeople took hold of the ropes and wound them round their bodies and then they just waited in the sea – all of them staring up and opening and shutting their giant mouths. The wind dropped and the air around the mast-top seemed to… crackle. It was like a storm without thunder."

"I felt that too. I couldn't sleep thinking about

you two up there so I came out on deck. I was with Mingan when it happened."

"He was there last night?"

Jem nodded. "I… I think he saved me from running into her."

"That was probably a good thing, considering what I saw next. See that gap in the rail over there?" He pointed with his good hand. "She pulled something out from the other side of this stack and dragged it across the deck, then she rolled it from there into the sea. It was a body, Jem – a man's body – and the merpeople fell on it, ripping it to pieces in seconds. It was disgusting. I saw them fighting over it, tearing it apart with their hands and mouths, blood spattering around them."

"*Mange bien, mes soeurs. Mange tout!*" With a jolt Jem realised exactly what those words meant. "Eat well, my sisters. Eat everything!" He remembered what Spider had told him about a man going overboard. Now he was certain – the crewman hadn't slipped on the ice. And last night he'd heard Captain Trevanion say another man had gone missing.

And then there was Ann… He didn't want to think about that in case it made it true.

"Why is she feeding them?"

"Because I think they are doing her bidding." Tolly rubbed his bandaged fingers as he continued. "After they'd... *fed*, they all swarmed forward and the silver ropes seemed to lengthen and tighten around the *Fortuna*. When the ropes stretched so far out across the sea that I couldn't see the merpeople any more, the ship reared up. We were almost thrown out of the cradle, but I managed to tie us to the mast with the blanket. The ship rose up..."

"Right out of the water!" Jem cut in quickly. "I was almost thrown overboard too, but Mingan caught hold of me. And then it started plunging forward and moving incredibly fast like it was being... *dragged behind something!*"

"Exactly!" Tolly slapped the canvas side of the shelter with his left hand and Cleo squealed. "She *feeds* them and they pull the ship for her. No wonder the sailors are muttering about the unnatural speed of this crossing."

"They think we are travelling on a witch wind," Jem said, "but it's something much worse." He pushed his long dark hair back and knotted it into a matted ball at the nape of his neck. It was so thick with salt and grease now that it stayed in place. He stared grimly at his friend.

"That's not all, Tolly. I found something in the hold."

✻ ☰ ✺

"The blood on the glass – do you think it was Ann's?"

Jem finished describing his terrifying encounter in the hold with the question that had been repeating itself over and over in his mind. Saying it aloud made it seem even more likely. Cleo nestled silently between the boys, anxiously watching their faces.

Tolly drew a deep breath. "Do you remember the blood bridge?"

"Of course, how could I forget it? Cazalon used Ann's blood to open a channel to the dead lands, so he could talk to her mother. But he's d—" Jem remembered the room in the mirror and felt a stab of pain from the Eye of Ra on his heel. "Do you think *someone* is doing that again, here on the ship?"

Tolly didn't answer. Instead he reached forward to move the lantern a little closer. Shadow and light distorted his even features as he looked up again. "Remember what I said about this being a trap?"

As Jem thought about the bony hand that had gripped his through the glass of the mirror, the red strips between his fingers and across his knuckles began to burn. "Do you really think he – Cazalon, I mean – is here on board with us, Tolly?"

The dark boy slumped forward and stared dejectedly at the flickering flame. "I don't know what I think any more. The one thing I am certain of is that Ann is nearby." The words sounded strangely hollow. Jem was surprised to see his friend clench his fists as he continued. "She *must* be. Someone is shielding her from us." His expression hardened. "What do you make of Mingan?"

Jem frowned. He might not have special gifts like his friends, but he could still sense when it was right to trust someone. And the man had saved his life last night, hadn't he?

He shook his head decisively. "Why would he hide me from that woman, and why would he save me from the sea? No – Mingan's not Cazalon. I'm sure of it."

"Then who is he? I can't read him at all, Jem. There's something very wrong about him, something he's keeping hidden. I don't trust him and neither does Cleo."

"Here, girl." Jem reached forward to offer Cleo a handful of gravelly biscuit crumbs saved in his pocket. She crammed them into her mouth, licked her paws and eyed his pocket hungrily. "Sorry, that's all I have." Jem rolled a tiny nugget she'd overlooked towards her. "I've seen her watching Mingan, but she's not scared. She's *interested* in him – and that's different. Spider says the captain trusts him – he's sailed with him before, many times."

Tolly nodded. "I don't doubt the captain is kind and fair. But he is troubled. Do you remember when he talked about his daughter?"

Jem nodded. "He said something about giving her a pet dog? I thought for a moment that he might take Cleo for her."

"I was worried about that too – it's why I tried to read him." Tolly scratched Cleo's head. "All I could sense in him was deep sadness." Tolly paused. "That was when it started, I think."

"When what started?"

Tolly didn't answer immediately, but stroked Cleo's rounded back. Eventually he spoke. "You know I'm not a mind-reader exactly?"

Jem shifted uncertainly. "You… you pick up echoes. Like seeing the ripples on a pond after someone has thrown a stone into the water. But the more you care, the stronger the connection. It's why we can mind talk and it's why you can *feel* Ann here with us on the ship?"

"Yes, that's... right." Tolly hesitated, his face crumpled with doubt. "I don't really understand it myself. If I'm bonded to a person – or a creature, like Cleo – it's quite easy to read them without even thinking about it. After we got away from Malfurneaux Place, the power, or whatever it is, became stronger. Since I've been with Gabriel I've sometimes had to close myself off to stop looking into people's thoughts so easily. I don't feel right about prying, but sometimes I can't help it." He smiled grimly. "Ann said... *says* that I must be coming into my inheritance, into my power, but that I must learn to control it. She is going to help me. Looking back I think that house fed off me – it drained me."

Jem's back prickled. "Malfurneaux Place was evil." He thought again about the room he'd seen in the mirror. It was *definitely* Cazalon's chamber.

"The thing is," Tolly said, huddling Cleo beneath his cloak as a splatter of briny water crashed onto the deck, "there is something about the *Fortuna* that reminds me of that house. Ever since we've been on board my... skills have faded. At first I thought that it was my fear of being on a ship again. I wondered if my mind was clouded by panic. But now I don't think that's true."

Jem stared intently at his friend. "Um... I tried to connect to you last night, when you were up in the lookout cradle."

"Did you?" Tolly looked stricken. "I didn't hear you. But it's not just you. I can't hear anyone's thoughts like before. Everything is muffled. It began with the captain and then I wasn't able to read Mingan at all, and now..."

He brought his fingers to his temples and closed his eyes. Cleo cocked her head to one side and stared at him, her black eyes unblinking.

"What about Ann, Tolly? Can you still sense her?" Jem gripped his friend's shoulder. If Tolly had lost all sense of her he didn't know what they were going to do. "Is she here? Is she still... alive?"

Tolly's opened his eyes and stared bleakly at the candle lantern. He swallowed hard. "I... That's the worst thing... I didn't know how to tell you. I haven't managed to pick up a trace of her, not a single thing, for two days now."

Jem thought about the red mark on the mirror. The dry bloody print of a small hand. A girl's hand.

"I've still got this – would it help?" Jem reached under his cloak to pull Ann's shawl free from his belt. There was a ripping sound as the red wool tore at the edge.

"I'm not one of your tracker dogs, Jem." Tolly's voice was flat.

A single harsh cry came from somewhere overhead.

Startled, Jem leaned out from the nest and looked up. A vast dark shape flickered briefly across one of the grey sails, moving swiftly to another and then upward again. The great curved shadow reminded him of a hunting hawk. He blinked as the shadow disappeared, only to come into view again much higher up, outlined starkly for just a second in the moonlight.

Tolly shuffled forward and peered upward, following the line of Jem's gaze. "W-what's that?"

Every hair on the back of Jem's neck rose. He tried to track the little light of Pocket's lantern swinging backwards and forwards in the lookout. Through the forest of ropes and canvas he saw the yellow glow appear and disappear, moving with the rhythm of the ship. It twinkled faintly, then vanished – only to return several seconds later.

The vast shadow flitted across the topsail once more and Jem saw the ragged outline of something that looked like a single giant wing.

Pocket's light swung into view and dipped out of sight. Jem waited. He began to count. One, two, three, four, five, six, seven, eight, nine… Surely he should have seen it again by now? Ten, eleven, twelve, thirteen…

A scream split the air. Seconds later something heavy splashed into the water just beyond the prow of the boat. Jem leaped up but Tolly caught his arm.

"No – you can't… The merfolk!"

A terrible wailing rose from the water. The agonised sound came in choked, muffled snatches as if something, or someone, was being dragged beneath the waves and struggling free, only to be caught again.

"Help me, for pity's sake! Hel—" The words turned into a shriek of terror. Jem tried to pull away.

"It's Pocket! We can't leave him. He can't swim!"

Tolly held tight. "Those things, Jem. You haven't seen them – I have. They'll tear you to shreds."

A pitiful gurgling wail came from the water. Cleo covered her ears and her fur rose along her back.

It was intolerable. "I don't care. We can't do nothing." Jem shrugged off his cloak. For some reason the thought of Pocket's mother and her good meaty stew ran through his mind. Tolly still kept hold. "Let me go! I can swim, even if you can't. I'm not going to leave him." But as Jem yanked at the sleeves of his jerkin, the screaming stopped abruptly. Tolly released his grip and shook his head.

"It's too late." The *Fortuna* was utterly still for a second, then it bucked and plunged forward. A great wave broke over the prow, knocking Jem to the deck. He rolled into the side of the canvas stack and only just managed to catch Cleo as the receding foaming waters threatened to carry the little monkey overboard.

Clutching Cleo tightly his chest he braced himself against the rail and scanned the turbulent sea for any sign of Pocket. The huge white waves crashing against the bows of the ship were flecked with something black. Jem bit into his lip so hard he could taste blood on his tongue. Tolly was right – it was too late.

"Tolly!" Jem shouted. "Are you there?"

"Yes, I'm here – on the other side."

Soaked to the skin, Jem crawled around the stack and released Cleo. She scurried to her master who was flattened against the ship's black rail. She made little crooning noises as she burrowed into his arms. Tolly looked up, his eyes glistening. "I'm sorry, Jem, but you wouldn't have stood a chance. And I'm sorry for poor Pocket. He was good to me and Cleo." He huddled her close and shivered. "That was terrible – the sound of him out there in the water."

Jem nodded grimly. "If only we could have done something to…" He froze as a heavy whooshing noise and then a thump sounded from the other side of the stack. The boys shrank together as they heard the all too familiar sound of scratching, scraping and ticking across the deck timbers.

"*Mange bien, mes soeurs. Mange tout.*" Madame's diamond-hard voice cut through the night. Jem couldn't see the woman, but he knew she was standing just yards away. The peculiar ticking noise was loud now, fast and regular. He glanced anxiously at Cleo, but Tolly was holding her tight and rocking her, willing her to be silent. The halting, scratching noise came again. Jem held his breath as it passed the stack and faded as the woman moved back down the ship to her cabin beyond the Medusa doorway. When he heard the sound of a door closing he rested his head on his knees and took a gulp of air.

"She just *fed* Pocket to the merfolk, Tolly. What are we going to do?"

"Indeed. What are *we* going to do?"

The words jangled every nerve in Jem's body. His head snapped up.

A tall, indistinct shape was silhouetted against moonlight. For a split second he thought it was a great bird, but it shuddered and rearranged itself into a horribly recognisable form.

CHAPTER
EIGHTEEN

"*Bonsoir, mes amis*, or perhaps I should say, good evening?" Madame de Chouette twitched, ruffled her cloak and took a scraping step towards them. Moonlight gleamed on the fat coils of auburn hair that surrounded her pointed face.

She folded her arms and smiled. Her dark lips parted and the eye-patch rose a little higher on her bone-white cheek. "I do not believe the captain introduced me to you at the beginning of our voyage and I was *most* particular that I should know every member of my crew and hear their pledges to me. Stand."

Jem hauled himself to his feet. His back was rigid and his mouth felt as if it were filled with sand. Beside him, Tolly stood too.

The woman's single eye narrowed as she regarded them. "Come out. I want to see you clearly." The boys shuffled out from behind the stack. Cleo followed them a little way, making a high-pitched keening noise.

Jem could actually feel the woman's eye flickering over his face as she stared intently at him.

After a moment she nodded. "You will both follow me, and bring the animal."

Madame de Chouette turned and stalked down the deck. Jem shot a glance at Tolly. His friend shook his head and held out his palms. Jem felt cold as he realised Tolly hadn't spoken into his mind. He paused, waiting for something, but there was only silence.

When she was just a few yards from the Medusa doorway the woman stopped, but didn't turn round.

"I said follow." Her voice sliced through the night.

Jem went first and Tolly bent to scoop Cleo into his arms. She was trembling and tried to hide her face in the folds of his cloak. Beneath his grimy shirt, jerkin and cloak, Jem felt his back prickle with sweat, although his breath misted the freezing air. The great shadow on the sail – had that been her? He thought of Pocket plucked from the lookout and torn apart by the hungry merfolk below. Did the same hideous fate await them now?

He stared frantically about. There was nowhere to go, nowhere to hide, and no one else on deck.

The woman didn't turn immediately as the boys approached. Instead she stood with her back to them, staring up at the Medusa mask.

Jem thought he heard her whispering words he didn't understand – maybe she was speaking to herself in French, he thought. She dipped her head forward and spun round to face them, her cloak swirling about, spreading to rest around her hidden feet like a pool of oil.

She reached out to Jem and took his chin in her gloved hand. The damson leather was heavily embroidered and soft, but Jem felt bony fingers beneath like iron pincers. She tipped back his head so that it caught more of the weak lamplight. Jem flinched, but not in pain. A horribly familiar fragrance filled his nostrils – a sickly, flower-sweet scent masking something bitter and putrid. It was the scent he'd smelled on Duchess Mary when Cazalon had bewitched her with mummia – and the rotting smell of the count himself.

"No!" He jerked his head and tried to free himself, but the woman slipped her hand down to his throat and held him so tightly that he struggled to breathe.

"I merely want to look at you, boy." Her slanting golden eye glinted in the lamplight and she smiled broadly, her perfect lips parting, revealing a mouth full of small, even, yellow teeth. Close to, although her pale face was beautiful, Jem thought it seemed like a painted mask covering something quite different.

"You would be handsome, if you were not so unclean."

Jem recoiled from her musty breath. Her fingers caught on the chain around his neck and she started to twist it. He could feel the metal cutting into his skin and he scrabbled at his collar to free himself, but she was unnaturally strong and her grip tightened.

Jem heard her give a little involuntary cry. Immediately she dropped the chain and released him. Her eye flicked to the medal, but he took a step back and tucked it quickly back into his shirt. Cleo made a whickering sound and the woman turned her attention to Tolly. "*Et l'Africain?* Another fine specimen." Cleo moaned and burrowed deeper into Tolly's arms. The woman stared at her. "*Un singe?.*" It sounded like a hiss.

The jewels sewn into a star shape on her eye-patch glittered. "Captain Trevanion has been most remiss. You were not shown to me at the beginning of this voyage with the rest of the crew. I wonder why that can be? Perhaps you are stowaways, *non?*" She smiled and the red paint on her lips crackled into spider legs around her mouth. "And yet there is something very familiar about you. I wonder…" She brought her gloved hands together as if she was about to pray.

The smile disappeared and her golden eye hardened. "Let me see... I think we have met before, my young friends." Her gloved hand suddenly darted towards Cleo. She snatched her from Tolly's arms, dangling her in mid-air by one of her back legs. Cleo, her eyes huge, clawed at the air and made a pitiful squeaking noise. Tolly grabbed at her but the woman took a step back. "Oh yes, I have seen you and this little —"

"That is impossible, Madame." Captain Trevanion stepped from the shadows beneath the steps. Behind him was the tall, dark shape of Mingan. The strange man's nostrils flared as he caught sight of Cleo flailing from Madame de Chouette's fist. Jem let out a long, shuddering gasp. For the last minute he had forgotten to breathe.

"This boy," Trevanion gestured at Jem, "is the son of an old family friend. I have promised his mother that I will introduce him to life at sea – him and his companion."

"Really?" Madame de Chouette stretched out her arm to one side and released Cleo. Mingan pounced forward to catch her in his cupped hands – saving her from cracking open her skull on the deck. It happened so fast that Jem hardly saw him move.

Cleo steadied herself in the man's large hands, looping her tail around his tattooed arm and turning to stare up at the woman. Jem saw the fur on Cleo's chest ripple as her heart beat double-time.

"Your own… *pet* has a way with animals, I see, Trevanion." She smiled again, but there was no warmth in her words. "I thought I'd made it clear that every member of crew should be shown to me. Why did you not introduce these boys with the rest of the men?"

Trevanion glanced at Jem and rubbed a hand across his forehead, pushing his ragged grey wig back. A line of fair stubble at the front of his head appeared. He looked like a man who hadn't slept in days. "There wasn't time, Madame. They arrived later than expected. And since then with so many other… concerns to attend to on board, I simply forgot to bring them to your attention. I hope you will forgive me. I can vouch for them both. I assure you."

"Indeed?" Madame de Chouette's metallic voice was cool.

"They are from a good house. I knew this boy's uncle – a man of title." Jem noticed Trevanion avoided looking at the woman directly as he spoke.

"Is that so?" Madame de Chouette nodded and held her head to one side. Jem became very aware of a peculiar silence around them. It felt as if the *Fortuna* was skimming or, more accurately, flying above the waves. The rocking and plunging had stopped and the ship was as steady as a table, but there was now a dizzying sense of driving, tumultuous speed that pulled at the pit of his stomach.

Jem saw the captain glance up at the stars and tighten his hand beneath the lace of his shirt cuffs. Trevanion felt it too.

Madame de Chouette didn't speak for several seconds. Jem became very aware of the odd ticking sound measuring the silence between them. She nodded again and he couldn't tell if she was listening to something or assessing the captain's words. At last she grinned broadly, revealing her tiny, ochre teeth once more.

"Well then, as it seems I have gentle company on board, perhaps it would be fitting to invite you and these boys to dine with me tomorrow. I think it is time we all became better acquainted. It will do you good, Captain, to spend time away from your maps and star charts – Mr Valentine too. Bring him. We will dine in style in my... chamber. Perhaps these fine boys and this... *charming* little creature will divert us all, *non?*"

Cleo bared her teeth and made a low throaty noise that sounded like a growl. Mingan ran a long finger down her back and she quietened. A look of confusion crossed Tolly's face.

Trevanion bowed his head. "As you wish, Madame. I will have something prepared."

"That will not be necessary. I will provide our *feast*. It will be my pleasure. Let me... surprise you." Madame de Chouette smiled again.

Trevanion looked up and frowned. "But surely you cannot..."

"That is all. I bid you good night." She brushed past him to the steps.

"Wait, Madame!"

"Yes?" She paused.

"I... I believe that it would be good for your nephew to have boys of his own quality to speak to. He has been shut in your cabin for days now."

Madame de Chouette's golden eye glinted. "He is an invalid, Captain, as I explained. That is why he cannot go on deck or mix with the crew."

"But surely it would be beneficial for him?" The captain sounded determined. "He cannot be more than a couple of years older than these two?"

"He is fifteen, as you say, but weak. The crossing is hard enough for him without further... disturbance."

Jem's mind reeled as he took in the conversation. The woman wasn't alone on the boat, there were *two* passengers. Something he'd overheard Spider say flashed into his mind. "They *came aboard in the early hours and went straight to the cabin... Master Grimscale says we're not to speak to* them *at any time."*

It was the snatch of conversation they'd caught just before the hold was sealed, trapping them on the boat. No wonder neither of them had marked it. They were too concerned about how to escape. But of course, it was obvious – Madame de Chouette didn't have a nephew on board. *Ann* was the other passenger! She had to be. His heart thumping, Jem glanced at Tolly, whose brown eyes were dancing with hope.

Although the link between them was broken, he could tell his friend was thinking exactly the same thing. Cleo chirruped and wriggled in Mingan's hands. Trevanion looked at her and cleared his throat.

"As you know, my own daughter is an invalid, Madame. The company of those of her own age always lifts her spirits and I believe a little creature like this could do nothing but good. Besides, I would like to meet your nephew properly. It is important for a captain to know his charges."

Madame de Chouette pursed her lips. The red paint puckered into a little twisted rose bud. She jerked her head to one side, closed her eye and once again seemed to listen to a silent voice.

"Very well. It will be as you wish, Captain." Her eyelid flicked open and the peculiar golden iris bored directly into Jem's face. "But I fear you will find him poor company. So, it is agreed. You and Master Valentine will accompany these boys and this... *animal*," she almost seemed to spit the last word, "at my table." Trevanion bowed, and she continued. "You will ensure that the man Grimscale works them well tomorrow. I would have them dine with an appetite."

With that, she stomped up the stairs and threw back the door to the cabin beyond the Medusa mask. Jem caught a rush of heat and a flash of glinting thread from a tapestry inside and then the door slammed shut behind her.

Mingan handed Cleo back to Tolly and turned to the captain. He made a swift chopping motion and moved his hand like a fish. He shook his great shaggy head and the bones in his hair clacked together. He pointed at the moon and held up six fingers.

"No, I don't understand either, old friend." Trevanion visibly shivered and pulled the sides of his long braided frock coat together. "There is nothing natural about this blighted voyage. But I promise you this: I will do everything in my power to keep everyone safe – as many of us as possible. You *will* see your home and your people again."

He turned to Jem and Tolly. "Mingan here came to fetch me out on deck when he saw Madame with you. If I had not intervened she —'

"She would have killed us – just like the others!" Jem's urgent voice came out louder than he intended. He lowered his words to a whisper. "We've seen her push bodies into the sea, haven't we, Tolly? The missing crewmen – they haven't been accidents at all. And tonight Pocket was thrown out of the cradle and we saw…"

Trevanion raised a hand to silence him. He turned swiftly to scan the doorway to the cabin and glanced at Mingan. The tall, silent man inclined his head.

"Come." The captain walked towards the prow of the ship and they followed.

He stood facing the open sea, the waves ahead

flecked with points of starlight. Once again Jem was aware of the flying motion of the *Fortuna*. The ship was unnaturally smooth and steady as it glided *above* the waves. Jem felt his stomach knot as he realised that every time Madame made a sacrifice to the merfolk, the Fortuna moved faster and smoother than before.

Mingan held up three fingers now. He moved it to his neck and made a swiping gesture.

"Three men gone?" Trevanion raised the heels of his hands to his forehead. He clenched his fists, tore off the wig and cast it into the sea. The grey curls spread like foam for a second or two before disappearing suddenly as if snatched by invisible hands?

Trevanion was quiet for a moment and then he spoke in a cracked voice. "My fault, it's all my fault. I should never have agreed to take charge of this vessel. I have made a terrible error and I have put many lives in danger." Mingan caught his arm, but the captain shook him off. "It's no good, old friend. You cannot deny it. Once I thought I would pay anything to cure my daughter, but this price is too much. I have been a fool." He turned to Jem. "Young Pocket, you say?"

Jem nodded. "He was aloft in the lookout and

then we saw... I don't know what exactly... but he plummeted into the sea and... we heard him scream. It was the most terrible sound, but we couldn't do anything."

Tolly stepped forward. "There are things in the water. She – Madame, I mean – she feeds them human flesh and afterwards they... pull the boat. Those incredible bursts of speed – it's the merfolk. We're not making it up."

Trevanion stared at Tolly's earnest face. He shook his head. "Before this voyage I would not have believed such stories, but now..." He looked at Mingan. "You have felt it all along?"

The tall man nodded.

Trevanion's face was ashen in the starlight. "The boy Pocket, he was just eleven years old. I am responsible for his death and for the others too —'

"No, you're not. She is!" Jem cut in, but the captain just stared blankly at the glinting sea.

"Well, I promise you this, no one else will be lost before we make land. I swear on my honour and on my life." His hand tightened on the rail. There was a crackling sound and Jem saw a faint greenish glow play around the outline of Trevanion's knuckles.

Jem glanced uncertainly at Tolly. "We'll be at sea

for weeks yet, sir. How will you make sure that —'

He stopped mid-sentence as the captain began to laugh bitterly. "Weeks, you say? I am afraid you are sadly mistaken. The *Fortuna* is making such *good speed*," he gave the words a hollow emphasis, "that I very much doubt it will be much more than a week before we sight land. Six days, that's what you think, isn't it, Mingan?"

The tall man inclined his head and the skull-threaded plaits fell forward.

Trevanion swung round, the dark pits beneath his eyes giving his face the look of a haunted man. "It is true — I almost wish it were not. We have checked the charts over and over again, but the stars never lie. We cannot be here already, yet we are. We should have met storms and navigated a passage through the ice islands and yet every day has dawned bright and the sea has been clear. This is a demon's vessel. I rue the day I agreed to be its captain. I am a cursed man."

He looked at Jem and stopped himself. "You boys will be ready to dine with Madame at six bells tomorrow. Remember the story we have agreed. Say nothing more. It will be better that way. I will protect you as best I can. Now you go below, and you back to your canvas foxhole, and get some rest." Jem saw Tolly start as Trevanion smiled weakly. "Oh yes, boy, I know where you've been sleeping. Mingan here has been keeping an eye on both of you."

He turned to the tall man. "Come with me, I want you to look at the charts too. Perhaps you can make some sense of this journey, for I cannot." The two men started back down the deck, their heads bowed together.

"It has to be Ann!" Tolly spoke in a rush of excitement once the two men disappeared into the shadows at the stern. "When we first came aboard, Jem – before all my... powers disappeared – do you remember I saw a room through Ann's eyes? It was the last real connection I made with her. She was frightened by something. She couldn't look – she turned to a window and there was water there. She didn't know who she was." Tolly's eyes gleamed. "But I think *we* do now!"

"And tomorrow we'll know for certain." Jem pushed a knot of salt-stiffened hair from his eyes. Master Jalbert's words came into his head again. "*Never drop your guard.*" He reached across to stroke Cleo's nose – the little monkey was curled in Tolly's arms. "But we must be careful. That woman is…" He bit his lip and looked up to the empty lookout.

Tolly finished the sentence for him. "…is like Count Cazalon?"

CHAPTER
NINETEEN

"That's it. Just one more and we'll have you nice and ready for her." Jem gasped for breath as Grimscale thrust his head into the bucket of seawater for a fourth time. He felt shards of broken ice scrape across the skin of his face and struggled as Grimscale held his head down.

Just when Jem thought his lungs would burst, the man's thick fingers loosened from the back of his neck. He scrambled to his feet, the salt burning his eyes.

Grimscale rubbed his meaty hands together. His fat grey tongue emerged to lick the corner of his lips. "It's your friend's turn next – and maybe I'll have a go at the monkey too. Filthy creatures, they are."

Grimscale caught Tolly roughly by the collar and forced him to kneel. "Come on, I haven't got all day. Let's shine you up for Madame."

"Leave them be, why don't you?" one of the older crewman shouted from across the deck. "They're just lads. Would you want to eat at her table? I wouldn't. Not for all the roast beef back home."

Grimscale ignored him. He was clearly furious that Jem and Tolly were being singled out. All day he'd set them the most difficult and painful tasks. Jem's fingers were raw from scrubbing and from sewing tears in the sails with a thick bone needle. The skin of both his hands was chapped and scaly from the cold and his right palm still stung after the encounter with the mirror. His back ached too. Tolly had been sent to the topmost masts of the ship to unfurl the largest sails alongside Spider. The skinny boy had almost had to do the work of two up there, because of the damage to Tolly's fingers.

One thought kept them both going through the day – Ann.

"Think you're above the rest of us, do you? Well, I've got something here to take you down a peg." Grimscale plunged Tolly's head into the bucket with a vicious shove to the back of his neck. Tolly's bandaged right hand scrabbled desperately on the deck boards as he struggled in the water.

Grimscale grinned. Just when Jem began to panic that Tolly wouldn't be able to hold his breath for so long, Grimscale pulled him free. The boy choked, arched his back and gasped for air as beads of water streaked down his cheeks and dripped from his chin. Cleo tried to wriggle free from Jem's arms to comfort her master.

Six bells sounded from the stern. Grimscale's smile dropped. He forced Tolly's head back into the bucket again with a tattooed hand and freed him several seconds later.

Tolly took great rasping breaths again as he came up for air, but Grimscale wasn't finished. "One more for luck, eh?"

Thump!

Jem spun round and was surprised to see Mingan crouching on all fours on the deck. After what had happened to Pocket, Trevanion had ordered that only the most experienced crewmen should man the lookout, and Mingan was supposed to be up there now scanning the waters for floating islands.

The man straightened up and took a step towards Grimscale. His mass of bone-threaded hair caught on the wind and clattered around his head. As Mingan towered over the mate, Jem saw a muscle twitch beneath Grimscale's left eye. He puckered out his thick lower lip so that it covered the gingery bristles that were beginning to thicken into an ugly moustache. For a moment Jem thought he was going to say something, but he merely grunted.

"Another time, my friend." Jem wasn't sure if he was talking to Mingan or to Tolly.

"Off you go then, *gentlemen*." Grimscale managed to make the word sound like an insult as he dragged Tolly to his feet and pushed him towards Jem and Cleo.

As the boys made their way to the steps, Jem glanced gratefully up at Mingan's long face. The man frowned at Jem, clamped his hand over his own mouth and shook his head.

�※ ⚊ ※

The door beneath the Medusa mask swung slowly shut behind them. It took a moment for Jem's eyes to become accustomed to the dim light. The passage was all wrong – surely it couldn't be that long and that high? He rubbed his eyes – had the saltwater distorted his vision?

But when he looked again the passage was the same. It seemed to continue ahead for an impossible distance, the curved walls meeting in shadow high above. The air was warm and musty with a cloying, sour-sweet fragrance.

He took an uncertain step forward. The red walls were lined with the brilliant tapestries he had glimpsed earlier. Glinting with threads of silver and gold, they depicted hunting scenes. The first one showed animals in a forest – shimmering white deer, russet foxes and long-bodied hares. He felt sharp a stab of longing for the woods around Goldings. Unexpectedly, his mother's face swam into his mind. What must she be thinking now? He tried to imagine the scene when all three of them – and Cleo too – rode into the courtyard at Goldings and it gave him courage. They were moments from finding Ann.

"It's not like a ship here at all." Tolly peered at the next tapestry and Jem saw his friend's eyes narrow. He held Cleo tight to his chest. "It's… it's like Malfurneaux Place. Look!" He gestured at the wall. "This is horrible."

Jem drew level with Tolly and looked at the tapestry. Instantly he wished he hadn't. It was a scene of carnage – all the animals shown in the first tapestry were now lying dead in the forest, their entrails spilling out across the fabric in looping trails of embroidered crimson and gold. Who would commission such a thing? He didn't want to look at it any more. He tore his eyes from the walls. "Come on."

They kept walking along the candlelit passageway. There were no doors.

"Where do we go?" Tolly whispered.

Jem shook his damp head. "Further along, I suppose. There must be a doorway somewhere leading to the cabin? Do you sense Ann at all, Tolly?"

As soon as he said the words the floor beneath their feet shifted, knocking both boys to their knees.

It wasn't the movement of the ship. The curved walls closed and billowed around them – one second the passage was incredibly cramped and tiny, the next it swelled to a cavernous space. A kaleidoscope of lights, colour and distorted images whirled about – faces, buildings, rooms, flames, creatures – and the air began to vibrate with a whumping sound, like the beating of a giant heart. The noise grew louder and louder.

Tolly curled forward and tried to shield Cleo with his chest. Jem closed his eyes and covered his ears with his hands. He had the most horrendous feeling that he was soaring above a bottomless pit and that at any moment he would plummet. His stomach somersaulted at the thought. The thumping noise was so loud now that every sinew of his body pulsed, as if the sound would tear him apart.

Then it all stopped.

He heard the sound of a door opening and the captain's voice. "Come on, Valentine – at last we'll get to meet the lad. That's something at least?"

Jem opened his eyes. Trevanion was staring down at him. "What the Devil are you two doing on the floor?"

Jem looked around in amazement. He and Tolly were crouching in a simple wood-panelled passageway. A single candle lantern swung from the low ceiling. Three arched wooden doorways – one to each side of the passage, the third surrounded by an elaborate carving of gilded vines – stood at the far end. The endless passage and the tapestries had vanished, replaced by exactly the sort of cramped, timber-lined space you would expect to find on a ship.

He scrambled to his feet. His head was still spinning and he had to lean against the wall to steady himself. Cleo wailed as Tolly tried to stand upright.

"Have you two been at the grog ration already?" Trevanion looked down at their drained faces.

Even Tolly looked grey.

Jem shook his head. "N-no, sir, we…"

"It's Grimscale, Captain. Before the boys were sent in he forced their heads into a bucket of water. I didn't catch it early enough to put a stop to it, but one of the men just told me." Valentine's voice was sharp with anger. "It was to clean them up, he said, although of course it was just for his own vicious pleasure. He's a brute. They're likely light-headed for want of air. Is that right, lads?"

Jem nodded, though he couldn't begin to make sense of what had just happened. Perhaps Valentine was right – maybe it had been a hallucination caused by lack of air?

Trevanion shook his now wigless close-cropped head. "The man is a monster." He shot a wary glance at the door at the end of the little passage. "Come then, we must dine with Madame. And remember, lads, what I said…"

He stared meaningfully at Jem and Tolly in turn. They both nodded.

"Manners, is that it?" Valentine grinned and winked at Jem. "You've had a lecture?" The young master mariner had a round, kind face and twinkling eyes. Jem wondered why he had agreed to come on this voyage, but the question was answered as Valentine continued. "He's always been a stickler for manners, has the captain here, but I'll tell you what, boys, there's no one finer to teach you the ropes. You're learning with the best. There's no man I'd rather put to sea with. When I am captain of my own vessel it will be thanks to him."

Jem saw a shadow cross Captain Trevanion's face as Valentine clapped him on the back.

A sound from the end of the short passage made them all turn. The narrow door clicked open and swung into the room beyond.

Madame's cold voice came from the darkness. "You may enter, gentlemen." She began to laugh girlishly, although to Jem's ears there was a jarring, tense quality to the sound.

Her voice came again.

"I come from an old family with many customs. I like to keep up the old ways, most especially in matters of hospitality. As you cross through the doorway into my room, I would like you all to say your name aloud and thank me for your invitation this night. Is that quite understood?"

Valentine snorted and spoke under his breath. "That's a new one. Must be an odd family."

Trevanion didn't answer. He squared his shoulders and stepped past Jem and Tolly. Jem heard him mutter, "If it will get us through this voyage, so be it..."

He paused at the door and stepped through.

"Captain Richard Trevanion. I thank you, Madame, for your invitation this night."

Valentine followed. "Ralph Valentine, Master Mariner. I, too, thank you, Madame, for your invitation."

Tolly pulled hard at Jem's arm. "I don't think we should..."

"And the boys – the young gentlemen? Are they also beyond my door? Come, I am hungry."

Jem looked back at Tolly and spoke in a whisper. "We have to go in – for Ann. This is our chance!"

Tolly nodded grimly. "I know, but it feels... wrong. *Really* wrong."

"I am waiting." Jem felt the Eye of Ra flare on his heel at Madame's voice, but almost immediately the sensation dwindled to an itch.

Tolly was right, this felt bad – it smacked of Cazalon's sorcery, but what option did they have? Ann was in there!

He wriggled his foot in his shoe and took a deep

breath. "Jeremy Green, deckhand. I thank you for your invitation this night." He stepped through the doorway into the room.

Tolly paused for a moment, then sighed as he followed on behind.

"Ptolemy, and this is Cleopatra, a monkey. We… thank you for our invitation this night."

CHAPTER
TWENTY

Madame de Chouette's chamber was grand. It ran across the whole width of the *Fortuna*'s stern and a wall of windows reflected the light from three candelabra on the wide oak table. On top of the embroidered black tablecloth, pewter bowls and platters were laden with meat, fruit, pastries, pies and bread. A set of large silver carving knives was laid out in the centre.

Jem's mouth began to water.

"I was not aware we had fare of this quality on board." Captain Trevanion scanned the table in evident surprise.

"I am very creative." Madame de Chouette smiled and reached forward to pluck a glistening grape from the bowl in front of her. She rolled the fleshy purple ball between her gloved fingers and then crushed it so that the juice ran down the fine green leather.

"How careless of me," she murmured. "Please be seated – all of you. I have been looking forward to this evening so very much."

Jem took an uncertain step forward. He glanced back. Tolly was frozen in the doorway, gawping up at the low-beamed ceiling of the chamber. Then he looked down at the floor, frowned and kicked at something on the rug just beyond the door. Jem couldn't make out what it was.

"Come in, *Ptolemy*, you are welcome at my table." It was an order, not an invitation. Madame de Chouette's mouth set into a line of something like disgust as Tolly and Cleo walked slowly forward and came to stand next to Jem. The atmosphere in the room seemed odd – it didn't feel like a meal, more like a ritual, like the time in the catacombs beneath St Paul's.

"*Never drop your guard.*" Jem repeated Jalbert's words silently to himself like a mantra.

"And so, all my guests are here and everything is ready." She smiled, took up a pewter goblet and leaned back in her chair. It was larger than the others round the table, like a throne, Jem thought. He was aware of the odd ticking noise again.

Trevanion cleared his throat. "And… er, the boy? Your nephew, Madame? I trust he will be joining us?"

She raised the goblet and grinned more broadly, her little yellow teeth glinting in the candlelight.

"He is here, as you requested. He has been resting. Step forward, child, let our guests see you."

There was a rustling sound from the left of the chamber.

Jem couldn't help but hold his breath as a figure stepped from behind a heavy curtain. His temples began to throb as he stared across the room.

A tall red-headed boy appeared.

Disappointment cut through Jem like a butcher's knife. This was not Ann.

"Come, sit at the head of the table, *mon cher*. I hope you have an appetite." Madame gestured to a cushioned chair. "And all of you, be seated, please. We shall dine."

Jem watched the boy walk towards the table. His stringy limbs were too long for his body and he appeared to have difficulty coordinating his steps. As he shambled towards the chair, his arms flailed at his sides and his head lolled forward so that his large chin rested on his breastbone. He looked a couple of years older than Jem and Tolly. There was a line of angry red spots across the back of his neck and faint red, downy hairs on his pallid cheeks.

Madame's nephew slumped formlessly into the chair. His heavy-lidded eyes were almost sealed.

The woman was staring intently at Jem now, and she raised one eyebrow just a fraction. "Why don't *you* come and sit here next to me." She patted the chair by her side. "And your friend with the little monkey can sit opposite you. Captain, opposite me, and Monsieur Valentine to the right at the end there. *Parfait! Alors* – we can begin. *Mange bien!*"

Jem shuddered as she spoke the familiar words. He sat down, staring at the boy's large, freckled white hands laid flat on the table. He took a swift side glance at the boy's face with its broad flat nose and heavy lips. He breathed oddly through his mouth and there was a speck of drool at the corner of his lips. Madame had been telling the truth all along. Her poor nephew was an invalid. He looked across at Tolly, but his friend's eyes were locked on the slouching form of the red-haired boy, no doubt feeling as dejected as Jem.

He saw Tolly tighten his grip on Cleo as she wriggled in his arms and stared at the boy.

As the captain took his seat he cleared his throat and steepled his hands together. "Perhaps, before we begin, it would be appropriate for me to say grace…"

"No!" Madame de Chouette almost screamed

the word. She lunged across the table and ripped his hands apart. The room fell completely silent. Jem saw the captain make his hand into fist, but he didn't say anything.

After a long pause she began to laugh in the odd girlish fashion again. "How foolish of me. I hope you will forgive my impetuous nature. In my family it was not our custom to say grace before a meal. And as I explained, I wish to keep the old ways alive – especially this evening... for Fabien's sake." She patted her nephew's hand and he made a small sound like a kitten's mew. Jem pitied the boy, but all he wanted to do now was leave.

Trevanion frowned. "F-Fabien? It is good to meet you at last."

The boy didn't answer or even register the fact that the captain had addressed him.

"Such a pity." Madame de Chouette's voice had a simpering quality. "My dear nephew has been stricken for a very long time now."

"Indeed?" The captain's voice was sharp with interest. "Do you know the cause of his malady? My own daughter Jane is —'

"— also afflicted. It is why you agreed to make this journey, isn't that right, Captain?"

Trevanion nodded grimly and reached to fill his pewter tankard. He took a great gulp and spoke again. "And your promise, Madame. You will make good? I have your word?"

She smiled again. "Of course! I always ensure those loyal to me get exactly what they deserve. And you have been very loyal, dear Captain... so far."

Trevanion shot a guilty look at Jem and took another swig from the goblet. He wiped his mouth and continued. "Forgive me, but one thing I would like to know is why you are making such a perilous journey at this time of year, especially with such a frail lad."

Madame de Chouette smoothed the green leather of her gloves and stroked the layers of lace that frothed around the crook of her elbow where the cuffs met the black velvet of her dress. Jem realised that, apart from her pointed, painted face, she did not choose to reveal a single inch of flesh in the way that women of fashion usually did.

She sighed. "Fabien is the last of his line. He is about to come into his inheritance. There are preparations to be made, bonds to seal...and transfers to complete. It is most important that he is there in person when the time comes. That is why we must make this journey, no matter the cost. Now, enough of us. Let me hear about your young friends." She turned slowly and fixed her penetrating eye on Jem again. "Jeremy, tell me something about yourself. Let us start with the medal about your neck – how did you come by such a thing?"

The Eye of Ra burned on Jem's heel and he gasped in pain. His mind was suddenly flooded with images of his mother, of Goldings, of his father the King, of Ludlow House, of the Great Fire, of Tolly, Ann and Cleo, of Gabriel and the players, of Malfurneaux Place, of Count Cazalon…

He was overwhelmed by the need to tell Madame about them all, to speak about everyone and everything he knew. He twisted in the chair, desperately trying to stop his tongue. He hunched forward, covered his mouth with a hand and started to make a choking noise.

Madame de Chouette smiled. "Take your time, boy." She ran a hand down the line of his spine. Even through the thick woven material of his jerkin he could feel the sharp, probing points of her fingertips. "There, it is passed. Perhaps some water?" She reached to a goblet set in front of him. He filled his mouth with a huge gulp only to splutter it across the table as a torrent of words began to stream from his lips.

"It… it was given to me. It belonged to my uncle once, but he's dead now so my mother passed it on to me. Her name is Sarah. We live at a house called Goldings near London. We haven't been there long. I only found out last year that my father is —'

A hollow clanging sound broke Jem's words. Cleo had knocked one of the three candelabras sideways on the table. Small flames licked at the embroidered cloth and a pool of hot wax began to spread.

"Clumsy girl!" Tolly spoke loudly as he doused the flames with water from a large pewter jug. "I'm sorry. I was trying to hold on to her, but it… it must have been the sight of the food. Come back here, Cleo. Fabien, your hand – the hot wax! That must burn terribly."

Tolly leaned across the table to place his bandaged right hand onto the large white hand of the other boy. As Tolly made contact with Fabien's skin, the sick boy's head shot up. He stared at Tolly and began to jerk and twitch in the chair, all the while making the high-pitched mewing sound, which grew louder and louder. He started to rub the back of his free hand against his eyes as if he was trying to clear something away.

Madame de Chouette glared at Tolly and lashed across the table, swiping his hand aside. She gripped Fabien's shoulder, her long green fingers tightening like a claw.

Fabien began to cough, the sound rattling in his chest. He hunched his narrow shoulders up to his fleshy ears as the choking fit wracked his body, then he quietened and sagged back. His head flopped forward again and he was completely still.

"Good boy, it is over now." Madame de Chouette relaxed her clasp and reached for another grape. She offered it to Cleo, who squawked and jumped from the tabletop into Tolly's lap.

Jem thought he heard the woman hiss between her teeth. Then she spoke. "Such a pretty creature, but so wild. While you are my guest you must endeavour to control her, *Ptolemy*." The woman narrowed her golden eye and turned to Trevanion. "I hear there are places on this earth where the savages eat monkeys, is that not so, Captain?"

Tolly's arms tightened around Cleo.

Trevanion shifted uncomfortably. "I am afraid I do not know, Madame. Perhaps it is possible, but I have not yet come across them."

"And you, Monsieur Valentine." She smiled coquettishly at the young man. "Have you heard of these customs?"

Valentine shook his head and reached for a goblet on the table. "No, Madame, but as yet I have only travelled with the captain here. Perhaps, one day, when I am master of my own ship, I will visit those countries."

"Indeed." The woman nodded and popped the grape into her mouth. She swallowed with a smile and continued. "I have also heard of lands where the flesh of children is considered to be a delicacy. Boys are sweeter than girls, I understand."

"I pray that I shall never set foot on such heathen soil." The captain set down his own goblet, but Jem noticed that his hand was shaking. The chamber was silent for an uncomfortably long moment until Trevanion tried a new topic. "This... feast is admirable, Madame. I would not have believed that such a banquet was possible at sea."

The woman cocked her head to one side. "I am always *resourceful*. You must eat – all of you. *Try* something." Once again, the words rang out like an order.

The captain reached forward and took a chicken

leg from a platter piled high with meat. He took a huge bite and, as he chewed, the tight, wary expression etched into his face was wiped clean away. "Why this is excellent," he said through a mouthful of flesh. "Quite the best chicken I've ever tasted."

Valentine reached for a glossy chop. His eyes glazed as he licked the salty sweetness from his fingers and rolled the taste around his mouth. "Superb!"

Madame de Chouette smiled and settled back in her chair. "And so we begin. I will be offended, Captain Trevanion and Master Valentine, if you leave my chamber this evening without trying *every* delicacy I have brought here for you." She regarded Jem with an appraising eye. "You, boy, are nothing but skin and bone. Eat… while you can." Her voice was musical and enticing.

Jem looked at the mounds of pies and platters of meat spread out before him and without thinking twice he reached forward to take a gleaming savoury tart. The golden pastry crumbled between his fingers as he raised it to his lips. He was desperate to cram it whole into his mouth. In fact, he wanted to eat everything on the table. A distant, muffled part of his mind asked how he could even think about food at such a moment, but he couldn't stop himself.

"No! Don't!" Tolly leaped to his feet and knocked the pastry from Jem's fingers.

The air in the chamber froze. Cleo scrambled to Tolly's shoulder and bared her teeth with a soft growl. Tolly took a sharp breath and glanced down at the pastry crumbs littered in front of Jem's place. His mouth twitched.

"That's twice now, boy." Madame de Chouette's voice was coiled tight as a spring. "I invited you to my table, yet you have disturbed my poor nephew and now you have insulted me by refusing my food." She rose from her chair and leaned forward, pressing her gloved knuckles on the embroidered cloth. Silhouetted in front of the windowpanes, the woman swayed above the table. The folds of her dress arranged themselves into two sweeping drapes that fell from each shoulder like curved wings.

Tolly hesitated. "I… I am sorry if I have offended you and your… nephew." He shot a look at the silent, slouching boy next to Jem. "I am afraid I am not used to such rich food."

Jem was confused. Across the table, the air around Tolly and Cleo wavered. It was like a point far ahead on a dusty road on a hot summer's day when a trick of the light offers a glimpse of a shimmering, distant, impossible land. Just for a second he thought he saw... He blinked and shook his head. No – there was just the door to the corridor in the wall behind Tolly. Alongside it was another great trestle heaped with even more fruit and elaborate pastries. His stomach began to rumble – the food over there looked delicious too. Perhaps he should take a grape?

Tolly's voice came again. "I'm sorry, Madame, but I am unwell and must go outside for air. I think my friend should come with me. Will you come *now*, Jem?"

Jem's head was muzzy. He was hungry and there was nothing more he wanted to do than eat Madame de Chouette's food. After all, he was her guest. Tolly *was* being rude.

"Let the boys go. More for us, eh, Captain?" Master Valentine's voice was thick and slurred. Jem looked along the table and saw that the skin of the young man's face was slack and his eyes were glazed and sleepy. He was mechanically shovelling handfuls of food into his mouth and Trevanion was doing the same. The captain's frock coat was now covered in greasy stains – he was eating like a starved beggar.

Somewhere in the depths of his mind, Jem

registered that this was all very wrong. He glanced at Madame de Chouette, but she was staring at Tolly and Cleo. Her single eye was huge, round and completely black, and she rocked gently on her curled fists.

"Jem, please." Tolly lunged forward and caught Jem's sleeve. As he dragged him roughly from his seat, a platter of meats crashed to the floor.

Tolly moved his grip and clutched Jem's hand. Instantly the room spun wildly.

Jem's head exploded with light and searing pain. He squeezed his eyes shut. When he opened them again he was almost sick. Lying at his feet was a lump of rotting fat. It twitched as an army of thick grey maggots burrowed through its surface. If the sight wasn't bad enough, the putrid smell made him bring his hand up to his cover his mouth and nose. He threw back his head to swallow some fresh air and was astonished to see that the low-beamed roof of Madame de Chouette's chamber had vanished. Above there was only empty blackness.

Tolly tightened his grip on Jem's hand and spoke again. "We thank you for your hospitality this night, Madame, but we must take our leave."

The words seem to come from somewhere far

away, as if Tolly was calling from the bottom of a well. Cleo chattered and clung to the collar of Tolly's jerkin as the boys stumbled across flagstones towards an arched doorway far ahead. Jem was dimly aware of Madame de Chouette calling their names over and over behind him. He felt compelled to turn back.

"Don't let go of my hand." Tolly gripped harder. It felt as if they were wading through a bog – Jem's legs were heavy and slow.

The woman's voice came again. "Jeremy Green, I command you."

It was no good, Jem couldn't stop himself.

Jem turned and saw Madame de Chouette towering above the table, but now she didn't look like a woman at all. Her dress was formed from jet-black feathers and the leather of her gloves had split to reveal curved bronze talons that clawed into the wood. She stretched out her arms and her sleeves unfurled like giant ragged wings.

"Return."

Every muscle in Jem's body ached to obey her.

"Get out! Get out now, wh–while you can." Fabien was sitting bolt upright at the table and staring at Jem. His slab-like features contorted with what Jem guessed was pain as he forced himself to speak. "Sh-she cannot compel you to enter this place again if you leave without her permission. You must…" Jem locked onto the boy's frantic, emerald eyes – and instantly knew who it was. Fabien was suddenly blocked from view by a huge black wing.

"It's not far," Tolly's voice came again, as he yanked at Jem's hand. Just before they reached the doorway, Jem saw a white powdery line on the stone-flagged floor, broken in the middle. The outline of a footprint glinted in the thin layer of crystals scattered beyond the break. Immediately he knew what he was looking at – salt.

He had crossed a line of salt at Madame de Chouette's invitation – just like that time at Malfurneaux Place when Cazalon had called him into his room. It was old magic used to bind a soul. No wonder he had lost control of his senses.

"One step more, Jem." He allowed Tolly to haul him over the threshold. A thud came as the oak door to Madame de Chouette's chamber closed behind them.

Jem stared in bewilderment at the plain wooden walls of the cramped passageway they had seen earlier, trying to make sense of what had just happened, but Tolly still tugged at his hand. "We have to get outside." He shoved the door ahead and the boys and the monkey tumbled down the steps and onto the deck as if the Medusa carved above the entrance was spitting them out.

CHAPTER
TWENTY-ONE

"It was Ann! Fabien was Ann!"

Jem crouched on the moonlit deck and fought for breath. "We've found her – she *is* on board the ship!"

"I didn't think you'd recognised her – you seemed completely under that woman's spell." Tolly gulped down a lungful of air. "I could see everything for what it really was, but the longer you, Trevanion and Valentine were there, the more Madame de Chouette was able to control you. You saw a ship's cabin?"

Jem nodded.

"Well, I didn't – just a vast, dark, cold space, like an old abbey or a ruined castle. There was a table set up for a feast all right, but the *delicacies* on it!" He shuddered. "Those grapes were some sort of round-bodied grub, like the grey things living in the ship's biscuits but ten times bigger. And there was other stuff too, like rotten meat. When you were about to take a bite out of a lump of it, I couldn't bear it any longer. I had to get us out. I wracked my brains trying to think of a way to get Trevanion and Valentine out

with us too, but they'd already eaten from her table –
I think that strengthened the spell."

"What about Fabien? Ann, I mean? We could
have taken her with us, Tolly. Why didn't you try?"

"Because she told me to go. She warned me. I saw
through that *shell* immediately but I had to find a
way to reach her. It was Cleo, really, she created a
diversion. Remember when I brushed *Fabien's* hand
and he started to twitch and make that odd high-
pitched noise? That's when I heard Ann's voice,
almost shouting at me. I think it was because I was
touching her. She told me that we had to get out."

"But we could have taken her too… or at least
tried."

Tolly shook his head. "And what would we have
done then? It wasn't the right time. Ann's life wasn't
in danger back there, but ours were."

"How can you say that? She's a prisoner up there!"
Jem's words steamed on the freezing air. He turned
to look down the deck at the hideous doorway. The
dead black eyes of the Medusa bored into him. "We
could have got her out."

"Didn't you understand what was happening,
Jem? *We* were about to become part of the feast.
Madame de Chouette was about to *serve us up* to the

captain and to Valentine. They were so far gone they would have eaten anything. And she wanted Ann to take part in the feast too. Remember what she said about 'appetite'?"

Jem felt a wave of nausea crash through his body as he stared at Tolly's face. He was right, of course. He remembered Madame de Chouette's words: "*I have also heard of lands where the flesh of children is considered to be a delicacy. Boys are sweeter than girls, I understand.*"

"Now do you see?" Jem nodded as Tolly went on, "Now we're out of that... room, or whatever it was, we still have a chance of getting off this ship and making sure Ann's with us when we do. For some reason, Ann's so important to Madame de Chouette that the woman has kidnapped her, disguised her, and set sail with her for the new colonies. So I think it's safe to say that she's not going to kill her..." Tolly paused. "Not yet, anyway. We've managed to thwart that woman once, Jem. We can do it again."

The *Fortuna* gave a great lurch and Jem clutched at the rail as a wave crashed across the deck. Jem looked up at the taut black ropes stretching overhead. He wasn't sure Tolly was right. They might have escaped from her chamber, but they hadn't escaped from Madame de Chouette. The *Fortuna* was *her* ship. Tolly might have outwitted the woman just then, but there was going to be a price to pay, Jem was certain of it.

"We can't give up hope. Did you hear what Ann called out?"

Jem frowned. "Something about her – Madame, I mean – not being able to make us enter that place again if we left without her permission. What did she mean?"

"I'm not sure. But I think that, somehow, we managed to break her power."

"*You* did, you mean." Jem chewed his lip. "Why didn't you fall under her spell too, like the rest of us?"

"Two reasons, I think. You saw the salt at the door? It was the first thing I noticed when I stood on the threshold. Because of what happened to you at Malfurneaux Place, I knew what it meant. I broke the circle with my foot as she called me in. The rest of you crossed the boundary at her invitation, so that gave her a hold over you – like that time with Cazalon."

Jem nodded again. "And the other thing?"

"Well, what was it like, then?" Spider's bony little face peered round Tolly's back and up at Jem

239

expectantly. He stepped between them. "Tell us about the grub. A lot better than weevil biscuits, I'll be bound? I didn't expect you two to be out yet. Ned reckoned there'd be at least six courses, decent grog and proper cheese at the end."

Spider sniffed and looked down at his feet. Jem saw something round and shiny plop to the timber deck. "Pocket would have liked that. He always loved cheese."

Jem hadn't told Spider what had really happened to his friend. Word had gone round that Pocket's fall from the lookout had been a terrible accident, but there were mutterings. Jem knew that sailors were a superstitious lot, but the men on board were talking openly now about the curse of the *Fortuna*.

Jem shuffled and glanced at Tolly. "I would have brought something back for you, Spider. But the food was —"

"Nothing special," Tolly cut in. "You wouldn't have enjoyed it. Trust me."

"And I dare say I wouldn't have the fancy manners for it, either." Spider looked up and grinned sadly. Once again the gap between his front teeth reminded Jem of Ann. Instantly, a tremendous rush of excitement shot through Jem. She was alive and on board!

"Anyways, I only came up for an essential and now I'm going down again. I nearly got knocked over the side myself when that last wave hit." Spider rubbed his hands together and slapped his arms. "I'm cold as a codfish tonight. I don't know how you two can sleep out here." He reached out to stroke Cleo's nose and she chirped softly. "You coming down to the bilge box now, Jemmie? It's not the same without Pocket. You can tell me about what you've just eaten and I'll dream all the sweeter for it."

Jem nodded. "I won't be long."

Spider turned to go.

"Wait," called Jem. "If… if you ever need to come up on deck again, for an essential at night, wake me and I'll come too. It's not safe out here."

Spider nodded. "I reckon someone should have told Pocket that, don't you?"

The doorway beneath the Medusa mask swung open then, spilling light across the deck. Captain Trevanion and Master Valentine staggered down the stairs. The pair of them were whey-faced and dishevelled. Valentine had to grip the rail. He looked as if he might be sick at any moment.

"There they are." Madame de Chouette stood

outlined in the doorway above. Slowly she raised a gloved hand and pointed down the deck to the place where Jem, Tolly and Spider stood. Her black dress flailed in the wind and tendrils of her auburn hair whipped around her shoulders, making it look as if the serpentine curls from the Medusa grew from her own head.

"Call Grimscale immediately. I want them searched."

The ring sat on top of a star chart across the captain's desk. The large round ruby in the broad golden band gleamed in the candlelight like a globule of fresh blood.

"Turn out your other pocket too," growled Grimscale. "Let's see what you're hiding there." Jem felt a vicious prod at his back.

"Nothing – there's nothing. I don't even know where that ring came from." Jem gasped as the jerkin was ripped from his shoulders, yanking his arms backwards so that his shoulders cracked. Grimscale shook the torn material and then delved into the pockets and lining. His face crumpled into a scowl of disappointment when it became obvious there was nothing to discover.

"Oh, I think you do, boy." Madame de Chouette sat in the captain's chair. She plucked the ring from the chart, pushed it over a gloved finger and held her hand out in front of her. She turned it from side to side so that the red stone sparked. "It is an old family heirloom. I knew it was missing almost from the moment you left my chamber. No wonder you were in such a hurry. I remarked on it, did I not, Captain?"

She glanced up at Trevanion, who was standing at the other end of the desk. The skin on his face had a greenish tinge. He passed a hand over his clammy brow. "I must confess I cannot remember a great deal of our evening. Perhaps the wine was over-strong? I know Master Valentine is also afflicted." It was true. After helping Grimscale to march Tolly and Jem along the deck to the captain's cabin, Valentine had been violently sick and asked to be excused.

Madame de Chouette smiled. Jem flinched at her tiny, pointed yellow teeth. "You may be right. It is an old and special vintage, Captain. An… acquired taste." Her golden eye flicked back to Jem. "I invited you to dine with me and you repaid my kindness by stealing. Master Grimscale, what would you do with thieves on board a ship of your own?"

Grimscale planted his fat hands on the table and leaned forward, grinning from ear to ear. "I'd keelhaul them, ma'am. Both of them, one after the other." Jem heard Tolly gasp. In a corner of the cabin Cleo cowered against the wall.

"No!" Trevanion thumped the other end of the desk. "Not on a ship under my command. I'll not allow such barbarity. The case isn't even proven against the pair of them. The other boy, you found nothing hidden about his person, did you?"

Madame de Chouette stared at Tolly for a long moment. She sighed deeply. "But how can we be sure he is not also guilty? They may have been working together. When the monkey frightened my poor nephew..." she glanced swiftly at Jem and just for a second her eye widened and darkened, "it was an opportunity, a diversion. I daresay that between them they have trained the creature to perform all manner of tricks to disguise their wickedness."

"That's true right enough, ma'am. This boy," Grimscale twisted Tolly's ear and forced him forward, "made the beast do cartwheels on deck a couple of days ago, to cover while his friend went ferreting about down below."

"To the hold?" Madame de Chouette was

suddenly very still. Jem now heard the ticking noise very clearly, faster than usual.

"I don't know where he went. Down to the mess deck for a good rummage is my guess. Not that he'd find much there. As I said to the Captain when they first came on board —"

"I think we have heard enough." Trevanion stepped forward and gripped Jem's shoulder. "Did you take the ring, boy? The truth now."

"No. I've never seen it before. I swear on my mother's life."

Trevanion's clear grey eyes looked troubled. "And you." He turned to Tolly. "What do you say?"

Tolly shook his head. "I've never seen it before either, sir. We are not thieves."

Jem took a deep breath. "It was Master Grimscale who found it there, just now. Why shouldn't it be him who took it? How can you be sure he didn't place it in my pocket?"

"Why you..." Grimscale released Tolly and lumbered around the table, but the captain blocked his path.

"Enough, I say!" He turned quickly to Madame de Chouette. "I apologise for having brought these two aboard the *Fortuna*. They are my responsibility and I will deal with them. I will personally ensure that they are handed over to a justice when we make land."

"Begging your pardon, Captain." Grimscale didn't sound as if he was begging a pardon at all. "I think we should make an example of them now."

Trevanion shook his head. "Morale is low enough as it is. We have lost three members of the crew since we set sail. A keelhauling or a beating would do nothing to improve things. If these two really are thieves, we will leave it to the law of the land. You know as well as I do how they treat wrong-doers in the new colonies. If these boys are guilty, they will be punished."

"This ship is mine, Captain. I believe *I* should be the one to decide their fate." There was a rustling sound as Madame de Chouette rose from the chair. "I think Grimscale may be right. An example must be set."

Jem felt Trevanion's grip tighten on his shoulder. "I am master of this ship, ma'am. While we are at sea, I am the embodiment of the law. I think you'll find that you agreed to this in our contract. All matters regarding the crew are my responsibility."

The woman walked round the desk and came to

stand in front of Jem. He noticed that she was taller than both Grimscale and Trevanion. She tapped the jewelled velvet eye-patch and tilted her head to one side. She plucked Jem's chin between her iron fingers again, forcing him to look into her golden, unblinking eye. Jem could feel the bones of his jaw crush together.

She continued to stare at Jem as she spoke. "Do not worry, Captain. I remember all the terms of our contract, as I trust you do. I can only think that your anxiety for your own child has softened your heart. Still, as the owner of this vessel, there are some things I can demand. Firstly, I *never* want to see these boys again. For the duration of the voyage they will not set foot on deck or feel sunlight on their skin. Their rations will be kept to the barest minimum. They will be bound together and locked away."

She paused for a moment as if listening to something. Jem thought he saw her nod. "I think… the hold might be just the place." She ran her tongue over the tips of her little teeth.

"Secondly, you will deliver them to the justice of Port Melas… after my nephew and I have left the ship for our estates. I will provide written evidence for their trial. And I trust poor Master

Grimscale here, who has been so foully abused by this treacherous boy, will be eager to appear on my behalf. I understand a boy may be hanged in the new colonies for the theft of a loaf of bread."

She loosened her grip on Jem's aching jaw and held up her hand so that the ruby glowed. The ticking was slower now.

"This ring is worth ten thousand loaves."

CHAPTER
TWENTY-TWO

The wide double doors in the *Fortuna*'s deck closed and everything went black.

Jem felt Tolly's shoulders stiffen. The boys were lashed together, bound back to back by the greasy ropes Grimscale had taken much pleasure in tightening round their bodies. Their arms were crushed against their sides beneath the thick cords. They had fallen, twelve, perhaps fifteen, feet, Jem guessed, but their landing had been cushioned by sacks of grain.

Grimscale's voice came down to them. "The rats will welcome your company, my lads. They're always looking for a bite to eat." Jem heard the man's heavy tread on the deck above. "And that's the last we'll be seeing of those two for the duration. Remember – no one is to speak to them or take them food. You, Spider, will be moving out from the bilge box tonight and the hatch will be locked. Can't have you near them when they cry out for their mothers, can we?"

Tolly's breathing was fast and ragged. The hold

echoed mournfully as huge waves thrashed against the wooden sides . Around them Jem could hear the packages and barrels creak and judder with the motion of the ship as they strained beneath their own ropes. The *Fortuna* rolled violently and the boys could do nothing as they toppled together from the sacking to the wet timbers below. The smell of tar, stagnant water and mildewed cloth filled Jem's lungs and the booming of the ocean filled his ears.

As they lay there locked together, shivering in a thin layer of stinking bilge water, Jem heard another noise – deep, soul-wracking sobs.

He felt Tolly's shoulders heave against his own. He didn't know what to do. He felt utterly useless. He knew that nothing he could say would make Tolly's misery go away. He wished Cleo was here with them. Tolly had said she was the only thing that kept him sane when Cazalon had brought them both as baggage on a ship from Alexandria to London.

"I don't know what I would have done without her company during that voyage."

He wondered what would happen to Cleo. He'd seen the way she cowered from Madame de Chouette in the captain's cabin and he was grateful that at the end of their interrogation, just before

Grimscale bundled them across the deck and pushed them down into the hold, Trevanion had called for Mingan to take her. But Tolly needed her now.

Jem clenched his hands tightly beneath the ropes. "You're not alone."

His voice sounded feeble against the hollow booming of the waves. He tried to sit up, but Tolly didn't move so Jem was forced to lie there. He knew his friend was paralysed by fear.

"Please try, Tolly. If we could sit up that would make it better. The water's freezing. I... I know how you feel."

Jem felt a great shudder ripple through his friend's back and heard Tolly fight to muffle another huge sob.

"You're... you're thinking about your parents and your sister and the time on the barge? It was terrible, and I know you only told me half of what happened to you all. No wonder this stinking place reminds you of that time. But I... I think I know how you feel down here... a little bit. It's like me with heights, but it's in reverse, isn't it? It eats away at your mind. You can't think about anything else. Your head is just full of... panic and darkness. You feel like you're going mad, losing control – and you feel utterly, miserably alone. But you're *not* alone. I'm here too."

Jem tried to wriggle his hand beneath the ropes so that he could reach Tolly's. He managed to link his little finger with his friend's.

"Remember the time you guided me down the wall at Ludlow House? I couldn't move because of the height, but you and Cleo helped me every step of the way. You were so calm and encouraging. It's a bit like that now, only it's my turn to help you. I can't guide you down exactly because... well, for one thing we can't go any lower, can we?"

Jem was grateful to hear a grunt that he hoped was a laugh. "But we are going to get out, I promise. We just have to work together and that means you must fight it – the fear, I mean. It's like Master Jalbert always says: never drop your guard. That's how the enemy wins. They find your weak spot and make it work to their advantage. Don't let it happen."

Jem felt Tolly's finger tighten around his own. Encouraged, he spoke again, more confidently now. "Look, Tolly, I think our strength has always come from being together, being a team. You have amazing mind skills and you're clever, and I am..." Jem paused, wondering what to say next.

"You are the bravest, most loyal and most honest person I know." Tolly spoke quietly in the darkness.

Jem was pulled to one side as the other boy struggled upright. The pair were now sitting back to back. Tolly took a deep breath. "Everything you say about fear is right. I know it's irrational, but after what happened to my family…"

Jem heard a muffled gulp and felt Tolly shift position.

"It's hard not to remember them when I'm in this place. It was terrible, Jem – the darkness, the stench of humans trapped together. The reek of fear – it's something so real you could trap it in a bottle. The memories fill my head. They make it difficult for me to think straight or remember to breathe." Tolly swallowed hard. "It was the last time I was with my father. He was such a fine man. He was…" His voice dwindled.

"A king! He was a king, just like mine," Jem continued for him. "That's how we beat Cazalon, wasn't it? We are the same, you and I, but he didn't know it. Don't you see, together we were able to defeat him. And we can defeat her – Madame de Chouette."

"It was the *three* of us together," Tolly corrected him gently.

"Exactly. We have to get Ann away from that

woman. I don't know how we are going to do that, but we have to try. I know it's hard for you down here, Tolly – and believe me, I'm not happy either – but we need all our wits about us. Don't let the fear win."

There was a long pause in the darkness before Tolly spoke again. Jem was relieved that his voice was firmer now, more controlled.

"So, what are we going to do?"

Now it was Jem's turn to fall silent. He shook his head and a strand of greasy hair got stuck across his eyes.

He blinked. "I… I… don't know."

Jem felt a tremor behind him and thought Tolly was trying to stifle another sob, but then realised he was laughing.

"You see. I said you were honest."

Jem smiled grimly in the dark. "All I know for sure is that we have to free Ann from the talons of that harpy. Why does she want her and why is she taking her to the new colonies? You're right that she must want… no – *need* her to be alive, otherwise she'd have…" He didn't want to finish the sentence.

Tolly straightened behind him. "Madame de Chouette is someone like Cazalon. She is incredibly

254

powerful. But Ann is too. Since we left Malfurneaux Place her... gifts have been getting stronger and stronger. Sometimes I think they frighten even her. I don't understand why she hasn't used her powers to break free. I think it must be something to do with this ship. If the *Fortuna* has clouded my mind, then it's likely blocked Ann's powers too."

Somewhere in the depths of Jem's mind a memory glimmered like a silvery fish leaping from a pool. He tried to catch it, but it disappeared into the murky waters. Then he caught another flash – it was something Tolly had just said, something about Ann using her powers.

He thought back to the time when Cazalon had led him along the gallery at Malfurneaux Place. As well as seeing a painting of Madame de Chouette, there had been the portrait of Ann's mother, Elizabeth Metcalf, as a girl. She had looked exactly like her daughter. Jem closed his eyes and fished deep into his memory. What had Cazalon said back then? It was something important...

"This portrait was commissioned on the eve of her thirteenth birthday – a very significant age for Metcalf girls, as it marked the time when they came into their..."

"Inheritance!" Jem shouted the word. "That's it, it

must be! Cazalon told me that Ann will come into her inheritance on her thirteenth birthday."

"But there's nothing left for her to inherit. When he became her guardian he took everything her family, the Metcalfs, owned." Tolly tried to turn as he spoke and Jem winced as the ropes dug into his arm.

"No, don't you see? It's not just money or possessions." Jem was excited to be one step ahead of his friend for once. The words came in a rush. "It's her powers. On her thirteenth birthday Ann will come into her full powers as a sorceress. When Cazalon showed me a painting of her mother, Elizabeth, at Malfurneaux Place, he told me that it was painted on the eve of her thirteenth birthday. He said that was when Metcalf girls..." he tried to remember the count's odd words, "inherited a... *a wisdom that most people would never possess in their entire lifetime.* But he meant power. I'm sure of it."

Tolly was quiet for a moment before he replied. "We know from what happened to you under St Paul's that thirteen was an important number to him."

Jem nodded, shuddering as Cazalon's words echoed again in his mind. *"A number of power, a number of magic, a number of completion... The point of balance between the light and the dark, between life and death.*"

"Ann is thirteen this year, isn't she?"

"On the first day of May." Tolly sat bolt upright, jerking Jem upward with him. "You're right. I didn't believe anyone could survive what happened to Cazalon under St Paul's. At least, I didn't want to believe it… but what if… what if a… *part* of him lived on? If Cazalon really is behind all this, he must want her very badly. There must be a reason. And I think I know what it is. You're right – he needs her *power*. And he needs to take it before she can fully control it. Do you remember what he said about the cavern beneath St Paul's being special?"

Jem nodded slowly. "He… he said it was a place where the powers of the earth could be harnessed?"

"Exactly!" Jem felt Tolly try to turn his head. "He said it was *a* place of power, not the only one. What if he has found another on the far side of the ocean? I was wrong. This isn't a trap at all – we were never meant to be here. No, it's a cargo ship… and the cargo is Ann."

CHAPTER
TWENTY-THREE

Jem yelped. Something had touched the tips of his fingers – something damp and furry. He flinched as wire-like whiskers brushed his flesh. There was a snuffling sound. He shunted to the side, pulling Tolly with him.

"Did you feel that?"

"And heard it. We have to free ourselves from these ropes, Jem. Remember what Grimscale said about the rats down here being hungry? Can you move either of your hands? I think I can move the left one a bit." Jem felt the side of Tolly's hand bump up against his.

"I'll try, but he's bound us together so tightly there's hardly any room to move my fingers."

The boys sat in silent concentration as they wriggled their fingers and hands beneath the bonds. The skin of Jem's wrist felt scraped raw as he struggled. He tried hard not to think about the starving rats scenting fresh blood. The bones in his right shoulder cracked loudly as he twisted his wrist and forced his hand down.

"There! I've got my right hand out. I can move all my fingers now, Tolly, how about you?"

"It's no good. Both my hands are caught. Can you pick at a knot like that?"

"I can try." Jem flexed his freed hand and tried to catch at the rope. His injured palm stung as he curled and wriggled his fingers. Tolly shuffled around to make it easier, but after a minute of scrabbling they gave up.

"What we need is something sharp to cut it with. If we could just find a nail or something poking out from the boards." Jem stared blindly into the darkness, trying to picture the layout of the hold. Beyond the grain sacks that had cushioned their fall there was a jumble of boxes, stacks of sail cloth, a pyramid of barrels lashed together and then the mirror.

The mirror!

"Tolly, stand up!" Jem pushed his shoulder against the grain sacks and struggled to rise.

"Ouch!" Tolly jerked upright and scuffled to his feet. "What are we doing?"

"Remember I told you about the mirror? That I kicked it and broke the glass? Some shards must be

259

on the floor of the hold. I'm sure I could use it to cut the ropes. I can move this hand, so I could hold the glass like a knife. It's this way – I'll lead, but we need to walk together. Are you ready? One, two, three…"

They bumped along the edge of the grain stacks and Jem turned cautiously to the left. After three or four steps Jem tripped over something and they clattered to the boards. "Sorry. It's a leather trunk, I think. Are you all right there?"

Tolly didn't answer, but Jem felt his friend's shoulders hunch together. He realised how difficult this was for him.

"I'm going to stand up again. That's it. Mind out for the trunk." He tried to sound reassuring. "It's not far down." The boys inched a few more yards along. With difficulty, because of their bonds, they scrambled over a mound of damp sacking and slipped to the boards on the far side. Both of them landed on their knees.

"Ow!" Tolly gasped. "I think I've found your broken mirror. There's a bit of it poking into my leg. It's just a nick – sharp, though. Here, if we move this way…"Tolly shuffled round so that Jem took his place. "Be careful. There – can you feel it?"

Jem's fingers closed around a jagged sliver of glass.

"Got it!"

"The light helps. I don't feel so bad now I can see you."

Tolly adjusted the little lantern. His even features were eerily illuminated by the soft yellow glow. Jem rubbed at his wrists where Grimscale's cords had dug deep into his skin. Once he had the shard of glass clutched firmly between his fingers and thumb it had been quite easy to tear at the ropes until gradually they weakened enough to free them. It had taken longer than Jem expected though, and in the darkness he had nicked Tolly's skin and his own several times. Now, in addition to the marks from Grimscale's knots, they both wore bracelets of tiny red wounds.

"It was a good thing you left these here when you came down last time." Tolly patted the tinderbox.

"It was Pocket's. I felt bad about leaving it here, but I had to get away from the mirror."

Tolly nodded and glanced up at the mirror. A crazed network of crackles showed through the gap Jem had ripped across its wrapping. He stood and pulled at the grey oilcloth so that even more of the glass was visible. "I don't know what this thing really is, Jem, but I'm certain it's broken. Look, it's

261

completely splintered."

The milky shattered surface of the glass glittered in the lamplight. It would never reflect anything again – and Jem was glad of that.

"It belongs to her – Madame, I mean," he said. "And I'm sure it was Ann's handprint on the glass. But how did it get there?"

Tolly was quiet for a moment. "Do you remember how Cazalon made the blood bridge to communicate with Ann's mother?"

Jem shuddered as he thought of the scars the count had inflicted on Ann's arms.

"What if Madame is doing something similar?" Tolly spoke slowly, as if he was sorting his thoughts. "What if she uses the mirror to connect with... someone?"

"Someone like Cazalon, you mean?"

Tolly suddenly thumped his fist against the wooden hull and Jem flinched. "It's useless. We are prisoners. I don't just mean prisoners down here in the hold, but prisoners aboard the ship. Even if we get out of here, what are we going to do? There's nowhere to hide, nowhere safe to take Ann, and nowhere to go."

"But what about the captain? Trevanion is on our side. I'm sure of it. If we could just —'

"Just what, Jem? I agree with you he is decent enough. But that woman has a hold over him – it's something to do with his daughter. Have you noticed the way she always reminds him about her?"

Jem rubbed the scratched skin of his wrist as Tolly continued.

"The only thing we can do is wait down here until we make land. That will be our best chance to take Ann back. Madame will have to bring her out on deck. If we can get out of the hold unnoticed when we arrive at… Port Melas, is it?"

Jem nodded. "In six days' time according to Mingan's reckoning. Wait – five now. But it's impossible to have travelled this fast, isn't it?"

Tolly laughed bitterly. "Nothing is impossible on the *Fortuna*, haven't you noticed? And there's Cleo – we have to find her too. Trevanion is right. This is a cursed voyage, but if we can bide our time and convince anyone who comes down here that we are still prisoners tied together then we stand a chance, don't we?"

Jem didn't answer. This was all hope, not a proper plan. He wasn't convinced that any of it would work.

Tolly continued, "Listen, we have the element of surprise on our side now. Once Grimscale takes us out on deck, we could make a sudden run for it."

Again, Jem didn't say anything. He could hear the desperation in Tolly's voice.

A thunderous boom reverberated through the hull. The ship tipped forward and Tolly snatched the lantern before it toppled to the boards. The contents of the hold rumbled and clattered. A stray barrel rolled free, missing Jem's legs by inches and thudding against the side. He was aware of a rushing, sucking sound from the timber wall and had to swallow hard to make his ears burst.

The *Fortuna* was travelling at great speed once more.

Something scraped along the outside of the ship. Then there came knocking, tapping and scratching from all sides. Something – many sharp-clawed somethings – trying to find a way in.

"The merfolk!" Jem jumped away from the hull wall and stared at the black wood in horror. Five inches, perhaps six at most, was all that separated them from Madame de Chouette's carnivorous servants.

"Can you feel the movement of the ship? She must have fed them again."

Tolly nodded. "I wonder who it was this time, poor soul, and who it will be next?"

"What if she comes down here?" Jem thought about the woman's clawed foot and imagined it rasping across the boards above them.

"Then we need to be ready for her." Tolly stood up. "Remember what I said about a weapon? The staff is down here somewhere... and I'm going to learn how to use it properly."

※ ⚒ ※

"It's no good. There's nothing."

Tolly flung Cazalon's staff aside in despair again. It clattered across the top of a pile of barrels before disappearing amongst the gloomy stacks. It hadn't been difficult to find, wedged between two long leather trunks.

Wearily, Jem went to collect the staff from the shadows. Just touching the blackened shark spine made his flesh crawl. As he held it up, the light of the lantern danced in the crystal eyes of the bird, making it seem alive and watchful.

"You have to try again – just once more." He held the staff out to Tolly, his arm heavy. He was tired – they both were.

Tolly's eyes drooped with misery, but he took it. Gripping it firmly in his right hand, he turned so that he was facing the sloping black wall of the hold. He took a deep breath, closed his eyes and tilted the staff forward.

Rows of furrowed lines crinkled across his wide dark forehead.

"I'd give anything to get her back, Jem, you know it." As if in answer, there was a crackling noise and a faint, greenish glow flickered around Tolly's clenched knuckles.

Suddenly he let out a howl of pain. His hand tightened around the staff just below the bird head. The eyes began to spark and Jem felt a jolt of excitement. At last something was happening.

The air around Tolly shimmered. His whole body began to glow with a pale luminescence.

"What do you see?" Jem whispered urgently, but the other boy held up his free hand.

A whipcrack snapped in the air. Jem's eyes widened as he saw a point on the tar-blackened timbers begin to pulse and glow. Then, just as before, in Ann's caravan, two beams of light arced from the crystal eyes. They hit the hold wall at exactly at the same spot. Jem could smell burning now. The beam singed a single red dot, but then it began to move, leaving a scorched trail as it twisted across the planks.

At first it was just a network of meaningless squiggles, then, like the last time, Jem began to recognise letters. The burning dot shot upwards and then downwards, moving jaggedly to form the letter "M". Within seconds, the word *MOON* glowed in the centre of the wall. The beam paused for a moment, circling and smouldering, then it began again, tracing a new pattern.

For a moment Jem thought it was just spinning on the spot, but it continued until a large disc was singed into the wood. The circle blazed brightly for a second, before dying away.

The beam raced on. Next the word *WHITC* appeared, then something that looked like *RW* – it was hard to make out as the planks were now covered in trailing scorch marks. There were hardly any clear spaces as the fiery point leaped to the right.

The number thirteen glowed briefly on the wall before the beam skipped down to scorch a long line across the top of a barrel, then returned to form a clear letter "W". It circled for a moment and Jem worried the wall might burst into flame. Instead the beam wavered and gathered pace, completing three more letters: *OLF*.

The whiplash sound cracked again and Tolly gasped. Jem tore his eyes from the smouldering timbers – and saw his friend tighten his hand around the staff. Now something glittered wetly on the shark spine.

"Stop! You're bleeding!" he shouted, but Tolly shook his head and grimaced. Jem tried to knock the staff from Tolly's hand but found that, just as before, he was rooted to the planks underfoot.

The burning dot leaped to a clear space and began to loop wildly. Tiny cinders of burning red wood flew up into the air as it circled and singed. It formed another "M" then an "A" then a "G". Now the beam began to flutter like a dying candle flame before lurching to mark four unevenly spaced stripes in the tar-coated wood: *IIII*.

The dot was suddenly motionless and the wood burned white hot.

Jem panicked, thinking that it would surely scorch through to the ocean, to the merfolk. He glanced at Tolly, whose eyes were still closed tight. Beads of silver sweat glinted on his friend's forehead. Gathering a last furious energy, the burning point leaped forward again leaving a distinct word in the last free space: *SING*.

Tolly let out a tremendous yell of pain and dropped the staff. He curled into a ball and clasped his right hand to his stomach.

Jem toppled to his knees and crawled over to crouch next to his friend. "Your hand, Tolly – show me your hand." He looked across at the staff on the floor, rolling precariously to one side as the ship moved. The nubbles were thickly streaked with something that glistened blackly in the lamplight. He turned back to his friend. "Please, let me see."

Tolly didn't make a sound. He rocked backwards and forwards, his back arched and his head dipped low. Eventually he straightened up. He took a deep, shuddering breath and looked down at his right hand, then without saying a word he held it out so that Jem could see.

Jem brought his hand to his mouth in horror. The first two fingers, the ones already damaged by the ice, were now twisted, blackened stumps. Tolly's thumb was nothing more than a shrivelled red lump of charred flesh.

Tolly stared down at his hand and then looked up at Jem. "I can't feel a thing. It doesn't even hurt... now. It's just numb." He ran the fingers of his good hand over the injured stumps and spoke softly. "I said I'd give anything, and the staff heard me."

Jem was about to ask what he meant, but Tolly continued hoarsely. "The words burned into the wood. What do you see?"

Jem tore his eyes from Tolly's hand and scanned the wall.

"I… I've got them – it goes… *moon*, then *whitc*." He frowned. "That could be a misspelling of witch? Then a word I don't recognise, something like *RW* then a 'W', then *olf*."

"Wolf," Tolly murmured. "I think it's just one word – *wolf*?"

"Of course!" Jem nodded. "But the last words are a jumble. *Mag*? I think that's what it is." He went over to the burned wall and reached out to touch the letters, running his fingertips over the four sharp lines scorched into the wood. He was amazed to find they were cold.

"Then there are these four deep marks and this last word, *sing*." Jem shook his head. "But it means nothing. It's gibberish." He narrowed his eyes and followed the letters again. "Is it a warning?" When he got no reply, Jem turned to see that Tolly had crawled over to a pile of grain sacks. He was curled against them, his injured hand cradled in the palm of the other hand. His eyes were closed.

"Tolly?"

Jem woke with a start.

Something was different. He raised his head from his knees and took a deep breath. The stink of tar and stagnant bilge was thinner somehow.

Thump!

Beside him, Tolly muttered in his sleep. The bumping noise came again. Now Jem was fully awake. Every nerve in his body jangled as he turned towards the direction of the sound.

A huge shadow loomed against the wall. Someone carrying a lantern had entered the hold from the little hatch in the bilge box. Jem heard footsteps. The pool of lamplight moved over the bulky piles. Someone was searching for something.

The little candle in their own lantern had sputtered out long ago. Jem shrank into the darkness and held his breath. If he tried to wake Tolly, he'd make a noise and that would bring whoever it was straight to them.

Something nearby sparked in reply to the moving light. It was the crystal head of Cazalon's staff, resting in a shallow pool of water. The staff was lodged in a gap just beyond the grain stacks where the boys had slept. Jem flexed his fingers. He might not be able to use it like Tolly, but it was still a weapon. Carefully, he reached out.

Something furry brushed his hand. Just as he was about to swipe the rat aside, Cleo's familiar chirrup came from the gap. Next moment she was scrambling across his lap towards Tolly. She squealed in delight and tried to burrow into Tolly's arms.

Tolly woke and blinked at the little creature at his side. "Cleo?" He shook his head and pushed himself upright. "Wh… What are you doing here, girl?"

"I've brought her back to you. We both have," came a deep voice.

Jem's head snapped up as Trevanion raised the lantern higher, casting a pool of light over their bodies. His thin face was worn and heavily lined and his grey eyes were dull. His fine velvet frock coat was shabby and stained. The captain looked like a man who had ceased to care about living.

There was a movement behind him and Mingan stepped into view. He bowed his head and folded his arms. Cleo whickered gently and Tolly held her close. They both stared up at the man.

"Thank heavens you are both alive." Trevanion paused. "I wasn't sure what we would find down here. I thought that she might…" He broke off and glanced at Mingan who nodded again.

"Listen to me carefully, boys. There isn't much time. The *Fortuna* will make land in two days." He laughed bitterly. "Oh yes, I have the great good fortune to be the master of the fastest vessel ever to have crossed the Atlantic Ocean. But at such a cost…" He stared bleakly down at the lamp. "Such a cost," he muttered again.

As if she had heard his words, the *Fortuna* bucked and plunged and her black timbers growled. She was suddenly like a ferocious rampaging beast, not a ship at all. Cleo cowered in Tolly's arms and Trevanion reached out to steady himself, clutching the edge of a chest. The lantern in his hands swung from side to side – one second his lean face was bathed in yellow light, the next it vanished into shadow. In that odd moment, something made Jem fear for Captain Trevanion. He knew without a doubt that the captain was slipping into the dark.

"When you hear us lower the anchor – and make

no mistake it is a sound you will know – the two of you must be ready. Mingan here will make sure that the small hatch is unlocked. You already know where that is. The rest is up to you. Make your way to the deck if you can – there will be so much activity that you will not be noticed if you hide. There will be a chance for you to slip away when the quay is crowded and busy. If you are fortunate, you might escape this… hell ship." Trevanion paused before adding quietly, "And if you do, you will be luckier than me. We have brought food and water for you. Here."

Mingan handed a small leather bag to Jem.

"I don't understand, sir. What about the justices? You promised Madame de Chouette that you would hand us over. And there's Grimscale too – he's itching to see us brought to trial." Jem looked from Trevanion to Mingan.

Trevanion drew a short breath. "Two more crewmen have gone missing since you were put down here. I have broken my promise and I will pay for that. I do not think this vessel will forget the oath I swore so rashly."

Jem remembered the captain promised *on his life* that no more lives would be lost before they made land. He thought about the strange glow that had played around the man's fingers as he spoke – as if the ship was listening to him, binding him.

The captain continued. "If I cannot save myself, I will save as many as I can. There is too much blood on my hands already. I'll not turn you over to the authorities at Port Melas, for I do not believe you are guilty. I won't endanger the nephew of an old friend. James Verrers was a good man. You, boy, for all your gypsy looks, have something of his quality."

He turned to Mingan. "Come, we will be missed. I will leave the lamp here. Save it and use it to light your way when the time comes." Trevanion turned to make his way back to the hatch, but Mingan lingered.

"Wait, sir!" Tolly stood up, Cleo cradled in his arms.

"Your daughter – what will happen to her if you let us go free? It's why you made this voyage, isn't it?"

Trevanion turned back and nodded. He face was strained. "But how did you know?"

Tolly took a step forward. "You spoke of her that first time when Grimscale found us and took us to you – and you've mentioned her since. She's ill, I think? Her condition has something to do with

Madame and this ship?"

Trevanion glanced at Mingan. "No one knows of this, except my old friend here. Mingan tried to help my daughter Jane with the remedies of his tribe, but the people in Swale, they —'

"Didn't trust him, because he was different?" Tolly stared hard at Mingan.

"Something of that nature, yes. It is a sea-faring port and they are used to strangers, but Mingan is very distinctive. They did not care for his looks and I sent him away. I was a fool to listen to them, but I was a bigger fool when I made a promise to that woman. The worst is that, deep down, I knew all along what she was."

Trevanion slumped against the wall. "It's a short tale and I'll tell it to you now. You will likely be the last people to hear my story. Perhaps, one day, you can use it to warn others, although I pray you never have to." He passed a hand over his brow. "Madame de Chouette arrived in her gilded coach at the end of November. It was during a great storm and she took rooms at the inn.

"For two months before she arrived the children of Swale had been afflicted by a curious malady – a sickness of spirit and body. Madame told us that in

276

her country she was considered to be something of a physician and she offered to... help. Within a week all the port was in her thrall. First it was the butcher's son – she cured him in a day. And then there were others too, the twins at the mill house, the baker's daughter, the rector's oldest boy. People called her the lady of miracles." Trevanion clenched a fist.

"And your daughter?" Tolly spoke gently.

"Jane had, no – *has* the sickness. She cannot talk, she cannot move, she lies on her bed staring at the canopy above. My sister Judith and Tam, her little companion, try to comfort her and rouse her, but she is lost to us. Jane is everything to me. I would give my life for her." The captain paused again and stared blankly ahead.

"When I heard of the cures I went to the inn and asked Madame to visit us. I fell into her trap, for I think it was me she was looking for all along. She had come to Swale in the depths of winter in search of a mariner desperate enough to do her bidding. I was that man. She told me she was looking for an experienced sea captain – someone who could guide her own ship across the Atlantic Ocean at the most dangerous time of the year. It had to be someone *respected*, she said," the word twisted from

Trevanion's lips, "someone men would trust with their lives.

"She promised that if I took her commission Jane's sickness would lift. She has sworn to me that the moment she and her nephew set foot in the new colonies my daughter will be well."

"And d-do you believe her?" Jem asked.

"It doesn't matter any more. I was a selfish wretch to risk so many lives. I love my child dearly, but I have made her the cause of so much harm. When we get to Port Melas I hope to have spared the lives of as many of my crew as possible – and that includes you two. I doubt that I will see my daughter again…" He hesitated for a moment, and then produced a letter from his coat and handed it to Jem. "If… no – *when* you get back to England, I would like you to take this to my daughter. I would consider it a great favour."

He straightened up and nodded at Mingan. "Come, we will be missed. We have been too long already. I'll not have Grimscale reporting behind our backs. Remember, boys: listen for the sound of the anchor chain. It is your chance."

Trevanion turned and began to climb the rungs to the hatch.

Before he reached up to open it, Jem had a terrible thought. "Sir, the crew who have gone missing – Spider's not one of them, is he?"

Trevanion stopped climbing, but he didn't turn back.

"No, Jem, it was not your young friend. The missing men are an old experienced hand from Swale who trusted me with his life… and Master Valentine. That is why I have entrusted my letter to you."

CHAPTER
TWENTY-FOUR

Just as Trevanion had said, they knew the sound instantly. A mighty clanking reverberated through the darkness as the anchor plunged to the ocean bed. The *Fortuna* juddered and bucked, every timber growling at the sudden restraint. Above them the boys could hear scores of feet thumping on the deck as crewmen raced to steady the ship and tend to the sails.

They had made landfall. Jem imagined Madame somewhere above making ready to leave. They *had* to get to Ann before the woman left Port Melas with her. He was certain Madame de Chouette was Cazalon's creature and that she was about to deliver Ann straight to him.

He fumbled to light the lantern left behind by the captain. The flame flickered to life, revealing Tolly already on his feet and staring in the direction of the rungs leading up to the bilge-box hatch.

"Now?"

Jem nodded. "I'll take the staff and you take Cleo.

I'll go first."

They were soon creeping into the dingy, low-ceilinged crew quarters where a row of empty hammocks bumped listlessly against the walls. Jem crouched at the bottom of the ladder steps leading up to the deck, listening intently. When he was sure no one was standing directly overhead, he climbed up and pushed at the slatted wooden door so that it opened a crack.

He watched a group of crewmen halfway down the ship pull on ropes to drag open the wide double doors to the hold. Above them the rigging was alive as other men swarmed up ropes and shinned out along mast spits to furl in the *Fortuna*'s flapping grey sails. Everyone was concentrating on a task. Jem took a deep breath and glanced down at Tolly. "Follow me. Keep low in the shadow and as soon as you come out on deck, squeeze behind the water barrels lashed to the rail on the right. There's a space behind them. It's where I hid from Madame with Mingan that time. We can watch for Ann from there."

Tolly nodded and folded his arms around Cleo. She chirruped softly.

Within a few seconds the three of them were wedged together behind the barrels. Jem's hands trembled as he laid Cazalon's staff down, careful to shield it from view. He looked over his shoulder at the foaming water against the side of the boat.

"Keep your head down, Cleo." Tolly tried to push the little monkey's black-and-white muzzle into the depths of his cloak with his good hand. It was no good; she was gulping down lungfuls of fresh clean air. After days in the darkness of the putrid hold, Jem couldn't blame her.

The sea-salted wind carried another odour now: earth and the sharp spice of fir trees. Jem was amazed at how good it felt to breathe in those familiar yet almost forgotten scents again.

He squinted, trying to adjust to the brilliant sunlight. To the left, beyond the ship's rail and through the cat's cradle of ropes, he could see a distant band of deepest green – a forest, covering the side of a hill, or perhaps it was a mountain? Jagged peaks of snow-covered rock punctured the line where the trees met clear blue sky. After the endless glass-grey ocean stretching to infinity on every side, not to mention the gloom of the hold, the view was wonderful – full of colour and promise. A tingling sensation coursed through his body, and Jem realised that he longed with every fibre of his body to stand on solid ground again.

He peered round the edge of the barrel. The long black deck swarmed with activity. The double doors of the hold stood wide open now and lines of crewmen tugged on ropes to haul swinging leather trunks from the *Fortuna*'s belly. The men worked in grim silence, the lusty shanties they had chorused together just a few days ago lost to them now. Like their friends, Jem thought sadly.

But there were other sounds – shouts of excitement and snatches of conversation from colony people crowding onto the jetty beside the ship. Jem leaned carefully to one side to take in more of the scene through a gap in the rail. He couldn't see the people jostling below, he was too high up for that, but further away, clustered around the end of a broad wooden jetty, scores of people pointed and chattered. Everyone seemed to be dressed in a shade of grey or brown.

Port Melas fanned out along the rocky edge of a gently curved, sheltering bay. More people were streaming out now from rows of low timber houses to see the *Fortuna*. Women and children watched from narrow doorways. Cattle ambled along a single icy track leading through the centre of the settlement and out into the trees beyond. Jem watched a small boy chase a herd of geese from their path. He wasn't sure what he'd expected of the new land, but he was surprised it was so ordinary and so familiar. Apart from the distant mountains, Port Melas looked like England.

"Speak your business." The deep voice belonged to a man somewhere down on the jetty. Jem recognised the West Country burr in his accent. The people here even spoke the same way as those at home.

Trevanion leaned over the side of the ship. "The *Fortuna* seeks safe haven. We have brought passengers from the old world to their estates and we have brought goods for you, the people of Port Melas. Will you grant us leave to stay awhile in exchange for grain and seed?"

The deep West Country voice came again. "A crossing, in January? Why 'tis impossible, sir. How do we know you're not pirates or spies sent to report on our ways?"

"I assure you that is not the case." Trevanion's breath misted on the frozen air. "We are men of Port Swale – you must know our reputation. We were commissioned to take this ship across the ocean so that our passenger can complete an urgent transaction. We have brought you supplies..." He broke off as a fat grain sack swung upward and out from the hold. It dangled tantalisingly over the side of the *Fortuna*. "We know that winter here is harsh and that your stores run low. In return for the safe berth of this vessel, our passenger offers the people of Port Melas these goods." He gestured at the swinging sack.

There was a long pause before the man on the quay spoke again. "I've not seen a ship like this before. Swale men, you say?"

"That is correct, but the *Fortuna* is..." Trevanion paused, "not of Swale. She belongs to our passenger who is anxious to travel on to estates in the north. Will you grant us safe haven?"

"I will confer."

Trevanion waited. Jem heard raised voices and snatches of muttered conversation.

The voice came again. "How many sacks are you carrying?"

"Fifty of grain and enough seed to sow thirty acres."

More muttering, then, "So be it. You are welcome here at Port Melas – in consideration of the supplies you have brought us. I will come aboard now."

Trevanion nodded to a knot of crewmen. They ran forward and released a wide plank from the rail, pushing it out over the side of the ship. It came to rest with a thump somewhere on the jetty below. Moments later, a bald, red-faced man clambered aboard. He was wearing a long brown coat and his boots were made from heavily stitched hide.

He pursed his lips as he shielded his eyes from the sun and viewed the ship. "And you are?"

"Captain Richard Trevanion, at your service, sir." Trevanion bowed.

The bald man nodded. "I am Goodman John Winterbourne. On behalf of the Council of Elders, I bid you welcome to Port Melas."

"You have made the right decision. I am grateful." Madame de Chouette's chilly voice rang out over the deck. Jem ducked down below the edge of the barrel. She was standing at the doorway to her chamber, just above their hiding place. He could just see the fluttering black edge of her gown. "My nephew and I will depart from this vessel today. Arrangements have already been made for us."

Jem felt Tolly go rigid beside him. He tried to catch sight of Ann, but she wasn't in view.

Goodman Winterbourne's eyes widened in

surprise. "You didn't say your passenger was a woman, Captain – a one-eyed woman and foreign at that."

"Do not concern yourself with such inconsequential matters, Goodman Winterbourne. I am not of any nation, I have no allegiances, but I do have estates in this land. Within the hour, I intend that my nephew and I will be travelling to them. We will be… collected."

Goodman Winterbourne frowned. "I was not aware of any estates in these parts, ma'am. There's Port Melas and five other settlements on the coast and the inlets to the south, but nothing else for many miles. Where are you heading?"

"North of this place. Far, far north. To a place you will not be familiar with. Our escort will be with us soon."

"Escort?" Tolly hissed the word.

"I will go now to prepare my nephew for the journey. Good day to you, Goodman Winterbourne. I must repeat myself: make no mistake, you have made the right decision today."

Above their hiding place, a door slammed.

"What are we going to do now?" Tolly whispered. "Once she gets Ann off the ship and out of Port

Melas, we'll lose her for ever."

Grimscale marched to the edge of the open hold, planted his hands on his leather belt and leaned forward. It was obvious he was scouring the gaping black space below for a sign of Tolly and Jem.

"Think yourselves safe down there, do you?" His voice was heavy with menace. "Enjoy the company of the rats while you can. Once we've emptied the hold, there'll be no place to hide. We have an appointment to keep with the Justices of Port Melas. I've already arranged it with Goodman Winterbourne. He tells me they have very particular ways of dealing with thievery here." He laughed and added, "Perhaps before that I'll introduce you to my cats, after all."

Jem shuddered as he thought about Grimscale's metal-tipped whips. He glanced at Tolly, who was struggling to keep Cleo hidden in the folds of his cloak. For the last half-hour they'd watched sacks, bundles, chests and trunks winched out from the hold and onto the jetty below, but Madame and "Fabien" hadn't left yet.

Tolly nudged Jem. "We should try to move somewhere else. They'll be unloading these barrels soon." He pushed Cleo's head out of sight for the hundredth time. "I don't think I can hold on to her much longer. I'm frightened she'll give us away."

"It's too busy at the moment." Jem tried to get a better view of the deck between the barrels. "If Grimscale wasn't out there overseeing everything, we'd stand a chance. I'm pretty sure the crew would let us go." He spotted Spider bent double beneath a bulging sack. The boy was almost invisible beneath the burden as he made his way to the gangway. Jem only recognised his spindly legs.

It gave him an idea. "Look! See that pile of sacks and bundles on deck over there? If you watch the crew carrying things off the ship you can't see their faces at all. They're bent double under the weight."

Tolly nodded.

"We can get off like that. You'll have to wrap your cloak tight around Cleo, almost tuck her in so she can't escape. I think it's our chance."

"Perhaps." Tolly spoke the word slowly – he didn't sound convinced. "But how can we get over there to the sacks without being seen? And what about Ann? She's still on board."

"Not for much longer though, you heard what Madame said." Jem gnawed at the skin around his thumbnail. What should they do? Spider appeared at the top of the gangway again. Despite the cold, the boy's forehead was covered with beads of sweat. He paused, spat on his hands and rubbed them together.

"That's it!" Jem sucked his teeth and spat a mouthful of saliva, landing a globule smack in front of Spider. The boy stopped, looked down at it and frowned. "You try too, Tolly, we need to get him over here."

Tolly followed Jem's lead. Soon Spider was being bombarded by sticky missiles.

He scowled and turned towards the water barrels. Jem heard him mutter, "Fink it's funny, do ya? Well, I'll teach you some manners." Spider rolled up his sleeves and marched towards them.

When he was just a yard or so away, Jem whispered urgently. "It's us – Jem and Tolly."

Spider's eyebrows shot up. He stopped and glanced anxiously back along the deck to where Grimscale directed the emptying of the hold.

"I thought you two were tied up down there somewhere. How did you get up here?" he spoke quietly.

"No time to explain. Please, Spider, don't give us away. We need your help to get off the ship."

Spider nodded and turned about nonchalantly so that he stood with his back to the barrels. He stretched his arms above his head and flexed his neck from side to side as if he was preparing his muscles for another heavy load. "What do you want me to do?" he whispered from the corner of his mouth.

"Can you move some of those sacks over here – as if you are sorting them? If you pile them in front of the barrels – six or seven maybe – it will make a sort of screen. Then, when we get a chance, we'll both hoist one over our shoulders and carry it off the boat. There's so much going on, no one will notice us, I'm certain."

Spider bent forward to touch his toes. It looked as if he was stretching his aching back, but actually it meant he could look Jem in the eye between a gap in the barrels.

"All right then. Let's give it a go, Jemmie."

CHAPTER
TWENTY-FIVE

Jem zigzagged across the last few feet of deck before reaching the top of the gangway. Smothered beneath the heavy hessian sack he couldn't see what was happening around him, although he could hear the muffled thump of feet and the rumble of rolling barrels.

Tolly had gone first with Cleo. From the hiding place, Jem had been relieved to watch his friend stagger through the gap in the *Fortuna*'s rail and then disappear from view.

Now it was his turn. At every step he expected to feel Grimscale's grip on his arm, hear his triumphant voice, and choke on the evil stench of his breath. If he was caught now, Jem knew Captain Trevanion wouldn't be able to protect him.

He cleared the edge of the deck and then felt the sloping gangway judder beneath him. Jem quickened his pace, but when his feet finally made contact with the solid wood of the jetty his head began to swim. Hunched beneath the sack, he thought he might be about to lose his balance and topple to his knees. He closed his eyes and paused for a moment.

"You all right back there?" Spider's voice came from somewhere ahead.

"It's… it's moving. Everything's moving," Jem moaned.

"That's land sickness, Jemmie. You been on water so long your head's got used to it. You've got to get the hang of terra firma again now. We all suffer first time out. Makes you feel sick, dunnit?"

"Yes." Jem opened his eyes again. He could see Spider's bony ankles poking out of a pair of ancient, badly scuffed leather shoes. Shoes that seemed to be at least three sizes too big for him.

"Tolly's over there." Spider indicated with his right foot. "He had it too, the land sickness, when he came off. I'd get over there sharp if I were you and keep low – the end of that stick is poking out from under the sack. I don't know why you brung it with you. Nasty-looking thing."

Jem staggered to the right, keeping to the line of the jetty.

"Here!" Tolly hissed. "We're here. Two more steps forward and one to the left. Then duck."

Jem followed Tolly's voice and found his friend crouched behind a stack of wicker lobster pots, all of them threaded with wide fronds of stinking seaweed. The pots were piled at the far end of the T-shaped jetty, far enough from the ship for them to remain unnoticed but near enough to see what was happening.

"Stash it there on top of my one." Tolly helped Jem shrug the sack from his shoulders. "There, if we balance it like this, it means we can't be seen easily from the land side either."

The boys knelt together, scanning the busy scene from their hiding place. Cleo squeezed in between them and wrinkled her nose – at the stench of the seaweed, Jem guessed. Crewmen moved up and down the *Fortuna*'s rattling gangplank. They looked like worker ants, each one bent double under a sack or a trunk. Meanwhile, bulky items swayed up and out from the hold, dangling precariously over the ship before being lowered to the jetty.

Captain Trevanion stood on the far side of the jetty with Goodman Winterbourne and a group of other Port Melas men – the councillors, Jem supposed. One of them had a sheet of paper and a quill pen, and as each bundle bumped ashore he made a mark on the sheet. Madame de Chouette was paying them handsomely for their welcome.

Jem looked up at the *Fortuna*. Her bulging black side loomed above the simple jetty of Port Melas, casting a giant shadow. As the ship rocked gently in the calm waters of the bay she looked like a sea monster, a leviathan, waiting to engulf the little settlement. No wonder Goodman Winterbourne and his council had been wary of granting them safe harbour.

In the sharp light of day he could now see odd carvings running across the *Fortuna*'s timbers, from the prow to the stern. Tiny figures fleeing from coiling serpents, misshapen creatures with an impossible number of limbs, twisted insect-like forms with ragged wings. Jem blinked as a memory stirred – he had seen something like it before.

He glanced up at the figurehead – the red-haired woman with the star in her hair.

"Tolly, look!" He nudged his friend. "Up there."

"Where?"

"The figurehead. It's different." Jem stared again. The painted woman's eyes were fully open now and her mouth yawned wide in a smile that revealed rows and rows of serrated teeth.

"Is it? I never got a clear view, but looking at it now, I'm glad."

A commotion on the jetty took their attention.

Jem peered round the edge of the wicker pots and saw a flash of brilliant green in the midst of the crowd at the foot of the gangway. As Madame de Chouette stalked along the jetty the wind caught at her cloak, blowing it apart so that the emerald silk lining showed clearly. People stood aside to let the hooded figure pass. She clasped the red-haired boy who was really Ann tightly to her side. Anyone who didn't know better would see a sickly youth supported by his loving aunt.

"Look! There's Ann. How can we get her away?" Jem clenched his fists so tightly that his knuckles hurt.

At the same moment a familiar oblong package was winched from the hold. The mirror.

Three crewmen stood ready on the jetty to guide it down into place. As it bumped onto the wood, there was a sharp crack. Madame de Chouette spun round, her single golden eye wide. There came a tinkling, splintering noise as every tiny fragment of mirror glass still set into the frame crumbled from its place. Some of it fell to the jetty where it glittered in the sunlight, some fell inside the torn grey oilskin wrapping.

"No!" It was almost a cry of pain. Madame de Chouette released Ann and swept back along the jetty to the mirror.

"Which of you has done this?" She threw back the hood of her cloak and turned her pointed white face from side to side, scanning the crewmen and the Port Melas folk. Her jewelled eye-patch glinted and Jem noticed that several of the folk formed the sign against the evil eye with their fingers.

"Captain! Where are you?"

All eyes turned towards Trevanion. She swirled round and began to advance towards him. "I thought my instructions were clear. The one thing I most specifically warned you to take great care of has been destroyed. You will pay dearly for this."

Madame de Chouette seemed to have forgotten her "nephew". Fabien stood alone on the jetty staring blankly at his feet. Except for his tufts of short red hair quivering in the wind, he was as motionless as a statue.

It was the chance Jem had been waiting for. "Now, Tolly! While Madame's attention is on the captain."

Grabbing the staff, he exploded from behind the lobster pots and pelted down the jetty. He heard the beat of Tolly's feet on the planks just behind him.

"I hope you're right about this," came his friend's

breathless voice.

Ann was just yards away. Jem wasn't sure what he was going to do exactly, but if he could reach out…

"Stop!"

The single word filled Jem's ears and made his head ring. The air around him thickened like porridge. He tried to catch Ann's hand, but it was like pushing through wool. He balled his fist to punch a way to her but it was hard to move his fingers.

Madame de Chouette's voice came again. "You will obey. Look at me."

He tried to force himself not to turn back, but it was impossible. The movement wrenched every muscle in his neck. As he twisted round he caught sight of Tolly's desperate face and then, outlined against the black hull of the *Fortuna*, Madame de Chouette.

Slowly she extended her arms. Brilliant green silk cascaded around her as the lining of her cloak spread wide. Then she smiled. "Did you really imagine it would be so easy to save your friend?"

Jem tried to run but he was rooted to the spot. He couldn't even close his eyes. Her outline wavered in the sunlight. At first it was as if a great green wave was rolling along the jetty to engulf them and then his vision blurred, leaching all the colours away. Madame de Chouette was now black as night, her cloak held apart like the wings of a massive bird. The folds of fabric billowed around her, rippling and rearranging themselves into jagged rows of sheeny black feathers.

Then slowly the woman's face hollowed and lengthened. Something hard and skeletal spread across her face – a mask of sharpened ochre bone erupting through the skin to replace her brows, her nose and her lips. The black pupil of her rounded amber eye was like a bottomless pit. She took a single step forward and Jem heard something tear: the bronze talons at the tips of her blackened claws ripping through the fabric hem of her dress.

She rolled her head, flexed her claws and gathered her wings into two sharp points that rose behind her back. Then she lowered her head.

Every atom of Jem's body screamed at him to run, but he couldn't move a muscle – even though he knew the owl was ready to hunt.

CHAPTER
TWENTY-SIX

Aroooo!

The long eerie howl echoing around the bay made the air shudder.

Then the wolf landed low with a mighty thump on the jetty planks in front of the hideous feathered creature. The muscles of its massive grey flanks flexed as it gathered itself. It was huge – bigger than any dog Jem had ever seen.

The wolf turned its ice-blue eyes on Jem and Tolly. It wrinkled its muzzle, snarled and then threw back its head and howled again. Jem's heart pounded like a hammer, and he could hear his breath come shallow and fast, like a cornered fox. There was silence for a long moment and then from every direction, answers came. It sounded as if a hundred wolves chorused in unison, their doleful cries rising and falling on the wind. The owl creature blinked once and jerked its head to one side.

Without taking its eyes from the boys, the wolf rolled its head and a new wave of terror rose through

Jem's body as its black scimitar claws scraped against the jetty. It was if the animal was testing them. The staff in Jem's right hand would be useless against such raw, muscular power.

It was the end, Jem knew it. Between them, the wolf and the owl would rip both him and Tolly apart. The wolf, narrowed its eyes and crouched, ready to spring.

Jem found himself thinking of his mother, of Goldings, of Gabriel, of little Simeon, of Master Jalbert, of the king, of Ann, of Tolly, of Cleo. Every person and everything he had ever cared about crowded into his thoughts. A corner of his mind registered the fact that it was true what people said. When you were about to die, your life did flash in front of you.

With an ear-splitting howl, the wolf leaped... twisting in mid-air to fall upon the owl woman. There was a shrill screech of terror and then the creatures tore viciously at each other, their forms blurring to a heaving, tumbling mass of black and grey and red.

Growling and screeching, they slammed against the jetty planks, first one gaining advantage and then the other. Jem watched in amazement as the shrieking combatants melded into a rolling ball of fury.

The folk gathered on the jetty began to run, most of them covering their ears to block the terrifying sounds. A man almost knocked Jem into the water. Jem tried to turn and run too, but his legs were like lead weights. Another man caught him roughly by the shoulder.

"What have you brought to us on that Devil ship?" The man didn't wait for an answer, but raced on past, the sound of his heavy boots drumming on the timbers.

"Seal all the doors! Women and children to the meeting house. 'Tis witchcraft!"

Jem heard the tolling of a single bell. He tried to turn to look back at Port Melas, but it was impossible. Horribly, his eyes were locked on the battle. The wolf lashed out with a huge paw, swiping the feathered creature aside in a blizzard of blood and black feathers. Madame de Chouette crashed against the side of the ship with a sickening snap, then fell back onto the edge of the jetty in a broken, twitching heap. Now the wolf had control. It stood over its opponent and pinned the misshapen wings to the timbers with its paws. Jem watched the owl's bony, mask-like head straining upward to tear at wolf's muzzle – held out of reach.

To the left of his eyeline he caught a glimpse of movement – a blur of black and white. He just managed to drag his eyes to follow the little form of Cleo as she scampered past. Surely she would never abandon Tolly – where was she going? He glanced up and saw that Tolly, frozen to the spot just a few yards away, was watching her intently. Tolly's eyes widened and then Jem heard his friend *speaking into his mind*. "Behind you!"

Something caught his hand. Small fingers worked their way into his. He tried to turn but he was still locked, unable to budge. He heard a familiar voice.

"Hold on."

The hand tightened its grip. Jem felt heat rise up through his arm and flood his body. He fastened his own fingers about the hand. Something white flashed to the right. He turned his head, slowly at first, realising with a jolt of relief that he could move again. He heard Cleo chirrup as someone stepped forward.

Strands of pale waist-length hair flew about in the wind as the girl stretched out to take Tolly's hand in her own.

"Ann!"

As the three of them stood linked together, Jem was

aware of a thrumming sound. A single, trembling note, like the fading echo that lingers after musicians have laid down their instruments. His head was suddenly filled with lights and colours – little explosions of brilliance. For a split second he felt as if the three of them were at the very centre of everything – that this point, here on the jetty at Port Melas, was the most important and powerful place in the world.

Ann turned to look up at him. Her face was haggard, with shadowed pouches beneath her green eyes. Her small, slender frame was lost in Fabien's clothes.

"Can you move now, Jem?"

He nodded. "But how…?"

She turned to Tolly. "And you?"

An anguished howl of pain split the air and, despite themselves, they all looked back. The unearthly creatures were nearing the end of their brutal struggle. The wolf flattened itself to the jetty as it tried to dislodge the owl woman from its neck, its muscular sides shuddering as it fought to breathe. Vast broken wings unfurled, shielding the struggling wolf from view.

Madame de Chouette opened her curved beak and let out a harsh cry of triumph. She paused for a moment, jerking her massive head from side to side.

Ann dropped their hands. "Now run, run! Before it is too late. Whatever you do, don't look back." She whirled about and started up the jetty towards the settlement, struggling to move at speed in Fabien's bulky jerkin and wrinkled breeches. Without question Jem and Tolly followed, Cleo darting between their legs. Ann shrugged off the jerkin and pelted forwards, springing from the end of the jetty and onto the frosted mud of the track. She paused to give Jem, Tolly and Cleo the chance to catch her.

"Where now?" Jem gasped out the words. The muddy pathways of Port Melas were deserted. Every window and every door was barred to them.

One last long, terrible howl split the air.

From somewhere behind there was a thunderous explosion. A bolt of lightning threw the world into sharp relief – every house, every tree, every stone was revealed in a moment of dazzling clarity. The booming came again and they ducked.

"Don't look back!" Ann repeated the words over the deafening bellow of splitting, groaning timbers, then came a sucking, wailing sound that blocked their ears. As the ground rocked beneath their feet, she reached for their hands again. "Don't!"

It was as if day became night. Something brushed

Jem's face and he looked up. Fine snow was beginning to fall, mixed with black feathers and spots of blood. As the flakes began to settle on the land, the red droplets gleamed like the ruby of Madame de Chouette's ring. There were shouts and screams from somewhere behind.

Jem fought the urge to turn back and felt Ann's grip tighten. "You mustn't, believe me."

He swallowed hard and repeated his question. "Where now?"

Tolly reached down to gather Cleo into his arms. "There's only one road out from Port Melas and it's straight ahead. We don't have any other option. Run!"

CHAPTER
TWENTY-SEVEN

The track disappeared beneath the snow, but they still ran on, pushing through bracken, scrambling over rocks, slipping and sliding – all the time pressing deeper and deeper into the silence of the soaring fir trees. When the ground began to rise beneath their feet they used jutting rocks and rotting stumps to haul themselves upward. Stones and thorns tore at their flesh, but nothing stopped them. If they paused it was to draw breath; if they spoke it was to decide which way to go. Fabien's undershirt hung loosely on Ann's narrow shoulders. When Jem saw her trembling he took off his cloak, wrapped it round her and tucked her red shawl about her neck like a scarf.

The trio were driven by one unspoken thought: the most important thing in all the world was to get as far away from the *Fortuna* – and from Madame – as it was possible to be, and then to keep on running.

It was only when they came to a narrow outcrop high above the forest that they halted. It was dusk.

The snow had petered out some time ago and the clouds were clearing in the east. A sliver of moon hung low in the purple sky.

"We've been climbing for hours," said Tolly, panting. "We can't go any further in the dark and we must be a long way from Port Melas now."

Jem thrust his hands under his armpits and stamped his feet. He might not have special powers like his friends, he thought, but at least he was practical.

"You're right," he said. "It'll be pitch black under the trees soon. We won't be able to see a thing, but all the same..." He frowned. If Madame de Chouette had won the battle with the wolf, she would be on their trail, he was certain of it. Half of him wanted to keep going, but the other half said they should take cover and wait for daylight.

"We can take shelter here." Ann's voice echoed from the rocky wall at their back. "Look – there's an opening. It goes back quite a long way, I think. If we could build a fire just inside no one would see the light. We should be safe here – at least overnight. Then we can get going again at first light. We all need some rest – although first we need to talk."

"I can't begin to imagine how it made you feel. The darkness, the memories…" Ann reached across to take Tolly's hand. "And this too…" She brushed the tips of her fingers over the twisted stump of his thumb and shook her head. She frowned at Cazalon's staff propped against the wall and turned to Jem. "That thing is evil, but I can't help thinking it's important too. It's why I never destroyed it." She put a hand on his shoulder. "I don't know what would have happened if you two hadn't come after me. Thank you."

Jem poked another stick into the glowing heart of the little fire Ann had made from nothing. "That… woman, Madame de Chouette, do you know who she is?" He pushed away the awful thought that she could be tracking them down right at this moment. They were safe in the cave, weren't they?

Ann pulled her thick white hair back from her face and knotted it at the nape of her neck.

"I know *what* she is – a witch and a dark one." Her wide green eyes sparked, then she sighed, looked down at the floor of the cave and traced patterns in the dust with a finger. "But that's all. I wish I could tell you more. The last thing I remember clearly is

Cleo finding the bean in the Twelfth Night cake. There was dancing and laughter. I watched you both and felt so happy. And then the door opened and darkness came in…" She shivered and stared into the flames. "After that, everything gets so confused." Lines of concentration furrowed her brow. "There… there was a meal. Tolly, you were opposite me at a long table? Something happened…"

"That's right," said Jem. "She forced us both to dine with her, Cleo as well. It was disgusting. If it wasn't for Tolly, we would have been part of the meal too!"

"When was that?" Ann's voice was a whisper.

"On the *Fortuna* – not three days ago."

"That can't be right." She shook her head. "The feast was laid out in an old house. I can see it now. You were both there and when Tolly touched my hand it broke that woman's power over me, just for a moment. It was like waking from a nightmare. I tried to warn you to get out. In old magic, if you leave the table of a dark witch without her express permission she can never invite you into her home again or enchant you within its walls."

"It was on the ship." Jem glanced uncertainly at Tolly. He thought about Madame de Chouette's cabin. The room had at first been oak-lined, but when

Tolly pulled him free there had been flagstones on the floor and a great arched space above their heads. Where had they *really* been?

"How did you manage to outwit her?" Ann scanned their faces with interest. Jem was pleased to see that something of her old spirit was returning.

"That was Tolly again." He grinned at his friend.

"I didn't tell her my true name. It was Cazalon who gave me the name Ptolemy, not my mother and father. When she called us into the room she asked us to repeat our names aloud and thank her for the invitation. She said it was an old family custom, but it felt wrong to me."

Ann smiled broadly, revealing the little gap between her front teeth. "You were right. If you willingly offer your name to a witch she can control you. It's a simple but effective binding spell."

Tolly nodded. "Binding, yes! There was a semi-circle of salt on the floor too, just inside the door. It all seemed so familiar. It reminded me of Malfurneaux Place – something Cazalon would —"

"The mirror!" Ann gasped. "I remember – after the Twelfth Night feast. I was taken to an old house. She forced me upstairs to a dark room and there was a mirror. It was twice my height and it was set in a gilded frame. It was old – the glass was smoked and pitted. She made me put my hand flat against the glass and then… then…"

She broke off and brought her hand to her mouth. "Look." Fumbling with her sleeve, she pushed up the flapping cuffs of Fabien's shirt, baring her left arm to the elbow. She held it forward for Jem and Tolly to see.

The translucent skin of Ann's arm was criss-crossed by a network of fine, raised scars – the legacy of the terrible magical rite Cazalon had used to communicate with her dead mother.

But there were three fresh, blood-crusted wounds on her arm now too. Someone had used Ann to make the blood bridge to the dead lands once again – recently. Jem felt a sick, plummeting sensation in the pit of his stomach.

Only one person would dare to undertake such a dangerous journey. They didn't need any more proof.

Cazalon was most definitely alive.

CHAPTER
TWENTY-EIGHT

"What do we do now? If Cazalon is here, we need to get away fast." Jem rubbed his hands together over the flames, but nothing seemed to warm him.

"We have to find a ship returning to England." Tolly shuffled closer to the fire. "Did you see any other vessels moored at Port Melas or standing off the coast?"

Jem shook his head. "I didn't really take much in. When the wolf appeared so much started to happen so fast and then Ann told us not to look back, remember? I... I'm glad I didn't. Those noises we heard – it must have been the *Fortuna*."

He stared into the fire and wondered what had really happened back at the little settlement. Where had the huge wolf come from? Had it defeated Madame and if that was the case...

Jem shook his head, trying to knit some sense from what they had seen and not seen.

Ann stroked Cleo's rounded back. The little monkey was nestled in her lap. "Never look into the heart of a dark working for it will leave a stain on your soul – my mother told me that once."

Jem thought of his own mother back at Goldings. He blinked hard and told himself his eyes were stinging from the smoke of the fire.

"You'll see her again, Jem." Tolly's voice was warm. Jem spun round. Tolly smiled apologetically. "Sorry, it was an accident. But I agree – we need to keep moving. If Cazalon is already here, waiting for Madame to deliver Ann straight to him, we need to make sure that neither of them find her. I don't think we should go back to Port Melas, do you?"

"No." Jem shook his head. "I don't think they'll welcome us. Goodman Winterbourne said something about other settlements, didn't he?"

"But even if we find a ship, how will we pay for our passage?" Ann frowned.

"I'll sell this." Jem reached into his collar and pulled out the golden medal given to him by Sarah. It gleamed in the firelight as it twisted about on the chain. "It's old-fashioned, but I think it's gold and these gems must be valuable. It's been in our family for generations."

"What does that writing say, there on the rim? May I?" Ann reached over to tilt the medallion so that she could see the letters more clearly. She pulled the chain to bring it close and Jem had to bend so that their heads almost touched. He noticed that Ann smelled sweet, like a fresh-cut meadow.

"I can't make it out. Did you ever notice the patterns?" She turned the medallion in her hand. "It looks like a triangle on this side, and on this side…" she held it up, "there are three figures, each with a tiny jewel in their hand."

Jem shook his head. "I haven't looked that closely. What do you think, Tolly, is it enough to buy our passage home?"

"It should be. People are always ready to buy gold."

As Tolly leaned forward to peer at the medal, Cleo jumped towards it. She chattered excitedly as the yellow metal glinted in the light. "She loves shiny things. She's like a magpie." Tolly grinned at Ann. "Do you remember how she stole the glass jewels sewn onto Juno's costume when we were in Colchester? Every night she crept back and took as many as she could carry, until by the end of the week there were hardly any left."

Ann laughed. "And Juno thought there were rats living under her caravan. She got Gabriel to crawl underneath to scare them off and then he got wedged between the wheel struts and Cornelius had to…" She stopped. "Do you really think we'll see them again?" Her voice was small and muffled.

"Yes, you will." Jem pushed the medal back into the neck of his shirt, feeling more confident now they could pay. They'd escaped Cazalon before, and they could do it again. "We all will."

They were silent for a minute before Ann's next question. "What makes you so certain Cazalon's in the new colonies?" She looked from Jem to Tolly in turn, her eyes full of confusion.

"Because Madame de Chouette took you prisoner for him." Jem reached out to the fire again. "Your birthday is in May, isn't it?"

"Yes, on the Feast of Beltane – the first day of the month."

"And how old will you be this year?"

"Thirteen."

"Do you ever think about your inheritance?"

She smiled wanly. "There's nothing left to inherit. Cazalon took it all when he became my guardian. Everything – except this shawl. My grandmother made it." She pulled the red woollen cloth tight around her shoulders. When she spoke again her voice was defiant. "But I don't care about possessions.

I have my memories and the stories my mother and grandmother told me. No one can take those away…"

"Think hard." Jem's mind was racing. "Did your ~~mother and grandmother ever tell~~ you anything about a special birthday?"

Ann sighed and began to draw patterns in the dust again. "They made every birthday special." Her voice was almost a whisper. When she looked up tears glistened in her eyes. "We always sang a song together on the morning of my birthday. My grandmother had sung it to my mother and my grandmother's mother had sung it to her. It was a nursery song, the same every year. I deliberately try not to remember everything because it hurts so much.."

She began to sing in a clear voice.

"One for the child who is yet to know
Two for the child who begins to grow
Three for the laughter in each day
Four for the games she loves to play
Five for the stories she is told
Six for the joy of being bold
Seven for the child who needs no charm
Eight for the child kept close from harm

Nine for the day she learns to spell
Ten for the lessons learned so well
Eleven for all that she will see
Twelve for the lady she will be
And of these years the happy morn
Thirteen when she will be born."

The notes rang around the cave, lingering long after Ann came to the end. Only when the last note faded away completely did Jem feel able to speak.

"It's in the song, Ann. Your inheritance, I mean."

She shook her head and rubbed her eyes roughly with the heels of her hands. "But it's just an old song."

"No, listen: '*And of these years the happy morn, thirteen when she will be born.*' Tolly and I think we know what it means. You will be 'born' on your thirteenth birthday – you will come into your full power as a sorceress. And that's why Cazalon wants you."

"And why Madame de Chouette was bringing you to him in good time." Tolly rose to his feet. "Now do you see, Ann?"

She didn't answer and Tolly continued. "He *is* already here somewhere. He means to take your newborn powers."

For a moment no one spoke. Outside, somewhere

in the forest, a wolf howled. The long eerie sound echoed in the cave.

Jem stood and took a deep breath. "We have to get you away from this land before that can happen."

At daybreak they stood at the mouth of the cave and scanned the snow-capped forest below.

"Which way?" Ann knotted her hair back again to keep it from flying about in the wind. She now wore Tolly's cloak over her ill-fitting clothes, but she had given him the red woollen shawl to tuck around his shoulders and to shield Cleo.

The day was bitingly cold. Skeins of white cloud unravelled across the blue sky.

"That's the sunrise, so we're facing east. We need to head that way." Jem pointed with Cazalon's staff. "Goodman Winterbourne said the other settlements on the coast were to the south."

Tolly nodded. "So we need to make our way back down through the forest until we reach the coast and then follow it until we find somewhere?" He looked up at the sky. "At least it's not snowing."

"But it's still bitter." Ann blew on her fingers and rubbed her hands together. "I can't believe we are so far from home. That everything is carrying on back there without us." She took a deep breath. "It's very beautiful here, isn't it? Miles and miles of forest and not a soul in sight. It's like England, but not like England. It feels so... so... huge."

Jem stared down at the shrouded land. "It feels so empty too, but *he's* here somewhere. We have to get back to England, Ann. We have to get you away before..." He stopped.

Before *what* exactly?

He glanced across. Ann's green eyes danced as she drank in the view. Madame had been clever, he thought. Fabien was Ann's opposite in every way. He looked over the trees again at the distant sea. Cazalon had to be out there somewhere. Why else would Madame have stolen Ann, enchanted her and made that terrible voyage?

But then again...

A spark flickered into his mind. Madame hadn't been so clever after all, had she? Ann was with them now. Perhaps Cazalon didn't even know she was here in the new colonies?

He continued more confidently. "As soon as we reach a settlement we'll buy a passage on the first ship out. We'll be home before your birthday."

There was a sharp cracking sound overhead. Jem glanced up and saw a splinter jag across the snow-covered rockface above the cave entrance. Slowly the snow began to move.

"Duck!" He dropped the staff to grab Ann's hand and pulled her away. Tolly leaped forward too, clasping Cleo to his shoulder with his good hand. Behind them they heard the soft whumph of heavy snow, and the rumble and rattle of stones.

A couple of seconds later, the mouth of the cave was completely sealed. White flakes flew up in the air around them.

"Look." Jem brushed powdery snow from his head and shoulders. "There are rocks in the fall. We might have been trapped inside." He shuddered. They could easily have died in there, sealed together forever in a stone tomb. That really would have been the end. At least now they had a chance, even if Cazalon, or Madame de Chouette – or both – was on their tail.

As he bent to retrieve the staff a huge ragged shadow fell across the snowy ledge. Jem sprang up, but the bird had gone.

He shot a look at Tolly. He was staring up into the wide blue sky and seemed to be listening. Jem knew why. Suddenly, the vast landscape didn't seem empty at all. He felt the hairs on the back of his neck stiffen as he tightened his grasp on Cazalon's staff and began to walk.

"Come on. We're going to find a port and we are going home."

CHAPTER
TWENTY-NINE

Jem stepped into a shadowy clearing, allowing himself a brief pause. Which way now? Everywhere looked exactly the same. He stepped up onto a flat rock and craned his neck. He needed to track the path of the sun, but the sky was now a strange leaden yellow. Night was coming already. He brushed snowflakes from his cheek.

Tolly crunched alongside. "We have to find shelter soon. Ann can't go much further today. She keeps falling behind and we'd be better off hiding than moving slowly at dusk – we're easy prey for Cazalon out here." He lowered his voice to a whisper. "Owls hunt at night."

Jem turned. Ann was twenty yards behind, just emerging from the treeline and into the clearing. Her face was almost translucent.

Tolly continued quietly. "She won't say anything, but she's exhausted and hungry. We all are." He patted Cleo's nose, which poked out from the shawl at his neck. "Not long, girl," he whispered unconvincingly.

"What are we going to do, Jem?

Jem rubbed at his chapped lips. "We've got to keep going. It's all we *can* do. Surely, we must reach the coast soon? Then we'll be on a ship, and away. Safe." He looked up into the dark cathedral of trees and his heart plummeted as he remembered Spider's words: *Beats me why the fancy Madame's so keen to make the crossing in winter. Never been done before.*

How long would they have to wait?

Their journey that day hadn't been as simple as he'd thought.

At first, after they scrambled down from the rocky outcrop, the sun had penetrated the forest, but the deeper they went, the darker it became. Snatches of blue sky overhead had disappeared hours ago, replaced by the dense, dark canopy of firs. Jem didn't like to admit it, but for a long time now he hadn't even been certain that they were heading in the right direction.

A distant howling made them both scan the trees around the clearing.

"The forest must be full of wolves… and they hunt at night too." Tolly reached down to haul Ann up beside them.

"It's not the wolves I'm worried about." She

clambered onto the rock.

Tolly clutched her arm to steady her. "You sense it as well?"

She nodded. "We're being followed. Ever since we came down into the forest I've felt something nearby. Sometimes it's almost as if there's a voice in my head, but if I try to listen and make sense of it, there's nothing. Once or twice when I looked back I thought I saw something pale slipping among the trees, but when I stood still and looked properly, there was nothing. But I…"

"But you can feel something there?"

Ann answered Tolly's sharp question with a single nod.

"I can too – something has been watching us." Tolly's jaw clenched tight as he turned in a slow circle, his eyes searching the shadows beyond the trees.

"Is it… Do you think it's Cazalon?" Jem hardly dared to speak the name aloud. "Or is it her?"

Tolly shook his head. "I don't know. What do you say, Ann?"

She shivered. "All I know is that if we don't find food and shelter soon, it won't actually matter. Tolly, you can't go on like that. Here, take this back." She started to struggle out of the cloak, but Jem stopped her.

"No! You need it. We can share mine. I'll rip it in two, there's plenty of material. It's stupid of me – I should have thought of it earlier."

He dropped Cazalon's staff and fumbled at the neck of his cloak to loosen the tie. As he did so, the mournful cry of a hundred wolves ripped the air.

Jem froze. When the howling stopped abruptly he wasn't sure whether to be glad or terrified. "What should we do?" He glanced at Tolly. Cleo was scenting the air, her face pressed against the dark skin of her master's cheek, her button eyes darting wildly as if she expected a wolf to leap from the shadows at any moment.

Ann reached up to free her hair from the knot at her neck. She quickly plucked a couple of strands and held them out. "Instead of trying to run, I could try a sealing charm. It's simple. I just need a single hair from your heads and from Cleo's too, then I can build a circle barrier around this stone to shield us. What do you think?"

"I don't think we have much choice. Here." Jem yanked a hair from his right temple and Tolly winced as he pulled a springy black wiry strand free.

"This is going to be tricky," Tolly muttered as he turned his attention to Cleo. She stared at him as he reached to stroke her, then she squealed. "I haven't even it done it yet! Come on, girl." He tried again, but Cleo screeched and burrowed into the shawl.

"Cl—' Tolly halted as a thudding noise and the sound of fast, ragged breathing came from somewhere nearby.

Jem yelled. "Quickly, Ann!"

"I can't, it's too late." She pointed. "Look…"

Jem followed the line of her stricken gaze and gasped as he caught sight of a huge grey shape slinking between the trees. It was coming straight at them.

Jem's stomach knotted into a ball. They were defenceless, exposed and about to be torn to shreds by a wolf the size of a bull. His mind whirled with jumbled thoughts and questions. He found himself thinking of Dr Speight and wished he was at Goldings right now doing one of the man's deadly equations. But he'd never see Goldings again, would he?

Probably not.

What would his mother think?

She won't even know.

What would Master Jalbert do?

He wouldn't have dropped his guard.

That's it – he needed a weapon!

Perhaps they could hurl rocks at it? Jem scoured the ground for suitable pieces but instead caught sight of Cazalon's staff, lying like a twisting black serpent on the snow.

This was his weapon! He leaped down, snatched it up and brandished it forward, taking a fighting position just as Master Jalbert had taught him. He gripped the staff and felt the rough shark spine beneath his fingers.

He squared his shoulders. What if it wasn't just Tolly who had the power? What if he could make it... *do* something too? He tightened his grip and concentrated. But there was nothing at all – not even the faintest tremor in his hands. He stared at the crystal bird-head. "Why not me?" he thought.

A shadowy form slumped across the treeline.

Jem saw something glinting in the fading light – teeth or claws?

The beast raised its head. Slanted blue eyes that the burned like candles narrowed, and a long muzzle wrinkled as the wolf opened its gaping jaws. Red drool dripped to the snow.

Jem heard Ann stifle a scream. Without thinking

he swung the staff and lunged, but she caught his arm. "No, wait. Look at Cleo!"

The little creature had wriggled from the shawl and jumped to the ground in front of the rock. She twitched her head from side to side, all the while keeping her eyes locked onto the wolf.

"No! Come back, girl." Tolly tried to catch her, but she scampered away from his hands.

Jem watched in horror as Cleo, tail erect, slowly approached the wolf. He could hear a low rumble from the beast's throat and brought a hand to his mouth as the monkey whickered softly and reached out to prod a huge, splayed paw.

The wolf lowered its massive head.

"Cleo!" Tolly roared her name, his cry echoed round the clearing.

There was a soft, pattering sound and then a muffled crump as a blanket of snow slipped from the branches overhead and enveloped both animals.

Moments later, Cleo's head, dusted in snow, poked out from the white mound. She chirruped, freed herself and began to dig frantically. After a few seconds she stopped, stared back at them and chattered angrily before burrowing into the snow again.

"What is she doing?" Ann jumped down and

began to walk slowly towards the mound.

"You mustn't." Tolly sprang from the rock, but Ann raised her hand.

"Wait. She's always right." Kneeling beside Cleo, Ann began to scoop away handfuls of snow. After a few moments she halted and turned to them.

"It's… it's a man – and he's wounded. Help us."

Despite his confusion, Jem followed Tolly as he began to dig alongside Ann. Cleo chirped and nuzzled against Tolly's side as he worked.

They soon revealed a man with swirling tattoos etched into the bronze skin of his naked torso and all along his broad shoulders and arms. His legs were encased in tattered skins and his long grey hair was divided into a hundred plaits threaded with little skulls – their bony whiteness gleamed in the half light.

Jem wiped flakes of snow from the man's scarred face and sat back on his haunches. "It's Mingan."

"You know him?" Ann dabbed at a deep scratch on Mingan's arm with the edge of her cloak.

Jem nodded. "He was on the ship. He… he helped me. He saved my life."

"Well, his life is in danger now. He's breathing, but look at the gashes in his side. His skin has been ripped apart."

Cleo chirped again. She batted an affectionate paw against Mingan's arm as if she was trying to rouse him.

Ann looked at Tolly. "She trusts him?"

After a long pause he nodded. "He cared for her when we were locked in the hold. But I can't read him, Ann. Even now, away from the ship…"

"Well, that's hardly surprising – the man is half dead!" Ann's voice was crisp. "He needs warmth – we all do." She looked up at the circle of darkening sky above the clearing and lines crinkled between her brows. "We'll have to stay here tonight. We don't have a choice now. If we move him over there beneath the trees…" she pointed, "it will shield us all from the snow. And I can make a sealing charm, too, to protect us from wolves… and from anything else out there."

Together they hauled Mingan to the fir trees at the far edge of the clearing. The dense canopy of interlocking branches overhead provided a sort of shelter. Ann made the sealing charm successfully this time – even Cleo allowed her to pluck a hair with little complaint. Then, whispering some words over a pile of twigs, she made a fire whose warmth soon began to penetrate their aching bones.

Jem had torn his cloak in two. Tolly sat opposite, wrapped in the other half. He was silent as the flames made shadows dance on his dark skin. Jem noticed that he never took his eyes off Mingan, who lay between them.

"Do you think it was him who was following us?" Jem fed a twig into the fire and watched it burn. "That's what you and Ann sensed?"

Tolly didn't answer for a moment. "I can't be sure, but..."

A sudden cracking sound came from above. Lumps of snow slid from the branches, pattering down in a circle around them.

Tolly shook his head slowly. "But I just hope it *was* Mingan."

CHAPTER THIRTY

When Jem opened his eyes he was confused. Surely there should be steam billowing about below the arched ceiling in the laundry at Goldings? And where were the great wooden barrels filled to the brim with hot lavender-scented water?

He blinked and shook his head.

A dusting of snow fell onto his nose and it all came rushing back. He wasn't in the laundry, but huddled on a frozen forest floor. He'd been dreaming about the warmest place he knew. On cold winter mornings he loved to sneak across the courtyard to help Eliza stir the tangled sheets.

Jem rubbed his face and struggled to sit up.

At the other side of the fading fire, Ann leaned over Mingan, pushing the matted hair back from his forehead. He moaned and opened his eyes.

At first he didn't seem aware of anything, he just stared upward. Ann soothed his brow. "You are with friends," she murmured.

Mingan moved his head a little so that he was

looking at the fire. Jem saw his eyes clear gradually and then widen. He tried to sit up, but a spasm of pain shot across his face. Instead he clasped Ann's hand.

"Moon Child…" he whispered. "*Moon Child*."

She shook her head and smiled. "Drink this." She helped Mingan to sip something from a sort of cup made of rolled bark.

"You're awake then? I swear you could sleep anywhere, Jem Green. It's a rare gift." Ann grinned at him. "I made a poultice for his wounds and a tonic from some leaves and herbs. Tolly helped me to find them under the snow. It seems to be working." She raised her eyebrows and jerked her head at Mingan, mouthing, "He heals so fast."

She helped Mingan to tip back the bark cone so that he swallowed the last dregs of liquid. He wiped his mouth. "Good," he whispered.

"You can talk?" Jem's knees cracked as he stood in surprise.

Mingan gazed up at Jem from beneath hooded eyes.

"It's just that on the ship you never…"

"Sometimes it is better to be silent." Mingan glanced at Tolly, who was sitting watching from the far side of the fire. Jem thought of the way Tolly had protected himself from Cazalon by pretending to be a mute. The count had believed Tolly to be little more than a pet, but he had been so wrong.

Mingan pulled himself into a more upright position, resting his back against a tree trunk. He winced as he moved, clutching a hand to his side as the leaves covering his wounds slipped.

"I thank you." He looked at each of them in turn and his ice-blue eyes flickered.

"I followed your trail, but I was weakened by these wounds. I would not have survived another night if I had not found you." He spoke in a deep, rasping voice. Jem noticed that his words were clipped and sharp, as if he didn't want to waste them.

"Who are you?" Tolly shuffled round the fire so that he had a clearer view.

"I think you must know that already." Mingan looked at Ann and bowed his head.

"You're a weren?" Ann didn't look frightened at all. In fact, Jem thought she looked excited. He felt something knot in the pit of his stomach. He was standing next to a werewolf!

Mingan stared up at him, his pale blue eyes

unblinking. "Now you understand?"

Jem nodded slowly. "Y-yes. I think so – some of it, at least. The battle with Madame – the owl – on the jetty. That was you?"

Mingan nodded.

Jem took in the deep scratches across the man's face and shoulders and thought about Madame's curved talons. He had felt sure that she had triumphed on the jetty, but now...

He felt a jolt of excitement and glanced at Tolly, who had stood up too. "So you killed her?"

Mingan shook his head and Jem's relief evaporated as quickly as it had come. "I do not know. The witch threw herself into the sea. That was the last I saw of her before I followed you." With a grimace of pain, Mingan hauled himself to his feet. Cleo chirped and scampered from Tolly's side. The man smiled and bent to allow her to jump onto his shoulder.

Ann nudged Jem. "I've never seen her take to anyone so quickly before, except you."

Mingan straightened up. "I am of this land, but there is danger here for those who do not know the paths. Where are you going?"

Jem gathered his shred of cloak together. "We've

been trying to get to the coast – to find a ship. Will you guide us to the sea, Mingan – if you are well enough?"

Mingan stared back at him blankly. "Why do you wish to go to the sea again?"

"Because we need to go back to England. Ann's life is in danger. We think there's... *someone* here who wants to take her from us. Madame was bringing her to him. With your help, perhaps even in the next couple of days, we could be on our way." Jem felt the flicker of hope again.

Mingan shook his head and the bones plaited into his hair clicked. "It is impossible."

"Why?" Jem demanded hotly.

"It's not that I won't help you. I *cannot* help you. The ports are far to the south – many days walking. The white season is with us – soon the paths through the forest will be gone." Mingan looked up at the sky. "And there will be no ships until the days grow long. Two, maybe three, months more."

Three months?

Mingan blinked his odd blue eyes. "You will not survive alone. I will take you to my home. There will be warmth and food. My people will make sure you are safe until the snow time passes. I give you my

337

promise. When the time is right, I will guide you to a ship for your passage back to England."

Everyone was silent for a moment.

"What should we do?" Jem looked at Tolly and then at Ann.

A single wolf howl, long and low, curled through the air.

"My brothers will not harm us." Mingan turned and strode into the trees. They watched his tall grey form slip between the trunks. Cleo chattered on his shoulder. She turned to look back at them, but she didn't jump down. Instead she flicked her tail and nestled into his shaggy mane.

"That's good enough for me." Ann swept Tolly's cloak around her shoulders and stamped on the embers of the fire. "Cleo has decided for us."

※ ⚎ ※

"So that huge thunderclap was the *Fortuna – dissolving*?" As he used the staff to trudge through the snow behind Mingan, Jem tried to imagine the scene the weren had described. "But how…?"

"I tore a wing from her back and it was the end. When the witch woman believed all was lost, she cast herself into the sea. At first there was nothing.

Then the water began to spin, faster and faster, until a dark whirlpool spread wide, rising from the bay in a spitting tower of fury. My friend, Captain Trevanion, ran from the jetty up the gangplank. He ordered every man to leave the *Fortuna*. To seek safety away from that… that place." Mingan closed his eyes for a moment. "My friend."

"What happened next?" Tolly's breath steamed in the cold air.

"Most of the crew escaped. Your friend, the small one —"

"Spider's safe?" Jem asked quickly.

Mingan nodded. "He was the last down the gangway before the *Fortuna* … vanished."

"But that's imp—' Jem stopped himself. He knew only too well that things he had once regarded as nightmares could be very real.

"And the captain was still aboard?" Jem recalled the odd encounter with Mingan and Trevanion in the hold. What did the captain say? Something like, "*I do not think this vessel will forget the oath I swore so rashly. If I cannot save myself, I will save as many as I can…*"

Mingan nodded. "We have travelled the world together. Now my oldest friend is lost and I will never see him again. He knew the price."

"His daughter, you mean?" Tolly quickened his pace as Mingan forged ahead. Cleo was now back with her master, nestled in the shawl at his neck. "You tried to help her – that's what Trevanion said."

Mingan growled. "It was the only time he betrayed me. He listened to the people of Swale who thought me a savage and he barred me from his house. He said my appearance frightened them, although compared to that woman..." Mingan stamped a foot into the snow. "He was desperate. Jane is... *was* everything to him. He would do anything to make his child well again. When we saw the ship for the first time – the *Fortuna* – we both knew it was like no vessel ever put to sea."

He shook his head. "I did not speak aloud on that ship because I knew it was listening. I was not willing to give it anything of mine. Not even my voice."

After a moment Tolly said quietly, "I don't think it was a ship at all."

"That's ridiculous – of course it was a ship. You even spent a night in the lookout. You can't have forgotten that. I haven't." Jem shuddered at the thought.

Mingan smiled. "Your dark friend is wiser than

you know."

Jem felt crushed and oddly stupid – as if he had missed something everyone had seen. "But I thought—"

"We need to know more about Madame." Ann's voice cut across his next question as they manoeuvred around a pile of rocks.

Mingan shrugged. "I know little, other than that she follows the shadow path." He grunted. "That first evening when the crew lined up for her inspection I did not look directly in her eyes for fear that she would know me for what I am. That was when I recognised you, Moon Child – not as a boy, but as you are. Those of our kind are able to see truly. I knew her for what she was as soon as she – as soon as you both – came aboard."

"You knew she was a witch?" Ann asked.

"I knew she was a shapeshifter… as are you, little sister. We are kin."

Ann frowned. "I… I can change into small things – cats, mice, birds. Actually, I'm getting much better at it, aren't I, Tolly? But I'm nothing like you or Madame de Chouette. You are both so much more powerful."

"You are wrong." Mingan stopped now and

turned to scan her face with his pale blue eyes. "You really do not know?"

"Know what?" Ann scuffled to a halt.

"Only the most powerful of our kind can shift to any form. To choose, as you are capable of doing, that is the highest rank. Who taught you?"

"No one." She smiled sadly. "My grandmother and my mother were... taken before they were able to show me anything more than simple skills. Later I...I studied their books and... practised."

Mingan smiled broadly. "Then you are extraordinary indeed, Moon Child."

"But what about you, Mingan?" Tolly halted abruptly and Cleo scrambled to stay on his shoulder. "You didn't answer my question earlier. I didn't ask *what* you are, I asked *who* you are."

Mingan swung round to face him. "You are right to ask, wise one. I am Mingan, son of Annawan, Prince of the Lake People. Like you I am a traveller, but I was not stolen from my family..."

Tolly started. "How did you know...?

Mingan smiled. "We share a gift. With you it is strong. In me it is more the sense of an animal. I know when there is danger and I know when to trust. Your little companion, the monkey, is the same.

She knows when a heart is true. Now, come, we must move on."

Tolly frowned, but stomped through the snow in Mingan's tracks and the man's clipped voice came back to them. "I was cast out by my people when they saw I was shadowed by the wolf spirit. I was young, just a little older than you, but they were frightened. My father took me to the sea and swapped good furs for my first passage. I was terrified on that ship, but I met Trevanion and he became my friend."

"But, in that case, why have you come back?" Jem heard the suspicion in Tolly's voice.

"Because it is time. I dreamed of my home for many years, but now I dream of my father too. He calls and I have come. Now I can control my wolf shadow my people will not fear me. When Trevanion asked me to sail with him, I was glad... until the day I saw the black ship. But then it was too late."

Not for the first time, Mingan paused, closed his eyes and threw back his head to scent the air like a wild creature, then adjusted direction slightly. They were heading into a thicker part of the forest now.

"So why *did* you follow us – after the battle on the jetty?" Jem scudded forward to keep alongside Mingan as he loped ahead.

"Because I know this land. You could not survive out here alone. I followed you because you have good hearts and for the sake of the Moon Child, my sister. Now, save your breath and follow. If we keep this pace, we will reach my home before dusk."

CHAPTER
THIRTY-ONE

They had been travelling for several hours. In the darkest part of the forest Mingan had led them to a hidden cleft in the rocks, where he'd retrieved warm cloaks for them to wear. "In winter our hunting parties leave furs and food in secret places, so that when the deep snow comes they will survive," he'd explained.

It had made the journey suddenly much more bearable. Snowflakes the size of sovereigns had begun to fall, adding a glistening, powdery layer to the snow that had already settled.

Jem thought that they were travelling north. They followed an overgrown trackway – to Jem the path was almost invisible, but Mingan seemed to trace it easily. Every so often he paused and studied the landscape, then nodded to himself and strode ahead. They didn't speak much now, the going was too hard, but Jem's head was full of uneasy questions. If Madame had survived the battle, where would she have gone next? If she wasn't on their trail then wasn't it likely that she'd gone to Cazalon? In which case both of them would be hunting for Ann.

Madame had taken so much trouble to bring her to this land, surely she wouldn't give up now? He already knew that Cazalon would never give up. The sour taste of fear made Jem's mouth go dry.

His breathing suddenly became fast and shallow and he fumbled to loosen the bone toggle of the fur cloak. Its sharply pointed end cut into the skin beneath his chin. Gulping down a lungful of air, Jem shoved the tangle of his fringe back into the the hood and peered through the snow at Mingan's fur-clad back.

Safety, that's what he'd promised. But could you ever be safe from a man like Cazalon?

Tolly stopped and turned back to stare at him. Jem realised that his friend had heard his thoughts.

3Y I Y2

Jem hunched his shoulders and leaned forward so that the hood of his brown cloak slipped down to cover his face. The snow was falling thickly now and their progress had become slower and slower. The ground rose sharply underfoot and the fir trees were becoming sparse. A ribbon of ice trailed through the rocks beside them. Mingan was leading them along a frozen stream.

"How much further?" Jem called, his voice muffled by the furs.

Mingan looked up and narrowed his eyes. "The snow will slow us, but by nightfall we will be sitting by the fire in my father's longhouse and eating good stew. I promise. Now, come."

Good stew. Pocket's face swam into Jem's mind and he remembered how the boy had spoken about his mother's cooking. Jem sighed heavily. Poor Pocket. He'd never taste that stew again now.

After the days on the ship and now here in the forest, the thought of sitting by a crackling fire and eating hot food again was wonderful, but Jem wished that Pocket could share it with them, and Spider too.

Mingan said Spider had escaped, hadn't he? Jem wondered where he was now.

They trudged upward in silence for an hour more until they came to a ridge. The snowfall was lighter here and Jem could see more clearly. Mingan moved to the edge of the outcrop and leaned forward.

"The path down will be icy – we must take great care. Shall I carry you on my back, Moon Child?"

Ann shook her head. "No. I'll be careful. Are we

near?"

Mingan nodded. "My people are below." A shaft of sunlight pierced the leaden clouds. He smiled and turned to look into the valley that spread below the rocky crags. Jem saw his expression darken and stepped forward to look too. Far below, long, curved hut-like structures were clustered around the edge of a wide lake. A thin plume of smoke coiled from one of the huts, but there were no other signs of life. It was silent. He glanced uncertainly at Mingan. This was his home?

Mingan's wide nostrils twitched. Gradually, Jem became aware of something too. The air coming up from the valley was laced with something sour, something rotten.

He looked down again and realised that the circular lake didn't reflect the weak, low sun now emerging from the clouds. The snow crusting the edges was dirty and the still, black water was utterly dead and frozen.

❄ ▄ ❄

Mingan turned in a slow circle at the centre of the desolate village. "There should be children playing. There should be laughing, singing, talking, smoke in the air and the smell of good food cooking."

Instead, the smell was vile. Jem gripped the staff and brought his other hand up to cover his nose and mouth. It made him want to retch. He glanced at Ann and Tolly. Ann had her back to him and was staring at the lake. Tolly was watching Mingan.

"Where are they?" Mingan's voice was barely audible as he continued speaking in a language none of them understood. Jem made a hasty count of the huts – there were over thirty. He could see that once they had been fine dwellings, expertly crafted from branches, packed with moss and covered by stretched hide. Each house was twelve yards or so in length and about six yards wide and they were all built to face the same direction – the lake.

"Look!" Ann pointed at the lake. Jem's neck prickled. The water was frozen into a series of jagged black furrows as if the rippling waves had been trapped in a single moment.

"What's wrong with it?"

"I don't know." Her small voice came from the depths of the silver fur hood. "But I can feel that something terrible has happened here."

Jem nodded. "The smell? It's…it's like…"

"Death." Tolly came to stand next to them. Cleo

poked her head from beneath his brown fur hood. Even she was silent.

A single long, low howl split the air. They all spun around to see Mingan kneeling on the soiled ice at the centre of the village. He thumped the ground and threw back his head. The grey fur hood slipped to his shoulders and he howled again.

Moments later, answering calls came from somewhere high above. A chorus of misery rang out across the valley – Mingan's wolf brothers were taking up his cry. The man listened now, head bowed.

There was a crackling, rustling sound from somewhere close by. Jem twisted about swiftly, brandishing the staff. He half expected to see a wolf, but instead a stooping fur-clad figure emerged from the longhouse nearest to the lake. The figure shuffled forward onto the grimy snow, a quiver full of arrows tied at the waist and a curved wooden bow slung over one shoulder.

Jem tightened his grip on Cazalon's staff. Mingan had told him they'd be safe here. This felt far from it.

The figure paused and tilted its head to one side. Jem knew that somewhere in the depths of the fur, eyes were scanning the three of them. He saw a gnarled hand move slowly towards the arrows. The person turned towards Mingan and suddenly froze. A parched voice called out a single word in a strange language.

Mingan scrambled to his feet as the stooping figure took another step forward and threw back its hood. It was an old woman with a rope of plaited grey hair and nut-brown skin covered in lines.

She spoke again to Mingan – a single cracked word – and he ran to her, enclosing her almost completely in the folds of his cloak. The old woman spoke rapidly and reached up to touch the scars on his face.

Mingan glanced at the children as the old woman continued to speak. He must have seen their bewilderment.

"She is my mother. This is my mother, Nadie."

⁂

Jem took another sip from the horn bowl. The meaty broth tasted better than anything he had eaten in a long while. After all those days on the ship with nothing but crumbled, maggot-riddled biscuits, he had almost forgotten what it felt like to have hot food in his belly. He could feel the warmth of it tingling through every limb.

Nadie's longhouse was lined with furs. A fire burned in a little stone hearth at the centre – the smoke curling up and out through an opening in the low-arched roof. Unlike the foul air outside, the comfortable dwelling smelled of herbs. The warm, spiced scent from Nadie's bone pipe reminded Jem of home.

Home!

He thought about his mother and swallowed hard. A lump of meat seemed to be caught in his throat. He looked up to blink the smoke from his eyes.

After they had entered the longhouse, Mingan and Nadie had exchanged a torrent of words. Their fast, guttural speech was completely impenetrable to the children – apart from one word that Nadie repeated again and again: *Witiko*.

Now Mingan's face was set in a grim mask as he stared silently into the hearth. Ann sat directly opposite Jem, her silver-white hair flowing loosely about her shoulders. No wonder Mingan called her Moon Child.

Tolly put down his bowl and let Cleo lick a dab of stew from the fingers of his good hand. "What's happened here, Mingan? What has Nadie told you?"

The weren had been silent while they ate, choosing not to take a bowl himself, but now he sighed and began to speak. As he did, Jem noticed he didn't take his eyes from the fire, as if he could see the story Nadie had told burning there.

"Four moons ago he came from the north – from the far north – and immediately my people knew him for a powerful shaman. He only ever came at night. They never saw his face, but they heard his voice and it seemed like a song to them. His cloak was made of thousands of pale feathers, so they called him White Crow.

"Just before he appeared in the valley, many of our children were struck by a sickness. They could not rise from their beds, they could not speak, they could not eat."

"Just like Trevanion's daughter!" Jem shuffled closer to the hearth so that he could catch every word.

Mingan nodded and his plaits clattered. "The people were frightened, but White Crow told the elders that he could cure our children. He said there would be a high price and asked if they were prepared to pay it. The elders believed we could meet any demand, for our currency is not like yours. We trade in meat and furs, spears and arrows. Our village was rich. Game is…" Mingan paused and corrected himself. "Game *was* abundant here. Our stores were filled and ready for the snow season.

"White Crow gave them a powder – a black powder – to be mixed with water from the lake and given to the afflicted children to drink.

"Within two days they were well again. The elders were so joyful, they offered to double whatever White Crow asked for."

A thought ran through Jem's mind. *White Crow –* why was that name familiar?

Mingan continued, "The shaman told the elders he needed time to decide a fair price. He said that he would come to the village in good time to name it. That was when it began."

"When what began?" Jem asked when Mingan fell silent.

Mingan breathed deeply. "It began with the birds. For three mornings when the people woke, they found dead, mutilated bodies of birds scattered at the edge of the lake. Next, small creatures from the forest were found hidden about the village – their throats torn, their entrails spilling from long wounds in their sides." Mingan gestured at Nadie. A tear slid down her wrinkled cheek. "My mother says that was when the silence came. No birds sing here any more.

"Then it was the dogs. Three good hunting hounds went missing on the same night. At first their owners thought they had been stolen by a jealous neighbour, but then the body of one of the dogs was found hidden in the trees at the edge of the lake. It had been torn apart."

"But could it have been attacked by another animal? One of the other dogs, or perhaps a wolf?" Jem regretted the word as soon as it left his lips, but if Mingan was insulted he didn't show it. Instead he turned his eyes on Jem and smiled grimly.

"There is not an animal alive able to dissect a body with the skill of a surgeon. The dog's tongue, heart, liver and lungs were gone and part of his skin had been removed – a perfect square was cut from his back."

Jem's blood froze. He remembered the experiments Cazalon had conducted on the pitiful creatures in Malfurneaux Place. On the far side of the fire Tolly sat up very straight and huddled Cleo to his side.

"But the dog was not the worst." Mingan took up the trailing end of one of his plaits and turned a little white skull between his fingers. "You must understand, we are a hunting people, but we only take what is necessary and we give thanks for it. These little creatures…" he rested the plait across his palm so that the skull knotted into it was cradled in the dip in the middle, "had made the great journey long before I found them. I did not kill them. I respected their earthly remains and made them a part of me. It is powerful magic."

"Like a protection charm?" Ann asked.

"Yes, Moon Child. I ask the spirits of these creatures to protect me."

Tolly leaned forward. "What did you mean, 'the dog was not the worst'?"

Mingan let the plait slip from his palm. "One of the young hunters went out alone. When he did not return that night his mother was not worried, but when two days had passed and there was still no word, she asked the other young hunters to search for him. Just before nightfall they found his body. It was like the dog."

He shuddered. "The next evening the shaman came again to the village. He named his price and at last the elders realised what they had done. White Crow demanded that the first-born child of every family should be sent to his longhouse on the far side of the lake. It did not matter if the children were male or female as long as they had seen no more than thirteen summers. One was to be delivered to him every three days until each family capable of making such a sacrifice had paid. Then, and only then, would he leave my people in peace. That was when they understood that the Witiko walked among them."

"Witiko?" Jem looked from Mingan to Nadie. "I heard you say that word over and over again. What is it?"

Mingan closed his eyes. "One who walks between the worlds. He hunts by night and feeds on the flesh of the living and the dead. He is the taker of souls. Even when he has fed he continues to destroy for pleasure. The story has been told by mothers to their children down many generations."

Mingan's eyes snapped open again. "But now I know it is not a story."

"What did they do about the payment, Mingan?" Ann's face was as white as her hair.

"The young hunters wanted to go to burn his longhouse to the ground and destroy him, but my father, Annawan, the chief and wise man of our elders, said it would only bring destruction upon all. Instead, he made careful plans for every man, woman and child in the village to leave. We are a nomadic people and this is our winter place. There are other hidden places, though, high in the mountains. At this time of year the living there will be harsh, but the choice was easy to make. In the course of a single day, one by one my people melted into the forest. Nadie has not seen them since. She believes they have escaped, that they are safe. But Annawan knew that a great sacrifice must still be made in order to ensure their safety. So when all had gone, he went to the Witiko to offer himself, wisest of all, in place of the children. My mother says that was the day the lake died."

"Why didn't your mother go with the others?" Jem looked at Nadie. The old woman was rocking back and forth, both hands folded at her chest.

"Because she is waiting for my father to return."

"But how does she know he is..." Jem faltered.

"Alive?" Mingan finished for him. He said something to Nadie. She opened the hand she held so close to her chest, revealing a polished black oval, smooth and rounded as a pebble that has lain in a stream. It was strung upon a leather thong around her neck.

"It is the custom for our people to swap love tokens when they are young. They wear them for the rest of their lives together. The tokens are always the same – an oval carved from specially chosen wood. It is meant to be a heart. This is the heart my father gave to her. She knows he is alive because her heart has not broken."

"But why hasn't the Witiko taken her too?"

"She believes it is because he wants to punish her for what my father did. Many times now she has waited at night by the shores of the lake, hoping that the Witiko would take her to Annawan. She has even watched him hunt – but he would not come near."

"So why didn't she go to the longhouse to find him?" Jem bit his tongue as he caught sight of Ann's expression. "I… I don't mean to be rude but…"

Mingan smiled sadly. "You are right to question. My father made her promise never to follow him there, made her swear an oath on her wooden heart. She cannot break that vow." He made a deep throaty noise like a growl. "But I have made no such promise.

"My mother says that by night he still hunts, but he can only move in the darkness. Since the deep snows have come he has exchanged his cape of feathers for a patchwork of furs. His hunger is insatiable. Each morning the land around the lake is spattered with fresh trails of blood and strewn with animal guts. But he is powerless by day. That is our protection."

"Protection!" Tolly laughed bitterly. "I don't call leading us to a village haunted by a creature that feeds on human flesh 'protection'. You told us we'd be safe here!" He turned to Jem. "*One who walks between the worlds* – does that remind you of anything?"

Jem stared blankly. There *was* something about those words… Of course! It was very like something Tolly had said after using Cazalon's staff that first time in Ann's caravan. *Beware the man of shadows. He who walks between the worlds.*

Tolly's eyes bored into Jem's. "There's only one person I can think of who walks between the worlds, and Mingan's brought us straight to him. The mutilated animals, the black medicine… Cazalon is White Crow. He is the Witiko – he *must* be – and we've brought Ann to his door."

Jem's heart bucked as he thought about the peculiar letters singed into the wall of the *Fortuna*'s hold: *WHITC RW*. Now he knew what they meant.

Tolly sprang to his feet. "Have you been working

with Cazalon all along, Mingan?"

Mingan frowned. "I don't understand. My only wish was to help you." He bowed his head and cupped his forehead. "I did not mean to bring you to a place of danger. Nor you, little sister, Moon Child."

"There you go again. Moon Child! Her name is Ann." Tolly almost spat the words. "And she is not your sister."

"Tolly!" Ann pushed her hair back from her shoulders. "If it wasn't for Mingan, who knows what would have happened to me – and to you two – back at Port Melas! He saved our lives."

"Only to put them in danger again!"

"He didn't know!" Ann turned to Mingan. "You thought you were bringing us to a safe place, didn't you?"

Mingan nodded grimly. "I am a man of honour. I would not harm you, any of you. I promised you shelter and to guide you to a ship when the snows end."

Jem's attention was taken by Nadie. The old woman was stroking Ann's hair and crooning softly. Tolly took a step towards them, but Ann shook her head violently. "Don't, Tolly. What is the song, Mingan?"

"The legend of the Moon Child. It is important to our people. When I first saw you on the ship your hair made me think of that story for the first time in many years. You remind my mother of it also."

"What is the legend?" Ann turned to allow Nadie to braid her hair.

"We have come here for hundreds of years to shelter during the time of snow. We did this even during the darkest days because the waters were warm; the lake never froze. The miracle was our secret. This has always been our sacred place – we call it The Lake of the Great Mother."

"And the Great Mother is the Moon?" Ann asked.

Mingan nodded. "Once each month her face is reflected in the water. It is our reminder of her promise. When our people face the greatest enemy we believe the Moon's Child will sing with the stars and the Great Mother will hear them."

Jem thought of the frozen black water of the lake outside. "It can't reflect anything now, can it?"

"No, it is dead. Like my village."

Nadie broke off from the song and spoke rapidly to Mingan. He shook his head and gave a sharp answer.

"What did Nadie just say?" Ann asked.

Mingan was silent for a moment. "My mother says

it was my destiny to bring you here, Moon Child."

"Destiny!" Tolly snorted and bent to take up his fur cloak. "That's it. We're leaving. We have to get you as far away from here as possible, Ann."

"Tolly's right." Jem flinched as Ann's green eyes flashed. "If Cazalon really is the Witiko, this is probably the worst place on earth we could have brought you."

"I've got the right to an opinion too, don't you think?" she demanded furiously.

"Please. I did not mean to cause you to argue." Mingan rose from the furs and raised his hands. "The wise one is right." He bowed his head towards Tolly. "At first light, you must leave the valley." He reached for his grey fur and swung it around his shoulders. He moved towards the door, but looked back over his shoulder at Jem and Tolly in turn.

"I am sorry. I should not have brought you here. Remember my words."

Jem sprang to his feet. "Where are you going?"

"I will stand guard outside tonight. You will be safe. I promise."

"We can stand with you." Jem reached for his own fur and for Cazalon's staff, but as he took it up, the sound of a hundred of wolves baying filled the air.

The skin around Mingan's blue eyes crinkled. "It will not be necessary. Listen – my brothers will be with me."

CHAPTER THIRTY-TWO

"Where has he gone?" Ann turned to scan the ruined village. It was dawn, but as Mingan had said, no birds sang here. It was as silent as the grave. She walked to the edge of the circular lake and knelt to touch the frozen black water. She gasped and swiftly pulled her hand away. "It's dry, like coal, but so cold that it burns."

Tolly crunched forward to stand beside her on the speckled snow and pulled back his fur hood. "There's nothing. Not a sound, not a movement. Even the trees don't move."

"But Mingan wouldn't have abandoned us, surely?" Jem glanced at Nadie who was standing beside him at the door of her longhouse. She turned the little carved heart over and over in her hands, her pale eyes locked on the frozen black water.

"We can't even ask Nadie where he's gone."

"Tolly could try!" Ann clasped his shoulder. "Perhaps you could look into her thoughts. She must know something."

Tolly nodded slowly. "She's sad and frightened. I

know that much already. I've felt it rolling from her in waves since we came out here."

"Does she know what's happened to him? Can you tell?" Jem released Cleo. She'd been wriggling and chattering in his arms. She scampered across the snow to the lake's edge.

Tolly watched her for a moment and then he spoke. "I was wrong about Mingan. When he said he was sorry last night, he truly meant it."

He turned and crunched the little way back to the longhouse. "I hope I'm wrong, but I think he's just made another mistake."

Nadie began speaking rapidly in her language with tears in her eyes. She clutched Tolly's injured hand, once or twice breaking free to point at the lake. When the old woman finished she covered her face with her hands and sobbed.

Ann put her arm around Nadie's shoulder. "Tolly?"

He rubbed his injured thumb. "She is frightened, terribly frightened… she… she wants us to leave, immediately. She promised Mingan last night that whatever happened, she would make sure we left the valley before nightfall."

"But what *has* happened, Tolly?"

Before he had a chance to answer Jem's question,

Cleo's frantic squeal made them all spin around. She was about thirty yards away on the snowy edge of the lake, her white-tipped tail thrashing above her head. They ran towards her.

"What's wrong? Here, girl, come to me." Cleo didn't answer Tolly's call, but stood alert, her black eyes unblinking.

"Look!" Jem pointed at the snow in front of her and then turned back towards the longhouse.

The footprints of a man with a long stride led from the longhouse to the shore where Cleo stood guard, and there they became the deep paw prints of a huge animal.

"Oh no." Tolly shook his head. "It's true then, the great fear I saw in Nadie's mind. Mingan has gone to save his father from the Witiko – from Cazalon."

Ann gasped. "But he doesn't know what he is – or what he can do."

Jem stared at the massive tracks in the snow. "But we do."

CHAPTER
THIRTY-THREE

Ann pulled Jem's hood around his head and fastened the bone toggle. "Remember, wait until he goes out to hunt – and then wait some more." Her voice was small and tight.

"We'll be back before sunrise." Jem wished he was sure of that. He shot an anxious look at Tolly, who was trying to entice Cleo from beneath the folds of his cloak. She was making furious chirping noises.

"She knows I'm leaving her," he muttered gloomily. "Are you ready?"

Jem pushed a wodge of snow-dusted fringe back into his hood. "This is the only way to make sure Ann's safe. We defeated him before, Tolly, we *must* remember that. Surely, we must have weakened him?" Jem wished he felt as confident as he sounded.

"But we could stick with the original plan. Get passage on a ship, get back across the Atlantic – far away from Cazalon." Tolly fumbled to fasten his own cloak.

"You know that we can't let Mingan face him

alone. He helped us on the boat and he saved us from Madame on the jetty. We can't leave him now. And this way, we'll no longer need to run – we'll make sure we defeat Cazalon for good. You agree with me, don't you, Ann?"

She nodded. "We owe Mingan our help. If he hadn't found us in the forest we would have frozen to death. Here, let me help with that." She threaded the bone toggle of Tolly's fur through a loop and continued quietly. "My grandmother taught me that every choice we make starts a chain, that I must always be careful to make the right choice, even if it is a hard one, because the chain can lead you into the dark or into the light. If we left now, then…"

"Then it would be the wrong choice," Jem finished for her. "We are the only people in the world who have thwarted Cazalon. That must mean something. And we have his staff." He looked into its crystal eyes.

Tolly sighed and buried his damaged hand in the folds of the cloak. Since that time in the *Fortuna*'s hold, he hadn't touched the staff.

Jem gripped the shark spine, grateful he was immune to its power.

He felt someone tug his hand and turned to look

down at Nadie's earnest face. She brought her hand to her heart and reached up to touch his forehead. Then, solemnly, she went to Tolly.

"She's thanking us." Tolly stooped to allow Nadie to gently touch his face. She took a step back and bowed to Ann, murmuring softly.

Ann caught Tolly's arm. "I want to come with you."

"No." Tolly pulled the fur hood over his head. "Look, if it really is Cazalon, it's bad enough bringing you so close. But to actually deliver you to his doorstep would be madness!"

"But what if you need me?" Ann spluttered out the words.

"We won't. This isn't about magic, it's about stealth. Besides, you have to look after Cleo. We can't take her with us – she might give us away. You're the only one she'll stay with. Come on, girl." Tolly delved under the folds of his cloak with his good hand and produced Cleo. The little monkey batted her paws frantically against his arm as he handed her gently but firmly to Ann. "Take care of her."

"Of course I will. And you take care of each other." Ann glanced imploringly at Jem. "Let me come at least some of the way. Please."

"You're not to leave the village – and that's final."
Jem wiped snow from his face. It was falling again,
but not heavily.

"Listen, we'll be back at daybreak." Tolly spoke
softly. "But if we're not, then Nadie will take you
to the rest of her people, as Mingan wanted. We'll
join you there."

Ann didn't answer.

"Promise me you'll do that?" Tolly stepped back
as Cleo tried to catch his cloak.

Ann gave a tiny nod and he turned to the lake
without another word. As Tolly crumped away,
Cleo squawked in the girl's arms.

Jem flicked his head forward so that the hood
shielded him completely, plunged the staff into the
snow and set off.

"*Never drop your guard.*"

He repeated his fencing master's words over and
over as he marched through the snow. But William
Jalbert had never faced anyone like Count Cazalon,
had he?

※ ⚊ ※

They crouched in the deep shadow at the edge of

the forest. The silent lake looked like a vast black pit, the shore stained with blood, feathers and rotting animal carcasses. Despite the band of stars twinkling overhead in the slowly clearing sky, nothing glittered or moved in its frozen depths.

It was almost dark. Jem peered through the trees. Thirty yards away, White Crow's longhouse was a sprawling, ramshackle affair squatting beside the edge of the lake. There was no mistaking it – there had been no other houses since they left the village.

Ragged hides flapped on the arched roof and broken branches set at odd angles poked out from its sides. It looked as if it had been flung upon the ground.

"What now?" Tolly shifted to get a clearer view.

"We wait until the Witiko goes out to hunt. Once he's gone, that's our chance. Can you sense Mingan?"

Tolly shook his head. "It's too dangerous. If the Witiko is Cazalon and I open my mind this close, he'll know we're here."

Jem craned his neck for a better view of the longhouse. "Mingan defeated Madame, remember? We need his help. If he's a prisoner inside, then we need to free him and his father too." He paused. "Do you think you could use the staff again?"

Tolly nodded. "If it's against Cazalon, I can."

"Good." Jem glanced at Tolly's face. He knew how much it had already cost his friend to wield the dark power of the staff. "He is weakest by day — that's what Nadie said. It's our protection and a weapon."

Tolly nodded again, but Jem saw him looking down at the staff. He needed to give Tolly the confidence he didn't feel himself.

"Listen, it's our best chance. When he comes back from hunting it will be almost dawn. If we have Mingan with us and if you use the staff, then we can drive him into the light and defeat him. If it really is Cazalon, we can finish what we started in the catacombs under St Paul's. And if it's just a Witiko, well, we've taken on worse and won, haven't we? What do you say?"

"Just a Witiko?" Jem was amazed to hear his friend laugh for the first time in days. Tolly stifled the sound and clapped Jem's shoulder. "I say that all sounds deceptively simple, but at least it sounds like a plan."

※ ⚊ ※

As they waited, the harsh screech of an owl sounded

overhead, emphasising the unnatural silence of the forest. Suddenly, there was a sharp cracking noise from close by. A twig broken underfoot?

Jem spun about.

"Oh no!" Tolly bent to scoop something from the snow – something that chattered with pleasure.

"What is she doing here?" Jem whispered urgently as Tolly stroked Cleo's nose and folded her into his cloak.

"Shhh." Tolly tried to muffle her excited chirrups. "It's always difficult to stop her from doing what she wants. She must have escaped and followed me. Like that time at St Paul's."

"But what if she gives us away?" Cleo's twitching nose poked out from Tolly's cloak as Jem continued. "We can't take her with us."

"We'll have to. I can make her stay quiet. As long as she stays hidden under my cloak... Down!" Tolly hissed the word as the tattered flap of the longhouse door jerked aside and a dark, bent figure came out onto the snow. It straightened up. Jem saw it was tall, very tall, and clothed in a patchwork of mismatched furs, just as Nadie had said.

But she hadn't told Mingan about the stench.

The unmistakable stink of rotting flesh carried

down to them on the wind. It was a dirty, pungent smell; a familiar odour, but now a hundred times stronger than the corrupted air that smothered Mingan's village like a soiled cloak. The hooded figure paused for a moment and then turned slowly in their direction. Jem felt the Eye of Ra burn on his heel and muffled a yelp of pain.

Tolly pulled his cloak tight around his body and Cleo.

The fur-clad figure took a faltering step towards them, but then it halted, raised its head and turned to look up at the trees behind the longhouse. It swayed uncertainly from foot to foot and then it started to move again.

Staggering rather than walking, it lumbered towards the distant trees, gaining speed as it went. After a minute or so it disappeared from view.

They waited for what seemed like a long time for some kind of sign. Finally, a distant blood-curdling screech made Jem's scalp prickle.

"He's feeding – it's our chance." He straightened up and retrieved the staff from the snow.

"*Never drop your guard.*"

He allowed himself a sour smile as he thought of Master Jalbert again. What would he make of a weapon like this? Jem looked at the bird-head. Its eyes glinted eerily in the starlight. He blinked – was there something moving, deep in the heart of the crystal? He held the staff higher. No, he was mistaken. There was nothing.

Tolly cleared his throat. "The Witiko – he won't come back, will he?"

"I don't think so…" Jem stopped as another piercing animal cry echoed across the valley. "Not yet anyway. Come on."

They slipped from the treeline and, crouching low, they loped along the shore until they reached a boulder ten yards from the longhouse. The only sound came from the flaps of hide on the roof – a dry rustling as the east wind caught them.

"I'll go first."

Jem sprinted out from behind the boulder and Tolly followed.

At the entrance to the longhouse he held back the flap and called softly, "Mingan?"

From somewhere inside there was a bumping, shuffling noise and then a muffled voice. Jem called again. "Mingan, is that you?"

The voice came again, stronger now, and thumping too. Jem turned to Tolly. "He *is* here. Quickly."

Jem ducked through the doorway, Tolly following close behind. But as the flap fell back into place behind them, Jem realised they had made a dreadful and deadly mistake.

CHAPTER THIRTY-FOUR

A hoarse, horribly familiar sing-song voice rang out across the black-and-white marble-tiled hall. "You are monstrously late. We have been expecting you for so long, it has almost become tedious. But I welcome you to my home once again."

Jem could feel the heat of the flames from the fire on his face and the cool, flat precision of the marble beneath his feet. A carved timber staircase rose into blackness from the centre of the echoing chamber. There was no mistake; it was not an illusion.

But how? Jem looked back at where they'd entered the longhouse. The towering double doors of Malfurneaux Place were closed behind them. He tried to run back to push them open but his feet were rooted to the stones.

Just as Jem had done, Tolly turned to the door, his eyes round with terror.

Tolly folded his cloak protectively around his body to shield a keening Cleo.

Mingan crouched in front of the fire. His body was hunched and twisted as if bound with invisible chains. He made the muffled sound Jem had heard from outside again. The firelight glinted on the little skulls bound into his hair and his terrified eyes darted to the staircase.

The air was foul. With great effort, Jem bundled the staff into the folds of his cloak, making sure it was hidden from view.

Though they couldn't see him, Count Cazalon's rasping voice came again. "How delightful it is to be reunited with... friends."

A dragging, rustling sound from above was followed by a harsh cry. Jem looked up. Osiris, Count Cazalon's albino raven, circled the chamber. He came to rest on one of the massive carved posts at the foot of the staircase, adjusted his feathers and rolled his ugly head from side to side. Then he opened his beak to reveal a fat yellow tongue that glimmered with slime.

Kraak!

Jem tore his eyes from the bird as the rustling came again. There was a creaking tread on the stairs.

First the trailing tips of pale feathers appeared in the firelight. Then, as the heavy, deliberate steps echoed around the hall, an entire figure, illuminated by the reddish glow, came slowly towards them down the staircase.

"Greetings." Count Cazalon tilted his head to one side.

Something like a smile rippled across his face, though it was difficult to tell because the skin stretched tight across his bones was formed from a patchwork of uneven sections, some of them covered with hair. Two raw pits gouged at the centre of his face were all that remained of his nose and his bald scalp was mottled and bumpy with moles. Only his eyes – slanted, black and glittering with malice – were unmistakably the same.

He jerked forward and Jem saw that he carried himself oddly, one shoulder twisted and almost level with his ragged mouth. Cazalon paused at the foot of the stairs and stared at them in turn. He ruffled the dirty white feathers of the cape that covered his entire body and Osiris mirrored the action.

The count made no attempt now to mask his smell with the sweetness of roses or spices from the East as he had done in London. No perfume on earth could disguise the stench of a living corpse. Jem flinched as the count leaned towards him and opened his black, sticky mouth. He tried to step back, but couldn't move from the spot.

"I trust you remember that simple magic, Jeremy, from our last *meeting*? Surely you cannot have forgotten the way I bound your feet to the stones of the cavern beneath St Paul's?" Jem ducked his head to avoid inhaling the foulness. He heard the man laugh.

"How disappointing. You do not seem as pleased to see me as I am to see you. And I have been planning our reunion with such care, have I not, Isabel?"

"You are always the most attentive of hosts, my lord."

Jem heard Tolly stifle a gasp as Madame de Chouette appeared from the shadows at the top of the stairs. She descended and came to stand just behind Cazalon, resting a gloved hand on his shoulder. Her black dress shimmered in the glow of the flames.

Madame smiled, but her mouth was now deformed by a deep scar that ran up from her chin, across her cheek and over the lid of her one eye, disappearing into her auburn hair. She glanced at Mingan and clawed at the folds of her dress with her gloved hands.

Jem felt beads of perspiration form on his forehead. How could this be happening?

Tolly's voice rang out in his head. "Jem! Can you try to —'

Cazalon twisted sharply, shooting an arm that was more bone than flesh from the folds of the feathered cape. Tolly yelled as something like a hand gripped his chin.

"I see that my servant has yet to learn manners. It is always so rude to *speak* without being asked, Ptolemy. You will *not* do so again." Cazalon's eyes flickered across Tolly's face. "Ah, but of course, I almost forgot. That is the name I gave you, not your *true* name. You told me that when you left me in the cavern beneath St Paul's, when we were last together." The probing tip of his black tongue moistened his flaking lips. "I have thought about you all often since that day. And about the promise I made."

"But how…?" Jem couldn't stop himself. He had to know.

"Don't speak to him…" Tolly's voice faded in his head as Madame de Chouette stepped over and enfolded him in a black embrace, pinning Tolly's arms to his sides.

"How did I escape? Is that what you were going to say?" Cazalon smiled. "I am an adept – probably the most powerful this world has ever known. Osiris!" He turned to the white bird bobbing on the stairpost. "Shall we show them?"

In answer, Osiris unfurled his wings and rose into the air. At the same moment Cazalon spread his arms wide so that the feathered cloak swirled about him. The raven circled the room twice and then swooped low. The count grinned as the bird extended his claws and came to rest on one of his outstretched arms. Instantly, the air around the count wrinkled. Jem blinked hard as his vision seemed to split in two. Part of him registered the twisted form of Cazalon standing at the foot of the stairs, but another part of his mind saw the wavering shape of Osiris lengthen until giant wings enveloped the count's entire body. Now the distorted outline of man and bird pulsed like a beating heart.

As Jem watched, the man's face blurred into a long, tapering skull. Then Osiris was gone and there was only Cazalon.

"Do you understand now?" The count held his

hideous head to one side. "Perhaps not – you're both such simple souls, after all. Little Ann might have been able to explain it to you, but unfortunately you will never see her again." He turned to Madame de Chouette. "It is not a skill everyone can perfect, is it, Isabel?"

Jem saw a glint of spite in his eyes as he continued.

"It is always dangerous to split the soul in two, but there is also a safety in it – as I have proved. Osiris is my Ba, my shadow self. My spirit. It was the highest magic of the temple priests at Thebes. Three thousand years ago I learned the secret of the rite of separation and it has been of great use."

He jerked his head towards Madame de Chouette. "Poor Isabel here begged me to teach her, but she could not achieve totality. At the final moment of the rite she could not divide body from soul. It is why you are so maimed, is it not, *ma cherie*? Cursed forever to walk on the feet of a bird."

"But you have promised, my lord." Madame de Chouette loosened her grip on Tolly and now Jem heard the familiar ticking noise. "When you take the girl's power, you will make me whole again, and more?"

Cazalon dipped his head, but Jem saw the fleeting amusement that flashed in his eyes. "When I take the power. Yes, that is right, Isabel. It is why we are here. Thank you for reminding me."

He turned to Jem. "I do not expect a simple boy like you to understand the high magic of Thebes, but when you left me to die beneath St Paul's, my shadow self, Osiris, escaped. This…" Cazalon passed a withered hand across his face, "is what is left of my earthly body and I have worked hard to keep it alive until the time is right. Many creatures have died to produce *the wonder* you see before you. I have used their bones, their skin, their blood, their life essence to become whole."

"Witiko." Mingan spat the word and Cazalon turned slowly to face him. He shook his head and began to laugh.

"Your dog has a voice again, I see. I wondered when he might whimper. I must thank you… Mingan, is it? The Grey Wolf? Well, I find I must thank you for bringing Lady Ann to the valley. I must admit, it was not quite what I intended, but the end is much the same." He limped forward and Jem saw Mingan flinch at the count's stench. "Do not attempt to change yourself. It will not work here within the boundaries of my home. The girl is with your mother, I believe."

When he didn't reply, Cazalon scraped a blackened fingernail across Mingan's scarred cheek. "You and I will go to meet them tomorrow. I know they are waiting – so trusting, so... vulnerable."

Blood trickled down Mingan's chin as Cazalon's nail gouged deep. "Betrayal – it is a sweet word. Tell me, Grey Wolf, you must have found it difficult to resist the call of your father? Such powerful things, dreams, are they not?"

Mingan growled and struggled to move, but like Jem and the others he seemed rooted to the marble floor.

Cazalon grinned slyly at Tolly and then at Jem. "These two are somewhat unexpected guests. You lost them, didn't you, Isabel, just as you lost my scrying mirror?" For a moment his eyes burned with fury as he turned slowly to look at Madame. When he spoke again his voice was laced with venom. "I told you, did I not, my dear, that it was among the most powerful and valuable of my possessions? Only three pairs of Venetian *Cadavere Tocco* mirrors were ever produced on the island of Murano, and at great cost I obtained the very last pair in existence. Now there is just one *corpse* mirror in the world and it is useless without its twin. Tell me, Isabel, do you feel regret for such wanton vandalism?"

He didn't wait for an answer but sighed heavily. "Well, that is of little matter for the time being. In fact, it is almost a neat conclusion that these boys are here. It seems, without knowing it, the wolf did your work."

Madame de Chouette stepped forward. "I am deeply sorry about the mirror, my lord. But I brought the girl to you and I guided your... *dwelling place* across the ocean for the time when you are whole. You will honour your promise, Lord Cazalon?"

"Ah yes, promises."

He stalked towards the fire and stared into the flames. When he spoke, his voice froze the blood in Jem's veins.

"I made a promise beneath the burning wreck of old St Paul's Cathedral. I wonder, Jeremy, do you recall it now?"

Jem couldn't bear to reply.

"Then let me refresh your memory. I swore that

I would hunt you down to the ends of the earth and beyond, and that when I found you I would ensure that the pain you inflicted upon me would be returned upon you sevenfold."

He paused.

"And so we meet again – at the ends of the earth."

CHAPTER
THIRTY-FIVE

Cazalon threw back the great double doors of Malfurneaux Place. With difficulty, Jem wrenched his neck to watch the count hobble into the night.

As a chill gust of wind was sucked through the doors, the fire in the hearth roared, flooding the hall with a blinding flash of light. Jem lowered his head to shield his eyes. When he looked again, the black-and-white marble floor beneath his feet had vanished. He was standing on blood-spattered snow. He tried to step forward, but it felt as if his feet were buried in the earth.

Now they were all outside the longhouse again, facing the tattered hide flap that served as an entrance. Beyond the roof Jem saw the edge of the forest and high above the trees a cleft in the distant mountains formed a V. There was a faint glow in the V's lowest point.

Jem pulled the folds of the cloak tight about him. It wasn't because of the cold; it was because he wanted to be certain that the staff was hidden. If only he could use it like Tolly. He wracked his brains trying to think of something to do.

Tolly fumbled with the folds of his own cloak.

"Give me the creature." Madame de Chouette swept between them and ripped Tolly's brown fur cloak apart. She plucked Cleo from his side and held her aloft by a hind leg, just as she had done on the ship. Cleo squealed and scrabbled uselessly at the air as the woman dangled her above the ice.

"Please – not Cleo," Tolly pleaded desperately, but Madame de Chouette whirled around and with a sudden vicious lunge hurled the little monkey into the air over the longhouse. They heard a screech of terror and then a sickening crunch.

"No!" Tolly's cry of misery tore into the night. He struggled to move, but his feet wouldn't obey. Instead he lashed out at the woman's head. She stepped neatly out of reach and smiled. Her tiny yellow teeth glinted in the light of the full moon now peering out between the mountains. "You will not miss her for long, boy."

Jem felt his eyes brim with tears and saw something leave a dark trail in the snow-dusted skin of Tolly's cheeks. He clutched the hidden staff. There had to be something he could do.

From somewhere behind, Cazalon laughed, but Jem couldn't turn to look at him.

"Do not waste your tears on an animal. You do not yet know the true meaning of misery. Now turn to face me – all of you."

Involuntarily, Jem, Tolly and Mingan moved as one, shuffling about in the snow so that they were facing Cazalon. He stood on the edge of the black lake and the feathers of his cape blew up around his patched bald head.

Cazalon's eyes narrowed. "It is a kindness. I am sure you would not want your little pet to see what I am going to do next."

Mingan bared his teeth and snarled. "Witiko."

Cazalon smiled in triumph. "You are mistaken. *I* am not a Witiko." He narrowed his eyes. "But your father, Annawan, now that is a different matter. I was blinded by fury when he came to me. I *needed* those children. Look at me – this face, this body is an abomination. I am ruined, but with young flesh, young lives, I could have —'

He stopped as his voice rose to a shriek of rage. He smoothed the feathered cape around his twisted shoulders.

"I thought of killing him, but that seemed too

391

kind. Instead I made *him* a Witiko – I condemned him forever to walk between the worlds of the living and the dead. He is entirely my creature now. Your wise old father, wolf prince, is a shambling, mindless wreck. He feeds like an animal and what he doesn't destroy he brings to me so that I may… restore my ravaged body as best I can."

Jem's gorge rose as Cazalon scratched thoughtfully at a tattered square of coarse dark hair beside his pitted nose. The man saw his disgust. His black eyes glittered.

"When Annawan returns before dawn I will feed Jeremy and my servant Ptolemy to him. And I will allow you to watch your father's hunger, Grey Wolf. It will not be pleasant."

He limped towards Jem and gripped a hank of his hair, yanking his head back. "To think I wasted time on you when all I needed to do was to wait until my ward came into her estate."

Even in the open air the rotting smell that rolled from Cazalon's body was almost too much to bear.

"Do you remember I told you how I travelled the world in search of knowledge, boy?" He released his grip and crunched away so that he stood on the lip of the lake with his back to them. He raised his arms and the tattered cloak flew up around him.

"I first found this place many years ago when the northmen came to this land in their long boats. I knew immediately what it was, even then. It is like the cavern beneath the cathedral, a place where the powers of the earth can be harnessed… in the right circumstances and at the right time."

"And that time is coming soon, my lord." Madame de Chouette rustled past Jem and knelt on the stained snow at Cazalon's feet. "The first day of May."

Cazalon rubbed his mottled cheek and to Jem's disgust a sliver of skin detached itself. He rolled it between his fingers and dropped it to the snow. "I have waited for so long, that three months will pass…" he clicked his fingers, "in the blink of an eye. I have walked this earth for three thousand years and now, I will be ready to meet the dark god, Set, when he comes for me. In the meantime, we will be… comfortable here in the valley with Lady Ann as our guest. There is no one to disturb us."

"And then we will take her power." Madame de Chouette reached for the hem of his feathered cloak.

"*We?*" Jem heard a dangerous snap in Cazalon's voice, but Madame de Chouette didn't seem to notice. Instead she turned her single amber eye on

Jem and Tolly.

"Did you know that on her thirteenth birthday little Ann will be as powerful as my Lord Cazalon – for the single minute he allows her to live? On the stroke of midnight he will absorb her – every atom of her being and every ounce of her new power." She turned to stare at Mingan and blinked slowly. "It is why I spared you, wolf prince. He will use your blood to awaken the power of this place and on that day he will become a true immortal. He will be a god. It is his destiny."

Jem's knuckles cracked beneath the cloak as he gripped the staff. He wanted to swing the wretched thing at the woman's head, but he couldn't move as she reached into the neck of her gown.

"And he has promised to reward me. Look what my lord Cazalon has already given me." She held something that glittered in her gloved hand. She raised it and turned it about so that it caught the starlight. It was Ann's crescent jewel. Jem thought the gem-studded moon brooch had been lost forever in the cavern beneath St Paul's Cathedral.

"Also a thing of power, I think. Perhaps I will force your friend to show me how to use it while we wait here to celebrate her coming of age... *Aaagh!*"

Madame de Chouette gasped, jerked forward and her eye widened. She flattened a hand against her chest and looked down as black droplets fell upon the snow.

Only now did Jem see the glowing arrow tip that pierced her back and emerged from her breast.

CHAPTER
THIRTY-SIX

"The pain! It burns! Help me, my lord!"

The woman tugged uselessly at the red hot point of the arrow and screeched in agony. She scuffled forward on her knees, her imploring hands reaching towards Cazalon. As the black material of her skirt parted, Jem caught a clear view of the talons. Her legs ended in two twisted, thickened stumps. The pale, lumpy flesh above her ankles was sparsely patched with dark feathers and grotesque claws twisted upwards behind her. He wanted to look away but he was mesmerised by the sight.

"My lord, will you not help me?" She gasped as she struggled forward, leaving a thin black trail in the snow. Confused, Jem glanced at Cazalon. He was simply staring at her.

There was a whistling sound. Without turning, Cazalon raised a corpse-like hand and a second arrow flared and burned to a cinder in the air behind him. Ashes pattered softly down on the snow.

Mingan twisted his hunched body about and

Jem tried to look too, but he couldn't quite turn his neck far enough. From the corner of his eye he saw Mingan's blue eyes widen and his nostrils flare.

"Your mother will not dare to come any closer." Cazalon's voice sounded bored. "Look what I have here." He reached into the neck of the feathered cloak and produced a smooth black oval held on a leather thong. He held it aloft and grinned. "While she believes your father to be alive, she will not come here, wolf prince. And of course, he *is* alive... in a manner of speaking."

Mingan growled, his tattoos rippling as he strained every muscle to spring at the count. But he was like a chained animal.

Cazalon smiled.

"Great magician, I beg you..." Madame de Chouette choked and crawled forward a little way more. "Have you forgotten our bargain, my lord? I have made myself a thing of horror for you. You promised."

Cazalon regarded her for a long moment and then he smiled so broadly that his distorted mouth spread like a wound across his face. He began to laugh – a croaking noise from the depths of his throat. When he stopped, his black eyes glinted and he spoke in a cold, deliberate voice.

"You have not *made* yourself a thing of horror, Isabel. You have *always* been one. Since the day I first met you – four hundred years ago now, was it? – you have been willing to do anything in return for power. I remember the day when you gave away your left eye. You plucked it out yourself, did you not?"

Her reply came in broken snatches between gulps of air. "Yes, b-because you told me to. You sh-showed me the rite of exchange. Everything I have sacrificed – my eye, my hands, the very skin of my back, has been for knowledge – you taught me well. Why would you do that, my lord, if you... did not intend me to sit beside you as your equal? And wh-when you take Ann's... power, you will be able to make me..."

"My equal?" Cazalon snorted. "You could never be that. You have been useful, Madame, but incautious, I fear. I *am* a great magician, as you say, and I kept our bargain. I gave you a *little* knowledge as you desired, but I am afraid you will never be great enough to use it. Your... deformity proved that. I cannot make you any more than your destiny allows, and your destiny is an inferior one."

"But you promised." Madame de Chouette repeated

the words, swaying as she tried to keep herself from slumping forward.

"Promised what exactly, Isabel?"

"My face, my hands, my feet… You said I would be whole again."

Cazalon shook his head. "But you can never be that, my dear, not now. Did you really think that I could make you young, beautiful – almost an immortal – when you have given away so much of your body over the years in exchange for power that there is nothing of value left to renew? No. You would always be a half-creature assembled from remnants."

Madame de Chouette stared wildly up at him. "But that is also true of you. You have remade yourself from many creatures and men too. Why would you condemn yourself to a life of such pain, allow yourself to become a living mockery when you could never reverse that horror?"

Cazalon smiled. "Because when I am a god I will be perfect. I will throw off this stinking patchwork carcass and be born anew. But, sadly, you would always be as you are now. Perhaps it is kinder this way. You must know what I say is true, Isabel. Look into your heart."

Her eye darkened with hatred. "I cannot. And

you know why." She spat out the words as if they were poison and ripped the black cloth from her breast, breaking the arrow in two. Jem started when he saw a gaping hole where her heart should be, and a glinting spider-like device twitching beneath her exposed, yellow ribs.

"I gave it to you…" Madame de Chouette began to cough. Something black and sticky oozed from the corner of her mouth and her whole body jerked violently. The ticking sound that Jem now knew to come from the clockwork heart became faster and faster.

Cazalon's sibilant voice came again. "*I always ensure those loyal to me get exactly what they deserve, do I not?*" He started to laugh.

Madame de Chouette stifled a cry of agony, then suddenly she went rigid, her amber eye locking onto a point behind Jem. A slow smile spread across her face.

With one last huge effort, she raised her arm. "This is yours, I believe?"

Jem saw something flash as it arced through the air, then caught his breath as a small figure cloaked in silver fur emerged from the shadow of the trees.

Deftly, Ann caught the jewel tossed to her by the

dying woman and held it aloft so that the moonlight glinted from its stones.

"Use it well." Madame de Chouette choked out the words and fell forward. Her body jerked mechanically on the snow as the ticking began to fade.

Cazalon didn't look at her but turned to face the silver-clad figure.

"Ah – Lady Ann has joined us at last, I see. I wondered if she could resist. Give it to me." Jem could feel the physical pull of the words as the man spoke. "Bring it to me, Ann Metcalf."

Ann shrugged back her hood and her white hair flew up around her head in the wind. "No. It is mine. It is part of my inheritance. You shall not have it – not one portion of it, Cazalon."

She raised the brooch high above her head and it sparked in the moonlight.

"Bring it to me now." The count's voice coiled like an adder about to strike.

Ann's voice came clear and strong. "It is mine and I will use it." The brooch began to glow in her hand and waves of light rippled out from the jewel. Soon Ann was enveloped in a brilliant halo that shone like a second moon.

Tolly's low voice came from beside him. "It's time,

Jem. Give it to me."

Jem knew what Tolly meant. Although his feet were still rooted to the spot he reached into the folds of his fur and pulled the staff free. He extended it to Tolly, who caught the end and planted it firmly into the ice, pointing the head of the crystal bird at Cazalon. He closed the remaining fingers of his damaged hand around the blackened stick.

Cazalon's ravaged face was unreadable. He folded his arms. "That is mine, boy. It is a useless weapon for you. You cannot wield its power…"

"You're wrong there, Cazalon. He can!" Jem was defiant, but the next moment he was horrified to see Tolly take a jolting step forward, his movements clearly forced by Cazalon.

"And you, Ann Metcalf. Bring me your toy."

Jem's hope dissolved as the light around Ann began to fade. She too took a halting step forward, twitching like a marionette. The strap across her body that held a quiver of arrows snapped and fell to the snow.

"Jem, I can't stop… I…" Ann began to move stiffly towards Cazalon, her face a mask of pain as she fought to resist.

She came so close to Jem that he was able to

snatch her free hand. As he made contact with her
~~bare skin, his ears filled with a familiar, thrumming~~
~~sound. Instantly he found that he could move his~~
~~feet. He dragged Ann towards Tolly, just managing~~
~~to catch hold of his friend's fingertips.~~

At the touch, a massive jolt of energy charged
through him. Like the moment when they linked
hands on the jetty, but a thousand times more
powerful. Jem's mind became a kaleidoscope of
whirling colours and little explosions of brilliance.

He heard Ann gasp and felt Tolly's good left
hand tighten around his own. The air shimmered
with silver sparks that danced and fluttered around
their heads like tiny moths.

Tolly's grip tightened. "It… it's working. Look,
Jem… Look!"

The bird-head was glowing faintly now. The light
deep within the crystal appeared to spin and gather
itself. Within seconds it was burning so fiercely that
Jem had to look away.

"Enough! Give that to me. I command you,"
Cazalon snarled in fury. He whirled about on
the edge of the lake and came forward, but Tolly
brandished the staff, warding him off. A beam of
light crackled from the bird's eyes, falling to point

between the children and the lake, where it began to burn a narrow path through the snow that singed towards the limping figure of the count.

Jem saw Cazalon's confusion. He paused and then he stepped back sharply, as the beam came closer to the trailing ends of his cloak.

"How is this possible?" He looked up, his coal black eyes burning with hatred. "When did you learn to use it?"

Tolly didn't answer. Instead he stepped forward, dragging Jem and Ann with him. He held the staff higher so that the sizzling beam forced Cazalon further onto the ice.

Jem saw something glistening on the knobbles of the staff. He glanced anxiously at Tolly's face. His friend's eyes were tightly closed and his forehead was creased with concentration.

"We're driving him away." Ann looked up at Jem. "But what do we do now?"

Jem shook his head. "Perhaps the ice is thinner the further out he goes. If we force him to go far enough perhaps it might break?"

"But it's not like any ice I've seen before. It's dead."

Cazalon raised his feathered arms at that moment, threw back his head and began to chant. The low rhythmic noise had a peculiar quality. It seemed to pull at the skin on Jem's scalp and scrape at his face. He tried to shake the horrible sensation away, but it came clawing again. The surface of the lake began to undulate, the frozen black ripples cracking and groaning. Then the dead lake began to creep towards them, moving slowly, like treacle.

"No!" Ann tugged forward and raised her left hand. The silver crescent moon gleamed as it scythed through the air, whipping past Cazalon's head to clatter to the ice beyond him. Without stopping his chant, he grinned and turned to see where it had fallen.

"I don't understand – I thought I could control it." Ann's voice was desperate. "I've lost it – again."

Everything went dark. On the lake, Cazalon disappeared, although they could still hear his voice rising and falling in a song that had no melody.

Jem twisted his head to search for the real moon. It was hidden by cloud, creating darkness so thick that he felt it tighten around his throat, and then, horribly, try to force its way into his mouth and nose. If only the moon would reappear.

The moon!

He remembered Mingan's story. *When our people face the greatest enemy we believe the Moon's Child will sing with the stars and the Great Mother will hear them."*

SING! That was another of the words burned into the side of the *Fortuna's* hold.

"Ann, you m…must sing!" he choked. "Sing to the m…moon. S… sing so that C… Cazalon's voice cannot be heard." Jem was certain he was right. "Sing!"

"B… but I can't even breathe." Ann coughed and Jem felt her grip loosen.

"W… we m… must." He clasped her tight.

"Sing… what, Jem?"

"Anything. I know! The T… Twelfth Night song from the feast at G… Goldings. I'll sing with you."

Jem began to splutter out the first line.

"We h…have travelled f…far and wide
To bring y…you joy on this dark n…night…"

By the third line Ann joined him. At first they sang with difficulty, gulping down painful lungfuls of air between the lines, but soon their voices strengthened and soared clear into the night.

"We link our hands and raise a cry
To turn away the evil eye…"

"Tolly, you too. You must sing with us." Jem broke off and glanced to the left. The beam from the staff was as faint as a candle stub now. Jem tightened his grip on Tolly's hand. "Together."

Tolly began to sing alongside them, his voice shattered with pain.

"*Now moon and stars shine bright and clear*
To banish bane and welcome cheer.
We link our hands and raise a cry
To turn away the evil eye.
Let no malice harm this place
For we celebrate with grace."

As they sang on, repeating the verses, the air began to quiver. The odd vibration made it seem as if a score of people, a hundred people, a thousand people, were singing at the lake's edge. The chorus echoed from the rocks and stones. When the howling of a wolf entwined with their song, rising and falling with the verses, Jem allowed himself a tiny smile.

The full moon emerged from the clouds, flooding the scene with silver light. The howling came again and Jem saw that Mingan was gone, leaving only scuffle marks in the dirty snow.

He continued to sing and turned back to the lake. Cazalon had disappeared too now – but he saw something silver glint out there in the blackness. Ann's crescent jewel!

As they sang on, the beam from the staff gathered a new strength and skipped out across the lake to ignite

407

the spark of the jewel into a ball of pale blue fire.

The ball hovered there for a moment, flickering and spitting off little points of light and then, gradually, it increased in size until it seemed five, no, six, times the size of the moon overhead. It spun and billowed and then quite suddenly it flattened – spreading out across the entire surface of the lake.

Jem watched in amazement as the eerie fire danced across the frozen water. Then it flared, sputtered and vanished from the smooth, clear ice that once more reflected the shimmering circle of the moon.

"We've done it!" Jem broke off from a verse and shouted excitedly. "We've done it. The moon has come back to the water. Do you see? It's what Mingan told us about – the promise in the legend…" He stopped as the moon's reflection began to quiver and expand.

"What's happening?" Ann turned to Jem, but he shook his head.

"*Sing* – we must keep singing. It's working – that's all I know."

He began again another verse and Ann and Tolly sang with him. Tolly's voice was becoming faint, and Jem squeezed his friend's hand. "Keep going, Tolly – look."

Now the moon's reflection pulsed in the ice, and

as it glowed, steam began to rise from its outline —
delicate tendrils of silvery vapour coiling into the air.
There was a tremendous cracking noise and a great
roaring whoosh as a towering column of blue water
erupted from the moon's reflection in the lake. Jem
could feel heat on his face as the sizzling jet spurted
upwards and the ice began to melt.

"Annawan, come forth!" Cazalon's voice was like
the tolling of a bell.

Without breaking the song Jem turned his head.

The count was behind them, facing the trees
beyond the longhouse. He spread his arms wide
beneath the feathered cloak and spoke again. "Come,
my creature. Do as I bid."

A lumbering form emerged from the forest.
Covered in tattered bandages of fur that trailed in
the snow, the Witiko staggered towards them. As it
moved, it swung its massive hooded head from side
to side.

As it came closer, the stink of sweat, blood, faeces
and decay filled Jem's nose and throat. He gagged
at the stench, even worse than that coming from
Cazalon.

The only part of the Witiko's body that was visible
was its hands. As it came level with the longhouse,

Jem saw fresh blood dripping to the snow from pointed black nails at the ends of fingers that constantly clenched and twitched. The thought of those fingers raking his flesh made Jem lose his place in the song. He felt Ann's fingers tighten round his as he rallied.

"*We link our hands and raise a cry*
To turn away the evil eye…"

The creature lurched around the edge of the longhouse and paused uncertainly. Jem felt Tolly's hand slip from his.

Cazalon didn't miss the weak moment, and immediately made a sign with his twisted hand. "Take the boys!"

The Witiko grunted and swung its shrouded head towards Jem. The song died on his lips as he caught sight of two points glowing like red-hot coals in the depths of the hood. Tolly and Ann fell silent too as the creature swayed from side to side.

It lowered its head and squared its shoulders, ready to charge.

But at the same moment there was an ear-splitting howl, a huge thud and a spatter of snow as a great grey blur blocked its path. A gigantic wolf crouched low before the Witiko, growling so loudly that the sound reverberated through Jem's feet.

The Witiko made to swipe the animal aside, but then it paused.

The wolf – Mingan – fell silent and arched his neck. The Witiko's threatening hand came down gently on the weren's head between his ears. Mingan twisted and licked the exposed skin of the creature's arm. As Jem watched, the Witiko trembled.

Cazalon hobbled forward, his slanted eyes brilliant with malice. "Tame your son, Annawan."

The Witiko gripped Mingan's throat, twitching as it tried to resist Cazalon's command. Black talons dug deep into the shaggy grey fur. Mingan snarled and then he whimpered.

Ann dropped Jem's hand. "Tolly!"

Of course! She was right. "Use the staff, Tolly," Jem cried out. When there was no reply he looked to the left. Tolly had collapsed, a heap of fur, the staff fallen from his hand. Ann was now kneeling beside him, but her eyes were on the terrible scene of the Witiko and Mingan, father and son, locked in battle.

"Good – that's good. Harder, deeper, Annawan."

Cazalon took a step towards them. He grinned, bent low and twisted his head so that he could look directly into Mingan's eyes. "Do not kill him… yet,

Annawan. I will do that when the time is right. Soon I will need the blood of the wolf prince to awaken the power of this place."

"*Never drop your guard.*" Master Jalbert's words sounded as clearly in Jem's head as if the fencing master had been standing next to him. Cazalon was completely engrossed – it was an opportunity!

Jem pelted across the snow and snatched up the staff. He turned, loped back and, brandishing it in two hands, hammered the crystal bird down with all his might onto Cazalon's patchwork skull.

There was a crunch of bone and sticky blackness spattered onto the snow.

At first Cazalon didn't move. Then he raised a claw-like hand to his broken head. His long fingernails probed the wound. His body began to tremble. He turned to look up at Jem, but his ink-black eyes didn't seem able to focus. Jem took a step back and raised the staff again as Cazalon struggled to stand. Instead, he fell forward so that he was crouching at Jem's feet on all fours.

Nadie's wooden heart fell free from the neck of Cazalon's feathered cape and swayed back and forth on its leather thong. Jem felt the Witiko's eyes move to it.

It watched for a moment, its head following the

motion of the heart, then it released its grip on Mingan and groped for the pendant, its black hand grabbing the leather thong.

"No!" Cazalon gasped, but the Witiko ignored him, jerking the thong to bring the pendant closer to its hidden eyes. As it did so it pulled Cazalon's deformed face closer to its own so that the two hideous creatures stared into each other's eyes.

Jem saw Cazalon's mouth twist in fear and wondered what was hidden in the furs to repel a man who was himself a living corpse.

The Witiko grunted and stood, bringing up the pendant. It was so tall, it lifted Cazalon from the ground and his fur-clad feet kicked out at nothing.

It bellowed with rage and flung the man roughly over its shoulder, then thundered towards the lake, moving with incredible speed.

"Stop! I command you. No... No!" Cazalon screeched in terror as the Witiko charged, sloshing and sliding across the melting ice towards the tower of steaming water. Jem saw the count's twisted hands beat upon the creature's back and watched in horror as the man and the monster he had created were engulfed by the scalding fountain.

A wail of terrible pain tore into the air. Jem couldn't

tell if the agonised scream came from Cazalon or Annawan, or both of them. As the sound intensified, Jem clamped his hands over his ears and sank to his knees. A wild, raw wind sprang from nowhere, ripping branches from the fir trees and pulling them into the spurting geyser that now began to spin and roar.

The column of whirling water rose even higher – and then it simply stopped. For a single, silent moment the world seemed to freeze and then the tower dissolved. Torrents of water crashed to the surface of the lake, creating steaming walls of waves that rolled towards the shore. Jem knew he couldn't outrun the deluge. He closed his eyes and waited for the waters to carry him away.

It felt like an age , but was probably only a minute later, when Jem took his hands from his ears again and looked at the calm, rippling surface of the lake. It sparkled in the moonlight as little waves lapped gently at the shore.

"Jem – come quickly. His hand – look at his hand." Ann stroked Tolly's brow. He was stretched out on the snow, his head cradled in her lap. Tears glittered in her eyes. "It's so badly damaged. Was it the staff?"

Jem nodded. He didn't know what to say. Tolly's right hand was almost unrecognisable. There were no fingers left at all now, just the stump of a thumb. His palm was shrivelled and black. He looked at the staff – the crystal bird was smeared with blood.

Jem swallowed and stared out across the lake. Had Cazalon perished in the scalding tower of water? He didn't want to think about the alternative. The man was almost an immortal – what if…?

Tolly moaned softly and Jem crouched down beside him. "Can you do anything, Ann?"

Ann stroked Tolly's head. "I can heal the wounds and treat the burns, but I can't make his hand whole again. And his hair! Oh, Jem, his hair."

Before Jem could say anything about his friend's changed appearance, one of Ann's tears fell on Tolly's forehead and he opened his eyes. "C-Cleo? We must find…"

"She is here." Mingan padded towards them on the snow. He was a man again now, but his long grey plaits couldn't conceal the vicious punctures in his neck from the Witiko's claws. Cleo was huddled against his tattooed chest.

Jem stood up. "No… She's not… Please…"

Mingan shook his head. The threaded bones

rattled and a black paw reached up to catch at one of the tiny skulls. Jem's heart leaped.

"She's alive!" Ann reached up to take Cleo from Mingan. "Let me hold her. I knew we should have left her at the longhouse. She ran off when she sensed Tolly nearby."

"*We?*" Jem asked, confused.

Ann nodded. "Nadie and I followed you. Neither of us were ever going to let you come here alone. Nadie gave me the bow for protection, not attack, but when I saw what that woman did to Cleo, I…" She paused and stared along the lake edge at the black heap in the stained snow. Madame de Chouette. She narrowed her eyes. "I think you'll agree, Jem, that I'm rather a good shot?" Ann smiled tightly. She cradled Cleo in her arms. "Oh little one, what are we going to do with you?"

Mingan knelt in the snow and Cleo tried again to catch one of his plaits. "I found her at the foot of a tree – it broke her fall. Her back leg is twisted, broken perhaps. But I think she has been lucky."

Ann nodded. "But your father, Annawan – I'm so sorry…"

Mingan ran a hand over the wounds on his neck. "He saved us, Moon Child. Do not grieve." Without looking at them he knelt and stretched out the hood of Tolly's cloak, arranging it carefully beneath his head. "Your healing skills will be needed here too. How is he?"

Tolly tried to smile. "Better already for seeing Cleo." He reached out to stroke her head, but stopped when he saw his hand. He held it up and turned it about in the moonlight.

"I can't even feel it," he murmured in amazement.

A rustling sound made Mingan leap to his feet. He scanned the shore and Jem saw a figure emerge from the trees. It walked slowly towards them and came to a halt a few yards away on the edge of the lake. Jem watched the silent figure bend down to pluck something from the water. It straightened up and rolled whatever it was about in its hands as it stared across the lake.

Then Nadie walked to her son and stood on tiptoe to hang Annawan's wooden heart around his neck. She delved into the folds of her fur cloak and took out her own love token.

It was broken in two.

EPILOGUE

Jem looked at the letter in his hands and wondered when he would be able to deliver it. As soon as they arrived in port he knew he would travel directly to Goldings. Every time he thought about his mother and that tumbling red-brick house he felt an ache deep beneath his ribs. The sensation was growing stronger every day.

According to Spider, they would be at sea for at least four weeks more, "this being a regular sort of vessel."

Jem squinted up into the rigging where his skinny friend was balanced precariously on a mast. He raised his hand and the boy waved back.

The *Magpie* was half the size of the *Fortuna*, but she was a stocky little ship and she was making good progress. They would be in England before April was out – just ahead of Ann's birthday.

Jem turned to look down the deck. Ann and Tolly were sitting on a pile of folded canvas playing a card game. Cleo was wedged between them, her bright inquisitive eyes following their every move. She would always limp a little now, but she didn't seem to mind. It certainly didn't stop her clambering around in the *Magpie*'s rigging. She was a favourite with the crew.

Ann had done as much as she could to heal Cleo and to soothe the charred skin of Tolly's right palm. Jem watched as Tolly deftly shuffled the pack and dealt the cards with his left hand. He always kept his maimed hand hidden from view now. Jem looked down at his own hands holding the letter. Four white stripes seared across the knuckles and over the olive skin of the back of his right hand were the only reminder of his encounter with Cazalon's mirror.

Ann and Tolly's plan was to accompany Jem back to Goldings and then to travel on to be reunited with Gabriel and the players.

As if she felt his gaze, Ann looked up, grinned and waved a fan of cards at him. "Come and join us. It's better with three."

"Yes, much better." Tolly laughed. "And I think she cheats! I need you to keep an eye on her."

"I'll be on my guard then." Jem felt a tightness in his chest again as he thought about seeing Master Jalbert and continuing his lessons in the courtyard.

He took a deep gulp of salt-laced air and rubbed something from his eye.

Mingan had kept his promise. At the earliest opportunity he had guided them through the softly melting landscape to a bustling port and he had insisted on paying for their passage – and for new clothes and provisions – with furs of the finest quality. On the day the *Magpie* set sail for England, he had watched from a rocky outcrop above the little harbour, before disappearing into the trees. They all heard the mournful howl of a lone wolf as the tidy vessel unfurled its mainyard. Mingan and Nadie would be with their people again now.

Finding Spider among the crew had been a wonderful surprise. In fact, at least two others on board the *Magpie* were Swale men, veterans from the *Fortuna* who had moved down the coast from Port Melas to seek work and a passage back to England. "We never speak of it. It was an unlucky ship for us all," Spider had confided on deck one evening. Then he fell silent and looked out to sea. Jem guessed he was thinking about Pocket.

After that they avoided talking about the past and concentrated on the future. Spider even promised to give Jem a guided tour of his beloved Port Swale when he returned to deliver Trevanion's letter.

Jem looked down at the folded paper in his hands once again and ran his thumb over the wax seal. He wondered about Jane. Would she be well now and, if she was, what should he tell her?

"I'll give you a ha'penny for 'em?" Spider had come down from the rigging to stand next to him. The boy nodded approvingly at the wisps of white cloud skudding across the blue sky. "I like this ship. She's got a good solid bottom and the captain's a fair man. I wouldn't mind travelling with him again. How about you?"

Jem shook his head. "I don't think a life at sea is for me."

Spider cocked his head. "What about your mate, Tolly, then? I'd say he was a natural."

Jem grinned. "I'll tell him that. But I think he has other plans too."

Spider looked back to where Ann and Tolly were sitting, their heads close over the cards.

"Funny that – from this angle you'd almost take them for twins, what with their hair being so white."

It was true. On that terrible night by the lake when Tolly had burned away half his hand on Cazalon's staff, every springy hair on his head had turned as white as snow.

"Moony – that's what some of the lads call him," said Spider, adding helpfully, "on account of his hair. What happened there, Jemmie?"

"It's a long story – and maybe one best left for when we reach England." Jem didn't meet Spider's inquisitive gaze; instead he found himself wondering about Cazalon again. He tried not to think of him, but the man kept insinuating himself into his mind. With an effort he forced him away.

"Moony, eh, Spider? It's a good nickname. I might use it." Jem smiled and looked down the deck again at his friends. As he watched Tolly select a card from the pack, an odd thought stepped into his mind.

What if, all along, Tolly and not Ann had been the Moon Child of Nadie's legend?

He must have started, because Spider tugged his sleeve. "You all right? Not gill sick?"

"No… no, I'm fine." Jem shrugged. "I just had a peculiar thought, that's all."

Spider grinned. "And I've a got a peculiar thought for you. The man on lookout duty last night reckons a great white crow came and sat on the top of the main mast. 'Orrible he said it was, stared right down at him for an hour and then it flew off due east – the direction we're going in, although there's no land for hundreds and hundreds of miles. Now, what do you make of that, Jemmie?"

ACKNOWLEDGEMENTS

When I was about eleven years old, the Cain family went on its first ever package holiday abroad, to Ibiza.

It was life-changing.

Until this momentous fortnight, the concept of a holiday had largely meant huddling behind a windbreak on a rain-lashed British beach, picking sand out of our luncheon meat sandwiches. On really bad days – when my younger brother and I couldn't persuade our parents to break open the pack-a-macs and shiver on the shingle – we wandered the streets, staring through misted shop windows at crumbling displays of grinning pink-and-white false teeth or giant, lurid baby dummies made of sweet, sticky rock.

Occasionally, when the rain was coming down so hard we couldn't see through the windows, we sheltered in a variety of very small, very dusty coastal town museums with displays on subjects such as the history of lobster pot construction. For some reason, I particularly remember an exhibition of local bus tickets: 'A fascinating trip from the Edwardian era to the present day.'

One bleak year in Broadstairs we went to see *Herbie Rides Again* on three separate afternoons. It was the only U-certificate film playing at the cinema and it allowed my parents to nap in the darkness.

I don't know if it was the constant drizzle, Herbie riding again and again and again or the bus tickets, but in 1975 my mother put her foot down. The Cain family boarded a Monarch TriStar at Luton airport and headed for the sun.

The main thing my parents and my brother discovered during those two weeks in Ibiza was that when it's glorious every day, you don't have to roam the streets looking for entertainment or shelter. Instead you can splash around in the hotel pool, order endless drinks and hot dogs from the outdoor bar, smother yourself in Ambre Solaire, stretch out on a sun-lounger and generally relax, secure in the knowledge that this really is a holiday.

I, however , discovered that I am terribly allergic

to high temperatures and bright sunlight. By day two the prickly heat bubbling over my face, arms and legs was so uncomfortable that I had to borrow my mum's black polo-neck jumper (packed 'just in case') and retreat to a shady corner on the far side of the pool.

The one bright side to my enforced exile from the sunshine paradise twenty yards away was the fact that I was able to read every book I'd taken with me (probably three or four). Then I started on the ones my brother hadn't even bothered to open because he was having such a great time in the pool with the younger members of a family from Manchester.

My dad had packed *The Three Musketeers* by Alexandre Dumas for my brother, hoping, I suspect, to wean him off his beloved Biggles books. Unsurprisingly, my brother hadn't shown the slightest interest.

But I was hooked from page one. I devoured *The Three Musketeers* in a day and a night, swept away by the thrilling adventure of d'Artagnan and his friends Aramis, Porthos and Athos. I admired the dastardly Cardinal Richelieu, but most of all I loved the thrillingly evil Milady de Winter. It was wonderful to find a rip-roaring story, where the baddest and bravest villain of them all was a beautiful, dangerous woman. *The Three Musketeers* is still one of my all-time favourite books.

Now, you might wonder why I've written about this here.

When the Templar team asked me where the idea for *The Moon Child* came from, I thought about the magical books I enjoyed as a child and the writers I loved to be scared by – Susan Cooper, Joan Aiken, John Masefield, Leon Garfield and Alan Garner sprang instantly to mind. In fact, I am sure I took books by Cooper and Garner on that same Ibiza holiday. For some reason, however, *The Three Musketeers* kept swashbuckling its way into my thoughts. I suspect there's quite a lot of its inspiration – and especially Milady – lurking in the shadowy recesses of *The Moon Child*. The two are very different beasts, but I know a seed for the story you've just read (and hopefully enjoyed), was sown during a blistering fortnight on a Spanish island back in 1975.

I'd like to thank everyone who helped bring *The Moon Child* to the page. My lovely, patient husband Stephen; the teams at Templar and Hot Key Books – especially Matilda Johnson, Debbie Hatfield and Olivia Mead; brilliant editor Catherine Coe, whose perceptive questions kept me on my toes; Melissa Hughes for her eagle eyes; and illustrator Levi Pinfold for his utterly breathtaking cover.

Last but not least, huge thanks to Helen Boyle, Emma Goldhawk and Will Steele – my own Three Musketeers!

Cate Cain, June 2014.

ABOUT THE AUTHOR

Cate Cain is a true Cockney, having been born within hearing distance of the church bells of St Mary-le-Bow in the City of London.

She studied English Literature at the University of London and trained to be a teacher. After leaving teaching, Cate became a journalist and worked in newspapers for more than ten years.

Cate has always loved history and now, appropriately, works for the Society for the Protection of Ancient Buildings in Spitalfields, London. Her office is in the attic of an old Georgian building and, like Jem, Cate often daydreams, looking out of the attic window over the London rooftops around her office.

Cate lives in St Albans with her husband, Stephen.